A SPY WALKS INTO THIS BAR

A Cold War Tale of Misdirection and Redemption

GENE COYLE

authorHOUSE®

AuthorHouse™
1663 Liberty Drive
Bloomington, IN 47403
www.authorhouse.com
Phone: 833-262-8899

This is a work of fiction. All of the characters, names, incidents, organizations, and dialogue in this novel are either the products of the author's imagination or are used fictitiously.

Published by AuthorHouse 08/15/2022

ISBN: 978-1-6655-6771-8 (sc)
ISBN: 978-1-6655-6770-1 (e)

Print information available on the last page.

This book is printed on acid-free paper.

Contents

**Dedicated to Richard Kobakoff, who bears credit
for my entering the Game, and for teaching me
much about espionage, people and the world.**

by indirections, find directions out

William Shakespeare
Hamlet Act 2, Scene 1

Prologue

While this is a story of one man's redemption, it is also sprinkled with instances wherein false "facts" lead to correct conclusions and good results. Also instances of true "facts" which lead to incorrect conclusions. This tale is indeed a fictional one, but the confusions portrayed in it do often occur in the real world of espionage. Nor am I hardly the first author to recognize such "misdirections" and thus the perfect quote from Shakespeare's Hamlet.

The characters described are fictional, but as with most things that come out of our imagination, their personalities and traits do reflect in part, real people I have known throughout my many years in the intriguing game of espionage. Some are composites and some have been borrowed from different years and various countries and placed in the country of Portugal as the Cold War is coming to an end. While the characters and events are indeed fictional, the reader should recognize similar behaviors by people from their own lives.

And as the saying goes, sometimes the truth is stranger and more amazing than fiction.

CHAPTER 1

Lisbon, Portugal — 1990

The faded yellow taxi rolled slowly to a stop in front of a nondescript, two-story building on one of the narrow, cobblestone side streets of the Bairro Alto district of Lisbon, Portugal. This neighborhood, on a hill above the downtown area, hosted sixty or seventy restaurants and bars. The foreign tourists generally frequented the more upscale restaurants on the two main streets of the area. The smaller establishments on the side streets, such as this one, attracted mostly locals and the more adventurous foreigners. The calendar might have said it was 1990, but from the appearance of these buildings it was still circa 1935 in the Bairro Alto.

"Aqui está Clube de Jazz," said the gray-haired driver to his four American passengers, all in their late-20s. A major tech firm had just bought out the small one that the two men had started straight out of college and they, along with their wives, were spending some of that newly acquired wealth on their first trip out of the country. The last one out of the ancient taxi overpaid the driver. The metal sign with the name of the bar hanging above the doorway was faded and about as dilapidated as the gray stucco-covered building itself. The rusted hinges creaked slightly in the wind as it swung slowly back and forth.

"You're sure this is the place?" asked one nervous wife of her husband. "It looks like a real dive and a good place to get knifed," she added in a low voice, as if not wanting to offend any mugger lurking in a nearby shadow.

"This is the name and address that the doorman at our hotel gave me when I asked for a bar with live music where locals went."

The four cautiously opened the front door. Social etiquette be damned, the two men entered first through the arched entrance, just in case. They passed by a glass-covered advertising case on one wall, which proudly proclaimed alleged "stars" who had performed at the club in the past. From the attire of the performers appearing in the faded 8 x 10 black-and-white, glossy photos with curled edges, it appeared as though the photos had been pinned there since the 1950s.

They then passed through a faded velvet curtain and found themselves in the main room of the club. Actually, it was the only room of the establishment. There was a long wooden bar along the wall to the left, with a brass foot rail, a dozen tall stools and two customers seated there. There were round wooden tables that could accommodate perhaps a hundred people spread around club. The tables and chairs had clearly led a hard life. Towards the back was a large alcove, which housed an upright piano and a small spotlight aimed at the keyboard.

The chipped and stained veneer of the piano made the tables look almost new. There were dim electric lights high up on the outer walls and on each occupied table burned a candle in a wine bottle covered with wax from many previous burnings. They provided almost no light, but added a nice atmosphere to the setting. Approximately thirty people were in the establishment that Tuesday night, most dressed very casually. No one turned to look as the four entered.

After their eyes had adjusted to the darkness, the Americans moved towards a table for four near the right-hand wall. All the walls were constructed of roughly hewn stone. A waiter in black pants and shirt, of perhaps thirty years, promptly came to their table with one cardboard drink menu for them to study. He lighted the candle on their table. The white apron tied around his waist, which came down to his knees, appeared as though it hadn't been washed that calendar year, but then it was November. Their waiter was experienced enough to have brought a menu in English and spoke to them in accented English. He looked like a typical Portuguese male. He was thin and only about five foot five, with short brown hair and heavy eyebrows. The waiter's nose had a slight bend in it as if it had been broken in a barroom brawl once or maybe even twice.

After handing them the menu, he said, "I be back soon to take your order." He might have smiled, but in the lowlight and with the thick cigarette smoke in the air, you couldn't really see his face that well to judge for certain. At least half of the people in the bar were smoking. If there was a ventilation system in the place, it wasn't working. There wasn't a filter-tipped cigarette in sight. The air was so thick and blue from the smoke it looked like a Hollywood movie set from the 1930s. They expected Marlena Dietrich to come out at any moment and lean against the piano. It reminded them of a small bistro they had recently visited in Paris. Apparently, Portugal and France were having a contest to see who could have the most cases of lung cancer in one year.

A few minutes after their arrival, a gentleman in his mid-50s, wearing a trench coat and a gray fedora, entered and headed straight for the back alcove. He hung his coat on a wall hook and tossed his hat on top of the piano. He immediately sat down and started playing *Stardust*. The individual had beautiful salt and pepper gray hair, trimmed short. Many of the customers applauded his arrival; obviously, they were regulars and knew the player well. He wore a navy-colored sport coat, and a white dress-shirt with open collar. The ladies all thought him quite handsome, with a rugged cheek line. The lines in his face gave him rather a sad look – clearly a face that had experienced a lot of life, probably much of it bad news. When standing up, he was six feet tall, with broad shoulders and a thin waist line. He had exceptionally long fingers, which no doubt allowed for his hands to effortlessly dance along the keyboard.

By the third song, customers started sending drinks over to the piano. By the end of the first set, there was a line of drink glasses standing on the narrow wooden space just above the piano keys. The waiters told inquiring clients that Oban single malt whiskey was Dooley's drink of choice. Four of the glasses were already empty and four more still full of the amber liquid that eased bad memories awaited his attention. Oban was the most expensive drink on the menu, so management was very happy with Dooley and his admirers. Initially, the bartender had tried sending him watered down drinks, in order to make such "gifts" to him even more profitable than the already inflated price provided, but Dooley quickly put an end to that practice. He threatened to announce to the customers at the start of each set that he was no longer accepting drinks. His glasses quickly returned to being pure whiskey. Dooley had been drinking a long time — a fact which showed on his face — and he could easily discern if a drink had been diluted.

The waiters and bartenders all liked Dooley and gently put him into a taxi at the end of every Tuesday and Thursday night when he played and drank at the club. All the staff really knew about him was that he was a widowed American living in Lisbon, who played the piano very well and seemed quite lonely and sad. There was probably a major tragedy somewhere in his past, but he never spoke of it. He had an excellent command of Portuguese and even occasionally sang in the language. The waiters, who thought they were helping him out, informed the single women customers who asked of his marital status that the handsome piano player was indeed "available." Some of those "single" ladies would send along with their song requests a note with their name and hotel room number or a phone number. Single meant either that they had no husband, or at least not one geographically in Lisbon that night. In either case, Dooley would sing the requested song, but nothing more.

His song selections focused mostly on love and sentimental tunes of the 1930s through the 1950s. He used no sheet music and simply relied on his memory to play songs by Cole Porter, Irving Berlin, Jerome Kern and many lesser known composers of that era, and particularly of the war years. The Portuguese had a musical art form called *fado*. These were songs of lost love and sadness caused by one reason or another, usually performed by a middle-aged woman dressed all in black. The locals were thus predisposed to enjoy Dooley's sentimental songs. His repertoire was full of sad and wistful tunes, made to sound even sadder by his playing style.

One of his regular fans in recent months was an attractive Brazilian woman named Olivia. She looked about forty years old, but still had her good looks. She was tall and thin with short, dark hair and that permanently bronze-colored skin of Brazilians and a thin face with high cheek bones. Probably, somewhere in her ancestry was some indigenous Indian blood. She had curves in the right places and usually wore a blouse with enough undone buttons to show that her breasts were real. Like most Brazilians, she was not shy at showing her natural attributes and she was always dressed impeccably — presumably one of the perks of working at a high-end dress shop. She was a little vague about her background or why she was in Lisbon. She simply said that she worked at Casa de Simone, a very exclusive dress shop and maker of women's clothing for the rich. William thought she might have been a designer or buyer, at least something above being a mere shop girl. They never really discussed her work. She'd mentioned once that there was a husband back in Brazil, but that it was mostly just a legal matter on paper. Of himself, he hadn't corrected her initial guess that he was simply a retired American who liked living in Portugal and enjoyed playing the piano.

At the club, the American went by the name of Dooley Wilson. Wilson was of course the famous black musician who appeared as Sam in the movie *Casablanca* with Humphrey Bogart and sang the memorable tune *You Must Remember This*. The Lisbon piano player's real name was William Wythe. He didn't figure Wilson would mind his using his name since he'd been dead almost forty years. He'd chosen that stage name as he liked the music performed in the movie and the fact that while Wilson did the singing, he only faked playing piano in the movie. Somebody else played piano offstage, as Wilson was a drummer. Wilson just pretended to play on screen and as a perverted homage to him, William chose that stage name as he was just faking most of his life. He was not a professional musician. He only played on Tuesday and Thursday nights as a hobby. The rest of the week he was a Second Secretary in the Political Section of the US Embassy in Lisbon. He was faking that as well. While William Wythe was his true name, his real job was that of an operations officer for the CIA. The bar didn't pay him much, but he didn't care. He just enjoyed the atmosphere and the free drinks. William did like to drink and technically would have been called a "functioning alcoholic", if anybody had ever had a chance to examine him.

He'd been an alcoholic for almost ten years, ever since his wife had been killed in a terrorist attack in Malta. He'd never gotten over her loss as he blamed himself for it happening and had found alcohol as his only comfort. Playing piano and drinking at the club was one of the few times that he could go for several hours without thinking about his dead wife. He functioned just well enough at his day job not to be fired, but not well enough to get promoted during that alcohol induced fog of a decade since her death. He continued to get overseas assignments because he'd take any posting anywhere and the Agency felt sorry for him. The CIA was quite a paternalistic place that took care of its own "weaker links", particularly in sad cases such as William's where he'd lost his wife to a terrorist. It also helped that a couple of years later he'd won the Agency's medal for valor while serving in Athens. He'd personally saved dozens of lives during a terrorist attack on a public restaurant frequented by American military personnel.

As long as William showed up for work, a man with that background could always get an assignment somewhere. He'd kept working overseas because he needed the money to finance his two daughters in private boarding schools and then in college. The U.S. Government had a policy that any federal official serving overseas got an "educational allowance" so that the official's children could attend a school back in America. William was already five years past the minimum retirement age of fifty, but he would need that educational allowance money for three more years. He'd told Chief/Europe Division when he got the Lisbon job that just one more three-year assignment and he would gladly retire. William caused no real screw ups overseas. He just didn't achieve much, but then that was true of some others as well. He wasn't a Chief of Station or even the Deputy, which he should have been by his age. He was just a lowly street ops officer. The Chief of Station didn't want him there, but the current Chief of Europe Division was a longtime friend of William's and of his wife's and looked out for him when he could. The COS gave William any shit task that came along, hoping he'd get fed up and leave – even though several people had explained to him the financial reason that William had for staying abroad. The other Station personnel all liked William, even if he wasn't much of an officer, in contrast to their general opinion of the COS as a first-class prick. William just took whatever tasks were assigned him and didn't care. If William did stumble across a promising target, the COS would instruct William to turn the target over to one of the other officers for further development.

A middle-aged, slightly overweight Portuguese male arrived that night at the bar shortly after the four American tourists. He took a seat near the back and ordered a bottle of Sagres beer. He'd been in the bar enough times in recent weeks that the waiters vaguely recognized him. He wore the same cheap sport coat every time he was there. He had thinning, black hair, which he strategically combed from one ear over to the other to create the illusion that he was not bald. A thin mustache completed his very forgettable image. He didn't fit the profile of the typical customer that frequented the club and he only ever came on a Tuesday or Thursday night. Carlos, the head waiter, had been serving drinks in dives like the Clube de Jazz for twenty years and he could generally divide the male customers into one of three categories. One, they came trying to pick up women. Two, they were heavy drinkers who didn't like to drink alone, or three, they were music aficionados. This guy never looked at or talked with women, he didn't drink much and he seemed fairly disinterested in the music. He just consumed two or three beers and watched people. Carlos finally began to wonder if the man was some sort of policeman or private detective. Aside from not having any real purpose for being there, Carlos noticed that the man always wore very thick-soled walking shoes. Shoes that a guy would wear if say he was on his feet a lot during the day. If a policeman or a P.I., maybe he had an interest in one of the club's employees. Alfredo sold a little weed from time to time to some of the younger customers, but that hardly merited such continual surveillance. Perhaps he was interested in one of the regular customers who came to hear Dooley play the piano. For that matter, maybe he was interested in Dooley, as the man always left shortly after Dooley finished his last set and departed for the night.

The owner of the jazz club, a gray-haired, dual-citizen of America and Portugal named Nick Haber, simply sat at the far end of the bar on most nights, slowly drinking beer and keeping an eye on the cash register. He liked to see that all the cash payments went into the till, not pockets of the employees. He was in his late sixties, but still looked as though he was in good shape and he had a face that told people without his uttering a word that you didn't want to cross Nick. He also had a few small scars on his face that indicated that on some occasions he'd had to back up his facial expression of toughness with his fists. Even after many years in the country, he still spoke the most God-awful Portuguese. Fortunately, he had a great sense of humor and his Portuguese employees all liked him. Nick had always been rather vague about why he'd moved to Portugal and eventually married a local gal. He'd never once travelled back to America since his arrival some twenty years earlier. Nobody was sure if that was because he couldn't or he simply had no desire to do so. Having a vague past did not make him stand out at the club. Most everyone working there was reticent to discuss much about their sad pasts. A couple of the waiters had done some time in jail for petty crimes and one had been in the French Foreign Legion. Like the Legion, Haber had a hiring policy of not asking any questions about a man's past. Everyone from the owner down to the elderly man who swept up in the mornings had reached equilibrium pretty near the bottom of life for one reason or the other – and weren't going anywhere. Nick saw in William, that same hopelessness of spirit and by the second week of becoming acquainted offered him a steady job because he fit in well with all the others.

It was Friday evening and the informal bar of the Marine Security Guard Detachment at the U.S. Embassy Lisbon had a pretty good crowd for November. Despite the growing threat of war with Iraq as 1990 was coming to a close, people were still in a holiday mood. The bar was in the same two-story building separate from the main chancery that housed the Embassy cafeteria on the compound. The ground floor was the kitchen and cafeteria, which served breakfast and lunch to Embassy staff Monday through Friday. The second floor was the residence for the Marines. The "bar" was open only on Friday nights for anyone connected with the Embassy. The Marines and American diplomats could also invite guests. The stone building was over one hundred and fifty years old and had been the private residence of a wealthy banking family until the 1950s. The inside was beautifully decorated on the walls with the original hand-painted ceramic tiles for which Portugal was famous. These were all in azure blue and had sailing motifs from centuries gone by. The floors were granite. The roof was red tile. The structure sat on top of a hill with a spectacular view of downtown Lisbon. Lower on the same hill, but facing away from downtown was a modern, ugly chancery made of concrete walls. The American Department of State seemed to specialize in building exceptionally tasteless embassies all around the world.

The Marine bar served several purposes. First, it generated money to be used to host the annual Marine Corps Ball every November 10th in Lisbon, as was the custom at embassies and military bases around the world. This was a celebration to mark the founding of the Marines on that date back in 1775. Second, it gave the Marines somewhere to party and blow off a little steam, but without going out to local bars and possibly getting into trouble. It also gave the young Marines some place to invite dates without going broke at local bars and restaurants. The Security detachment, which guarded the Embassy chancery 24/7, consisted of sixteen enlisted Marines and a Gunnery Sergeant as the commander. The enlisted men had to be single. The "Gunny" could be married, though the current occupant of the position was single. He was twice divorced and swore he'd never make that mistake again. Master Gunnery Sergeant Aloysius Murphy had twenty plus years in the Corps, including two tours in Vietnam and a Silver Star. Rumor had it that he'd deserved several more honors, but the American military required two U.S. military personnel to attest to actions for medals to be awarded – and for several engagements in which he participated, he was the only Marine still alive at the end of the fighting.

The eighteen and nineteen-year-old Marine corporals and sergeants under his command knew you didn't give the Gunny shit or question his commands on any topic. Actually, at six foot four and two hundred and forty pounds of all muscle, not many men, military or civilian, ever gave him anything but respect or a wide berth. He still wore a 1960s style flattop haircut, though it was getting a little thin on top. His face was permanently brown and wrinkled from so many years out in the sun. He needed glasses to read, but otherwise he still had twenty-twenty vision and still had a sparkle in his blue eyes, especially when he laughed like a triple-sized leprechaun. Life was very simple for Aloysius. Under his philosophical code, there was right, there was wrong and there were no excuses.

That particular Friday evening, Second Secretary William Wythe was enjoying his usual of eighteen-year-old Oban single malt whiskey on the rocks, which the bar stocked solely for him. He'd come straight from the Chancery over to the bar at the end of the Embassy's work day, as he generally did every Friday evening. He sat alone at the bar, as was his inclination. Over the months, his Embassy colleagues had come to learn of his preference for solitary drinking and respected his wishes. There was a sad look to his face that could have been the subject of a country-western song. His eyes were partially closed as he stared straight ahead at the liquor shelves behind the bar. His body was there at the bar, but his mind was floating longingly to places in times long past when his wife was still alive. William was a man who preferred living in the long ago over the present.

Embassy personnel and other diplomats in Lisbon couldn't decide if Wythe, who was fifty-five years old, was either the most incompetent officer in the American diplomatic service and that was the reason he was still only a second secretary at that age, or perhaps he was really the CIA's Chief of Station. Those appeared to be the only two plausible explanations for why William would be the oldest "second secretary" in the entire State Department. The local Portuguese staff at the Embassy jokingly referred to Wythe as being with the "Water Company." In Portuguese, the water company was the Campagna Industrial de Agua – the CIA. William was in fact with the CIA, but not the Chief. It really bothered the actual Chief of Station, Elliot Loken, that so many in the Embassy thought that Wythe was the head spook. William was probably ten years older than the real COS and so people just assumed he must be the head man. In fact, he was just a common street operations officer – just one of the braves, not a chief.

William told people early in their relationship with him that he preferred to be called William, not Dick or Bill. He would explain that his mother had named him after her favorite movie actor, William Powell, and so he generally went by William. In fact, it was a "tell" as to whether someone claiming to be a good acquaintance of his was or not. If they called him "Dick", they didn't really know him well.

As the Gunny neared Wythe at the bar, he said, "Good evening, William." William recognized the voice and immediately looked to his right, nodded in recognition and his face changed as if an electrical switch had been thrown. He'd been an Agency operations officer for enough years that he could instantly turn on the charm and a smile when needed.

"So, Gunny, what's new in the Marine Corps?" asked William.

"Nothing's ever new in the Corps. The faces change, but the Corps doesn't. You ought to know that William. Christ, you've been attending Marine Corps Balls since John Paul Jones was a midshipman.

"It's a vicious lie that I knew Jones. I knew his mother, but I never did meet him," was his droll reply. William and Gunny frequently exchanged such barbs about each other's age.

"And what's new in the world of diplomacy?" asked Gunny as his massive hand picked up the glass of tonic water and a lime that the bartender had just sat in front of him. "Has peace or sanity broken out anywhere in the world since last we spoke?"

"Not a chance. I got permanent job security. If peace broke out, the world wouldn't need diplomats."

"Any prediction for when the fighting's going to start down in Kuwait and Iraq? If I have to listen to that asshole Saddam say that the mother of all battles is coming much longer, I'm going to slit my wrists with a dull blade."

"Me make a prediction? Hell, you probably got connections higher up at the Pentagon than I do."

"Yeah, well I phoned General Gray earlier in the week and asked him, but he said it was a secret, known only to the President and the Washington Post."

"Well, I believe the part about the Washington Post. I'm not so sure about Bush. By the way, what are you going to do after you retire from the Corps? That date must be getting fairly close, isn't it? You going to find another job of some kind?"

"Hell, I've had a job. When I leave the Corps, I'll be looking for a position! Actually, I've been phoning every officer I ever bought a beer for to see if somebody couldn't get me pulled out of here and sent down to the Marine Expeditionary Force in time to be part of the upcoming invasion, but I've been getting nowhere. One colonel even suggested I was too old. Hell, I only weigh five pounds more today than the day I joined the Corps, can still run three miles with full pack in under twenty minutes and at the last qualifying round I was one point short of a perfect score with the M1 and a 9mm."

"Damn. Remind me to never get you mad at me," jokingly replied William.

"Anyway, as for retirement, I was hoping to get down to the Gulf and get killed, then I wouldn't have to worry about what to do after Lisbon. As it is, when I leave here this coming summer and take retirement, I might head down to somewhere around Camp LeJeune and open up a Thai massage parlor."

"You must have saved a lot of money over the years if you can afford to open a massage parlor in North Carolina?"

Gunny laughed. "I said I might. I didn't say I could afford to do it in style, though I do have a few bucks saved. What about yourself? I'm sure Uncle Sam's been paying you well for decades," he added with a smile.

William returned the smile. "Most of mine's been going to pay for the schooling of my two daughters over the years, so I'll probably just head back home to Virginia and see if I might be able to get one of those Walmart greeter jobs. Of course, I do buy a Lotto ticket whenever it gets up above two hundred million, so if I do get lucky one week, I might have to come up with a whole new plan. And if I ever do become a multi-millionaire, I'll probably need a personal bodyguard. You can send me your resume and I'll see if you meet my high standards."

"And have to spend every day of the week around your sorry-looking face. Hell, you'll never have that much money that you could afford to pay me what I'd demand to put up with that situation."

They both laughed.

"Excuse me, I have to go see a man about a horse," mumbled the Gunny as he silently slid off his bar stool and headed across the room.

William was always amazed at how smoothly Gunny moved for such a big man, with the grace of a dancer. He could easily picture the big Marine gliding silently through the Vietnamese jungle, just before he slit some Viet Cong's throat. While Gunny was off to the head, the corporal who was playing bartender that night started wiping down the bar near William. He leaned across the bar and said to him, "Gunny wasn't exaggerating. He almost fired a perfect score back in September at quals, and he hadn't even fired any practice rounds. Made the rest of us look sad. The day he has to retire from the Corps it will kill him. It's been his whole life since he joined at age seventeen from some small town in southern Virginia. He eats, drinks and dreams Corps. His picture should be on a recruitment poster."

"Yeah, if I ever had to go into battle, Gunny's the guy I'd want leading me." William held up his glass and said, "Semper Fi!"

"That's the way all of us feel as well. We'd follow him anywhere."

Gunny was just about back to his barstool and the corporal started to move on down the bar. William waved at him. "Bring me another double of this and a diet Sprite for my sister here."

"You know William, we'll hardly even need to do any fund raising for next year's Marine Corps Ball as long as you continue to come in here and drink that expensive eighteen-year-old single malt Scotch. We'll make enough off of you alone to pay for the whole event," teased Gunny with a grin as he settled back on his stool.

"Ah, and I thought you let me come in here to drink because of my charming personality." He tossed down the rest of what was in his glass and waited patiently for the next one.

Gunny never liked to tell people how much to drink or not to drink, but he liked William and hated to see him get blind drunk every Friday night. "Maybe you should go on home and drink there. But if you're going to keep drinking here, give me your car key now. I'll get one of the kids to drive you home in the duty car when you're ready."

William handed over his key and laid three more twenties on the bar. "When I've drunk up this, just call me a cab. No need for anyone to drive me clear out to Estoril."

Most all of the young Marines liked William and none of them minded driving him home when he was too drunk to drive, which was just about every Friday night. They did wonder what drove him to drink so heavily. Most guys with that much of a thirst had some serious issues in their life. However, a month earlier, one newly arrived sergeant made a comment on a Friday night from the other end of the bar about what a useless lush William was. Gunny went down to him and quietly told him to shut his pie hole before the Gunny did it for him. "That man's been through more shit than you could ever even read about – presuming that you know how to read."

Gunny in fact didn't know what caused William to drink so heavily, but suspected it might have something to do with a woman. He knew William's wife had been dead for some time, but didn't know the details. Gunny understood well the phenomenon of seeking solutions to problems in life from a bottle. By the end of his second one-year tour in Nam, he'd begun spending a lot of nights looking for answers at the bottom of bottles to the question of why several buddies two feet from him had been killed and he'd never had a scratch. And he'd lost count of how many men he'd killed. He hadn't really been in charge of other guys out in the jungle, but there were still times when his actions or his instructions to others might have caused their deaths. He'd spent a lot of time at night drinking back then, wondering if certain colleagues' deaths were on his shoulders. He married within a month of returning stateside after his second tour, to a stripper he'd met at a gentlemen's club in San Diego. The marriage only lasted two years, but she'd helped get him off the bourbon and he'd stayed sober ever since.

Since Gunny had personal experience with drinking too much, he knew it was probably pointless for him to offer William advice, but he made one subtle attempt. "You know, speaking as a man who used to drink so much that I totally missed 1970, I can tell you that there are no answers in liquor, no matter how expensive the brand."

William smiled and replied, "Hell, I know that. I just like the way I feel the following morning."

Gunny laughed. "Well, that's a good argument, but as an old, close personal friend of Jack Daniel, might I at least ask what it is you're trying to forget? Something you did or something you regret not doing?"

"Sorry, Gunny, but that's a topic that's classified way above your pay grade, but I do appreciate your concern."

"Understood, and I won't bring it up again, but I'll just say that you're still a relatively young man and you'd probably still have lots to contribute and more of life to enjoy if you spent more of your remaining days sober."

William raised his glass in a toast to the Gunny. "An astute observation, no wonder you're a Master Gunnery Sergeant." He then nodded to the young bartender to pour him another Scotch.

Once he had his next drink and it was again just the two of them, he turned and pointed at Gunny's glass of pure tonic water. "Just out of curiosity, what stopped your drinking?"

He first checked that no one else was near, then said, "In part, it was my first wife, the exotic dancer there in San Diego. She didn't know how to cook or clean, had no idea of what the word fidelity meant, and wrecked our car twice, but I do have to give her credit for helping me to stop drinking. But the biggest factor was my returning to my religion. I was raised a good Baptist as a child down in southern Virginia, but had drifted away from the church after joining the Corps. Then one evening I wandered into a black neighborhood of San Diego while drunk and came across a small Baptist church having a service. I could hear the singing and went inside. I started singing along with them. The thirty or so members of the congregation started staring at me."

"Because you were so tall," asked William with a grin.

"Yeah, that and the fact I was the only white boy there. Anyway, after the sermon, the minister asked me to stay and we started chatting. I went back on a few Sunday afternoons. I'll skip over the details, but one thing he talked about with me was my drinking and shouldn't I come back to Jesus. Well, since the third conversation with him, I've never had another drink of alcohol. I don't make a big public deal of it, but that's my story."

"Well, that was a good outcome."

Gunny laughed. "In most ways, except once I was sober, I realized what a horrible person my wife really was and that our marriage was a joke, so I got a divorce."

"Well, there's a dark lining to every silvery cloud. Gunny, while we're on philosophical topics, I have a personal question on warfare, if I may."

"Ask anything you like, as long as I don't have to answer truthfully if I don't like the question."

"Fair enough. Okay, here's the question. Do you remember the first man you killed in combat? I don't mean when you fired two hundred rounds into the jungle and probably hit somebody. I mean when you actually saw the face of the enemy you were about to kill."

Gunny's face turned taut and deadly serious. "Interesting question. Yes, I remember the first one perfectly. I'd only been in Nam about a month. It was at the time of the massive Tet offensive in 1968. The VC had infiltrated through the perimeter, probably with the help of some of our alleged South Vietnamese allies. I heard a lot of shooting one night and stepped into the hallway to go down to the small kitchen area. As I stepped through the kitchen doorway, there was a VC in his black pajamas with a rifle. I had on my sidearm and quickly pulled it out to shoot the little bastard. I was so scared that I forgot to cock it before the first pull on the trigger, so I had to use my thumb to cock it before I could shoot. He pulled his trigger, but his gun was empty. Otherwise, I'd have been dead. He looked awfully young and he was probably so scared that he hadn't kept track of how many shots he'd fired. I pulled the trigger of my handgun a second time and put a nice big hole right into his chest. Score: Aloysius 1— VC 0. By the end of that night, I'd killed ten or twelve, but I'll always remember that first one."

"You were a lucky man. That was quite a baptism by fire."

Gunny lowered his voice so that only William could hear him and stared down at the bar. "I occasionally still have nightmares about that night and will wake up in a cold sweat. I can still see his face as if it was yesterday. You can fire thousands of training rounds into paper targets, but the first time you put a bullet into another human being, it's a whole other story. You ever had to kill anybody, William?"

William paused. "Yes, some years back, but let me save that small story for another night."

"Sure, but I'm curious, what brought up this topic tonight? You thinking of shooting that little prick Elliot?" he asked with a grin.

"No, nobody in particular. I was just curious and thought I'd ask somebody who'd actually killed people and would honestly answer me."

Gunny nodded and took a long drink of his tonic water. "And one more thing. I've read a few autobiographies of guys talking about how time seemed to slow down and everything was moving as if in slow motion in a firefight. Total bullshit! Everything is moving fast and there's no time to think about anything. You have to rely on your training, so that you just instinctively react and do what's necessary to save your own life. That's why the Corps drills and drills the new recruits. I had a colonel who said once that we don't teach young men how to think like a Marine. We teach them to react to all sorts of scenarios like a Marine."

"Your colonel had an excellent point."

After another half hour of chatting with William and watching him down four more Scotches, Gunny signaled to one of his men to go bring the duty car to the side door of the building and then to two other Marines to discreetly help William out to the car via a passageway behind the bar. And so ended another typical Friday night for William Wythe. A man with no expectations nor hopes for better days ahead.

CHAPTER 2

Cia Headquarters — Langley, Virginia

The five members of a super-secret Counterintelligence Section known informally only as Committee XII officially began its weekly, all-hands meeting when Paul showed up with the box of goodies from the nearby McLean donut shop. In fact, even its existence within the Soviet and East European Division was known only to a handful of senior Agency officials who generally simply referred to it as "Paul's people." There were in fact no committees I through XI. Paul, who was head of the committee, had just pulled the number twelve out of the air, so as to make people wonder what committees one through eleven were doing. That action fit the sixty-year-old native of Boston's sense of humor.

The weather had changed for the worse on the East Coast and so Paul had switched that week's selection to heartier bear claws and cinnamon rolls. The duty of donut fetching rotated each week amongst the five members. A few members of the entity had changed since its original inception in 1986, but the little known group had been at work for four years. Its task was to try to figure out why the CIA had been losing an inordinate number of its Soviet assets, starting around 1985. One, or maybe even two cases getting wrapped up each year could be explained by just "bad luck." Maybe the Russian agent had done something "dumb", like ostentatiously spending too much of the money he was earning for his spying. Maybe a CIA officer handling an asset had made a mistake one night. But three or four cases going bad each year had to have a much more sinister explanation.

A number of reasons were being considered for all the loses, but the most alarming one was that the KGB had recruited a CIA officer within SE Division – and it was that mole that had been doing all the damage. Eventually, the search had been expanded outside of SE to other area divisions as well. In early 1990, the CIA had recruited a low-level Russian within the KGB's North America Department in Moscow who had an amazing story. He'd volunteered his services in return for money by shoving a note into the winter coat pocket of an American diplomat who was walking on the streets of Moscow one day. This volunteer claimed that there were actually several CIA moles, but that they were all handled by one senior officer within the KGB's Counterintelligence Department named Alexander Parshenko. This Russian asset, codenamed GOLDFISH, said that Parshenko had been handling these Americans for several years. He suggested that if the CIA could reconstruct what cities around the world Parshenko had visited and when, the Agency could then match that data against the postings of CIA officers and thus identify the moles. Committee XII had been working at constructing just such a chart for many months.

In his most recent secret communication to his case officer, GOLDFISH had advised that Parshenko would be traveling in December to Portugal and Spain. He didn't know in which country he was meeting a mole and which was just to obscure his travels. It had taken weeks of discreet record checking, but finally the Committee came up with the name of one officer who was now in Lisbon and had been posted in Athens back when Parshenko had visited there years earlier.

Jeanne lifted her reading glasses which always hung around her neck and did the honors of reading aloud for the other four members a quick synopsis of this one operations officer. "His name is William Wythe. He joined the Agency in 1960 after attending college at Indiana University and then his two-year mandatory stint in the U.S. Army. He has been a terminal GS-14 operations officer for almost a decade in Europe Division. His wife died in Malta ten years ago from a terrorist car bombing. Since that time, his career has gone nowhere, and he's reportedly a heavy drinker. He arrived in Lisbon early in 1990. He's also had money problems for a number of years. He has two daughters currently in college back in the States." She then passed out to each of them a summary sheet of what she'd just said about Mr. Wythe.

"Hmm," mumbled Paul. "So, we have a very marginal ops officer, who drinks heavily, needs money and whose career is going nowhere. Maybe we could get a star like him transferred to our committee," he added with his usual sarcastic wit.

"How does this guy keep getting assignments?" asked Sandy.

"I suspect he's been coasting quite a while on his wife's death," replied Jeanne. "He hasn't made a recruitment or been promoted in ten years. He continues to get assignments because he'll take any overseas posting."

"When was his last polygraph?" asked Paul.

"Same year he went to Malta a decade ago. He's always out of the country when it's time to be retested, so they just keep postponing his next test till he returns from overseas, which he never does."

"Sounds like we might have a pretty serious suspect here," added Paul.

Harry finished his jelly donut, wiped his fingers and brushed some powdered sugar off his tie. He spoke for the first time. "Before you four have the man shot at dawn, I'll repeat again that I still have serious doubts about anything GOLDFISH has told us to date. He has a great story about this master spy named Parshenko, but he hasn't yet given us one checkable fact. This may simply be one big deception operation, which the Russians love to run, just to get us seeing ghosts here and there. Besides, since he doesn't work in SE Division, how could Wythe have had knowledge about our Russian cases that have been wrapped up?"

The other four gave him their usual look of disapproval. Paul spoke up again. "I don't think the DCI would appreciate us being so parochial that we're only interested in catching Soviet moles working in our own Division, and not ones elsewhere in the Agency. As the vote would be four to one, if we took a vote, I say we immediately send one of our lesser known CI officers out to Lisbon, perhaps under the innocuous cover of doing some computer software upgrades. He'll stay there until Parshenko comes and goes. That will give us a good inside look at Wythe. I also want a ten-men and women surveillance team sent to Lisbon soon as possible to watch this guy out on the street for say a month, beginning immediately.

They'll need to get a feel for his usual behavior before Parshenko arrives, so that they can tell if anything changes once the Russian arrives there."

"What about watching Parshenko when he arrives in country?" asked Jeanne.

"No, we'll leave Parshenko alone. I don't want him getting spooked and canceling any planned meeting."

"What about advising the COS?"

"We tell no one at the Station. He might be Wythe's best buddy for all we know and tip him off. "Who is the COS anyway?"

Jeanne checked her file. "A fellow named Elliot Loken. From what I've heard, he's a pretty straight-laced GS-15 on his way up."

"Well, I still don't want him advised. Let's just do this coverage totally on the down-low. Bring people down from Scandinavia, so nobody at Lisbon Station will recognize any of the team." Paul then wrapped up the meeting and grabbed the last donut on the way out of the room.

Four days after the orders went out from Committee XII to several stations in Scandinavia, seven men and three women who were members of a special surveillance team that worked exclusively on Counterespionage issues were assembled in Lisbon. The women booked at one medium-sized hotel out at the far northern end of Cascais. They all had single rooms as one never knew who might work a day shift or a night shift, or both, and wouldn't want to be disturbed by a roommate when trying to get some sleep. Same for the men, who were split up at two more hotels. They had various cover stories ranging from a retiree on vacation, a man who had family money and thus he was always on holiday, an author doing background research and a woman who was waiting for her divorce to come through so she could go back home. They had five rented cars between them. They spent the first three days simply driving around Lisbon and its suburbs developing a feel for the city before they actually began attempting to surveil William. They determined that from his small neighborhood, there were two "choke points" through which he would have to drive, if he was going anywhere. Thus, by having a surveillant at those two locations, they could be sure of knowing if he was driving away from his home.

In the initial days, eight of them in four cars would follow him from home to work, and if he left the Embassy during the day. The latter activity was fairly rare. They would follow him home and then wait to see if he went back out in his car in the evening. They quickly learned of his Tuesday and Thursday night piano gig. For a few nights someone went in and drank beer and listened to his excellent playing, but they quickly decided that the physical layout of the place really didn't lend itself to holding secret meetings nor even brush passes, so they just waited for him outside. They also observed that he travelled to and from the jazz club in a taxi instead of his own car, so he probably wasn't doing anything clandestine on those two nights. For the journey home, he appeared quite intoxicated and one of the waiters would help get him into the cab. For nighttime coverage near his house, so that they could see if he left on foot, they put the man in his early fifties with the young lady of thirty in a car on a dark stretch of street with a view of the front of his house. They sat close with his arm around her. If anyone came by on foot, they'd pretend to start kissing. Clear to any passerby was the "story" that here was a young girl with an older man, who probably had a wife at home and he was too cheap to rent a motel room – thus they sat on dark streets and kissed. It wasn't ideal, but better than nothing to explain their presence on the street to neighbors who might walk by the car. Six other members were standing by nearby in three more cars, if William started out from home on foot or car.

On just the third night of their coverage, they thought that perhaps they had gotten lucky. Shortly after 2200 hours, William came out of his house in a black raincoat and a fedora slouched down on his head. Both hands were in his coat pockets and he was walking at a moderate pace. All eight of them were quickly spread in a circle around him, ready to follow him, regardless of which direction he took. He walked for close to an hour, never looking up, never putting a chalk mark on a pole or anything else that looked like "tradecraft" being practiced. Two nights later, same thing, except that he started closer to 2300 hours. The third night, he simply stayed in all evening.

The fourth night was piano night at the jazz club, but the next night he was back out walking. On that occasion, he walked further away from his house and arrived at a small shopping street, with five or six shops on it. It was almost 2300 hours and all the stores were closed and the street deserted of foot traffic. Just as Jane, the oldest surveillant, came around the corner of this street she observed that William had stopped for a moment to face the wall about 25 meters from the corner – and was then turning ninety degrees to his left to continue walking on down the sidewalk. When she got up to where William had stopped, she noted that there was a small metal mailbox on the wall. After that brief stop by the mailbox, William headed slowly, but directly back to his house.

Once William was back home, the team reassembled at a coffee shop. Jane reported what she'd seen.

"So, do you think our target mailed something?"

"I can't say for certain. If he did, he'd completed the act before I turned the corner. All I can positively say was that he had been facing the wall and was just turning back to his left to continue walking on down the street."

"But there was a mailbox on the wall at the spot where he'd stopped?" asked the team leader with a little frustration in his voice.

"Yes, there was, but there were also several advertisements on a billboard next to the mailbox. He might have mailed something or he might have just stopped for a few seconds to look at one of the flyers. From my point back at the corner, I couldn't say for certain which he'd been doing."

"Well, it's a classic "blind spot" in which to discreetly mail a letter or postcard without anyone who might have been following him being able see what he did."

They all nodded in agreement, but there was little point in discussing it any further. Jane was not going to change her conclusion, which was basically that she could draw no conclusion.

"Alright, I'll just write it up as Jane described it and we'll leave it to Headquarters to conclude whatever they want from the event", stated the team leader before sending everyone back to their hotels to get some sleep. Most of them were fairly excited by the "event." Following a suspect around for weeks or even months without spotting anything suspicious got boring and so they were inclined to interpret any unusual behavior by their target as a guilty action.

The following day back in Washington D.C., the Committee XII members spent twice as long debating the suspicious event in Lisbon as the surveillance team had, but in the end, they also came to no firm conclusion. They all agreed that it was a darn shame that the scheduled morning pickup hour at that box had come and gone before they could have cabled back to the team authorizing them to break open the mail box and take note of all its contents.

Paul finally summed up the debate. "OK, let's say he did mail a letter at that box. It's damned suspicious that he just happened to use a mailbox late at night when no one was around and approached it from the direction he did, which put him in a blind spot for ten or fifteen seconds from anyone who might have been following him. Thus, on top of our already existing suspicions of him, that mailing would be another black mark on his card. On the other hand, maybe he mailed something perfectly innocent, or maybe he didn't mail anything at all and had just stopped to look at a flyer on the bulletin board. Damn shame Jane didn't get around that corner just a few seconds sooner." They then all sat in silence for several long seconds.

"OK, Jeanne, send a cable back out to the team and instruct them to go discreetly take some photos of that billboard. Maybe if we see what flyers were on the board, we might feel more inclined to believe that's why he stopped there."

"Will do."

"And Harry, you send a clandestine message to the laptop of our CI man pretending to be installing new software in the Station. Ask him to try to get some insight as to William's personal habits, such as taking walks in his neighborhood."

"Sure, but I have a question for you while we're on the topic of Wythe."

"Go ahead," replied Paul as the others rolled their eyes in unpleasant anticipation.

"We know about his drinking problem ever since his wife was killed back in Malta and his need for money, but what would be his real motivation? I mean, he'd been a model, successful officer. How does becoming a Soviet mole help his pain over his wife's death?"

Jeanne spoke first. "His career has gone nowhere for many years. Perhaps the KGB promised to help him look good by arranging a top-grade recruitment for him."

"Sure, we've seen that over the years," replied Harry, "but where is his recruitment? He hasn't recruited even a safe house keeper in a decade.

Paul spoke up. "I'll tell you his motivation. I went over and spoke a couple of days ago to an old friend of mine in the Special Activities Division. He told me unofficially that shortly after the attack on the wife, the Agency had tracked down three guys who'd been in Malta at the right time and flew out the very night of the attack to Libya. NSA located them a month later at a terrorist training camp out in the desert. Plans for a squad of F-16s off a carrier in the Med to strike the camp were just about complete when President Carter issued a hold order. He was supposedly about to make a diplomatic breakthrough with some two-bit, Middle Eastern potentate or the other. By the time the attack hold was lifted a couple of months later when the diplomacy initiative had gone nowhere, the three suspects had moved on – destination unknown."

"That would have certainly made me pretty angry at the U.S. Government," conceded Harry.

"My friend said that Wythe was steaming mad that the peanut farmer had let his wife's killers slip away. His division chief at the time forced him to take several weeks paid administrative leave to go calm down. Ever since his return to duty, he's sought comfort in the bottle. So, I could see how in Wythe's mind that since he couldn't get revenge on those who killed his wife, he would get it on the Government who let them slip away."

There was silence around the table. "So, let's just continue our investigation of Wythe and see what turns up," concluded Paul, and then he stood up to signal the meeting over.

The next day out in Lisbon, coffee cup in hand, the thirty-five year old "computer tech" with short brown hair and ugly plastic frame glasses wandered into William's office, looking rather bored.

"William, have you got a minute for a question?"

William spun around from his computer terminal and said, "Sure, sit down. What can I do for you?"

"When I'm back home in Virginia, I like to go out and take walks at night – burns off a few calories and clears my head. Is it safe to go out at night here in Lisbon?"

"Well, I've been doing that several nights a week for over six months here, and nobody has mugged me yet." He gave Ed or Mark a big smile. He could never remember the fellow's name. "But I suppose it depends on your neighborhood. What hotel have they put you in?"

"I'm in the Sheraton, out towards Estoril, but I guess technically, I'm still in Lisbon."

"Oh, yeah, that should be a pretty safe area. Good lord, why the hell did they put you clear out there? There are four hotels within sight of the Embassy."

Mark's turn to laugh. "I guess they could get me a room for $3 cheaper out there. Maybe your Admin gal is dating the Manager of that hotel. Hey, I'm not joking, I went to Stockholm for several weeks last fall and it turned out that was exactly why visitors to the embassy from Washington were all being put at this one particular remote hotel. And there wasn't even a diplomatic discount at the place. I heard later that they fired her butt for that and other little things she had going on to make money on the side."

"Yeah, it's amazing what some people will do for money," replied William, somewhat nervously.

"Why you go walking so much?" asked Mark. "Does that help you sleep?"

"Oh, I've had trouble sleeping for years, so I guess that helps a little with that. I think mostly I just do it out of boredom. I live alone and I can only read so many good books or watch bad Portuguese TV. All they show all night long are these horrible Brazilian telenovelas. They're like American afternoon soap operas, but with more sex."

Mark laughed. "Hey, maybe I'll have to check those out – even if I don't understand the language! Well, thanks for the info on the safety of the streets." He looked at his watch. "Well, I'm going to go get some lunch. See you around."

"See you." William turned back to his computer.

That evening, from his hotel room, Mark used his laptop to send an encrypted cable back to Headquarters on his conversation with William. Aside from reporting on why he takes walks, he reported that the man was a heavy drinker. He never seemed to drink during the work hours, but nobody could look that hungover every morning who hadn't spent a lot of the previous evening doing serious drinking. A few other Station members had also discreetly confirmed that suspicion.

When his message was relayed on to the outside surveillance team, all of them agreed that the explanation seemed to fit William's walking pattern. Except for the night of the mailbox incident, he did generally appear as if he was just a man out wandering around for something to do and probably a bit drunk, given his staggering pace. However, they were paid to be suspicious. Walking as if bored could also just be a very clever ploy by William when he was out checking for signals to him that would trigger a meeting or some other clandestine operational act. He was also out of sight from the team for ten or fifteen second stretches. Perhaps he made a chalk mark somewhere, or put down a dead drop. In the daylight, on the days following his nighttime strolls, when he was at the Embassy, they tried to re-walk William's path – looking for telltale chalk marks or orange peels, but without success. Being a professional surveillant did make one paranoid over time. They got paid, whatever they observed or didn't observe, and so would continue on until told to do otherwise.

CHAPTER 3

Lisbon, Portugal

Shortly after 9:00 a.m. on a Monday morning in the middle of November, the local-employee phone operator for the American Embassy rang up to the Ambassador's American secretary, Lizzie Lee. Lizzie was a charming, elderly lady with pure white hair who had previously served as a secretary for four other ambassadors at different posts around Europe. She made everything run smoothly. There was little that the Iron Maiden of Ambassador Brown's outer office hadn't seen or heard in her forty years with the Department of State.

Lizzie saw that the incoming call was from the Embassy's main phone operator. "Good morning, Angelique. What can I do for you this morning?" asked Lizzie, with her soft, Southern accent. Ms. Lee was a native of Virginia and claimed to be a direct descendent of General Lee. Nobody ever contradicted her on any scheduling or protocol issue.

"I have a Portuguese woman on the phone, wanting to make an appointment with Ambassador Brown. Her family name is Braganza, which is an old, well-known Portuguese family name and she speaks in a very refined tone. She told me that she wishes to speak on a confidential matter with the Ambassador and that U.S. Marine Colonel North had recommended that she take up this matter directly with Ambassador Brown. Normally, I wouldn't bother you with such a call, but she sounds very upper class and a woman who is accustomed to getting her way."

"Hmmm, Colonel North you said. Yes, perhaps you'd better put her through to me. Does she speak English?"

"Yes, she does and very well."

"Alright, tell her that I am the Ambassador's personal secretary, that I make all his appointments and that she will first need to explain to me the nature of her business with Ambassador Brown." Lizzie Lee was also accustomed to getting her way.

After several seconds of silence on the line, a soft voice began speaking in British-accented English. It was indeed a very refined voice and clearly that of an elderly lady. "Good morning. I was told that you are the person who makes appointments for Ambassador Brown. Is that correct?"

"Yes, that is correct. With whom am I speaking?"

"I am Senhora Gabrielle Braganza. I was speaking recently with American Marine Colonel North about an issue and he said that I should take it up personally with Ambassador Brown. It is a very confidential matter and I would like to meet with him as soon as possible."

"The Ambassador is a very busy man. Perhaps you should tell me first what is the topic that you wish to discuss with him."

"No offense my dear, but this is a matter that I will only discuss with the Ambassador – not his secretary."

"Does Ambassador Brown know you?"

"He may know of me, but I don't recall ever meeting him previously."

Normally, Lizzie would have simply passed Sra. Braganza along to some junior diplomat, but she followed the news enough to recognize the name of Colonel North. He had become quite a household name as the Iran-Contra Affair had progressed in Washington D.C.

"I'll first have to discuss this directly with the Ambassador, before I can make you an appointment. Could you give me a phone number where you can be reached later today? It will be no later than this afternoon."

"Very well, but I shall expect to hear this afternoon."

After Senhora Braganza had provided her phone and suite number at the Henry the Navigator Hotel, Lizzie went directly in to speak to the Ambassador's Number Two, the Deputy Chief of Mission and thus began a growing domino effect. The name of Colonel North was the driving force.

At 11:30 a.m. the Ambassador called a meeting of his senior staff to decide on what to do with Sra. Braganza's request to discuss something confidential with him. Besides the Ambassador, the gathering included Deputy Chief of Mission Chesterbrook, head of the Political Section Hall, and the CIA Chief of Station, Elliot Loken. Before they all met, each of them had muttered an almost identical profanity upon being told that Marine Colonel North had told Sra. Braganza to come discuss something confidential with the Ambassador. They all wondered what on earth had Ollie been up to in Portugal? And even more importantly, how could they handle this matter, without actually getting involved and someday possibly having to appear before a Senate Committee! If they just sent her away and she instead wound up telling some journalist how she'd tried to bring the matter to the Ambassador's attention, but had been turned away, it could look equally bad. If on the other hand, the Ambassador, or any other senior Embassy official who had hopes of a rising career in the future, actually met with her and she told him God knows what about some other Ollie North scheme besides Nicaragua, he might wind up being dragged into a political scandal. Damned if they met her, damned if they didn't.

That was the main theme of the discussion at the meeting. After almost an hour, the COS finally proposed a solution that sounded good to all concerned.

"If we have one of my people meet with her, any necessary reporting afterwards can be kept much more controlled if done through Agency channels. And, I have just the right man who can handle the old lady tactfully and who has no career concerns, should it turn out to be a pile of dog shit."

The others looked intently at Elliot.

"I'm thinking of William Wythe."

The others then all smiled.

"He has excellent Portuguese and he's old enough to be relatively close to the old lady's estimated age." He paused for a few seconds. "And I'll make sure that he shows up sober for the meeting with Senhora Braganza."

Within five minutes of further discussion, it was decided that William was indeed the perfect man for the task of finding out just what Madame Braganza might have to say of importance. As Elliot walked back to his office, he silently congratulated himself on his brilliant choice. It was a win-win situation. If William came home with something important, Elliot could send it back to Headquarters making it look as though it had gone well thanks to the COS' personal guidance. If he came back with the smelly dog pile that they all feared, then it could all be laid off on William. And the added bonus, if it was the latter outcome, the COS could possibly be rid of William! Elliot was practically grinning with glee when he entered his office and buzzed for William to come see him. The COS could even claim that it was the Ambassador's idea.

A minute later, William sat down in an uncomfortable chair located in front of Elliot's desk. He'd been in the office many times previously, but had never before noticed just how many photos the COS had on the walls of himself alone or with minor government officials or celebrities during his lifetime. To the contrary, his desk was perfectly clean of anything except a small time piece and a calendar. William recalled the old cliché about how a cluttered desk indicated a cluttered mind. He was wondering what an empty desk indicated, but then the Chief began to speak, in his clipped, New England tone of voice.

"William, the Ambassador just came to me with an issue that he thought you were the perfect man to handle. An elderly Portuguese woman phoned the Embassy switchboard this morning seeking an appointment with the Ambassador on a confidential matter. She said that U.S. Marine Colonel North had told her to bring the matter directly to the Ambassador. She refused to disclose anything to Lizzie Lee as to the nature of the confidential matter, which she will only discuss with the Ambassador."

William smiled. "My, Ollie North does get around."

"I've just come from a Principles meeting to discuss this matter. The Ambassador suggested that you were the perfect man, given your age and excellent Portuguese, to meet with her first and get some idea of what she wants to discuss with him."

William seriously doubted if the Ambassador was the person who'd brought up his name.

"I see," replied William. "And what exactly is the Ambassador's plan?" He pronounced the word "Ambassador" with added emphasis.

"We have a phone number for the old gal, who's perhaps from a noble Portuguese family. He wants you to go meet with her and get some idea of what is the topic she wants to discuss with him. Explain that you're Ambassador Brown's special assistant, etc. and she must first talk with you before she can have a meeting with him. Come back with more details and then we can decide how to best handle this matter."

"I understand perfectly," is what came out of his mouth. What was going through his brain was that the little circle of top Embassy officials wanted a fall guy if this turned out to be the story of another illegal foreign policy initiative Colonel North had launched – maybe down in the former Portuguese colony of Angola where Cuban troops were fighting against guerrilla leader Jonas Savimba. At any possible future investigation, the Ambassador and other Embassy senior officials could all claim they only vaguely remembered the matter as it was William Wythe who'd actually met with her.

"I suggest you talk with Lizzie Lee to get any insights about Sra. Braganza she might have and to get the phone number."

"I'll do that right now." That gave William an excuse to end the meeting as quickly as possible. He glanced at one more picture on the office wall and read the caption as he was departing and thought to himself, "Good God, what man in his forties has a picture of himself up on his wall of when he was the captain of his high school debate team!"

He spoke briefly with Lizzie Lee and learned what he could of her impressions of Senhora Braganza. She also confirmed his suspicions of why he had been chosen when she told him in a lowered voice that the Ambassador had come out after the 11:30 meeting and told her to make no record of the call from the woman that day. She smiled as she told him this fact.

William saw no reason to delay and immediately upon returning to his own small office, he dialed the hotel of the woman. While listening to it ring, he observed that he had no personal photos or memorabilia of any kind in his office and wondered what that said about him. He didn't even have a photo of his dead wife, though he still carried one in his wallet.

Sra. Braganza was not thrilled at being told she would first have to meet with Ambassador Brown's "special assistant", but she did like William's solicitous manner and his pleasant voice as he spoke to her in excellent Portuguese. He at least sounded like an ambassador's special assistant. She reluctantly agreed to a meeting at her hotel suite on Tuesday morning at 10:00 a.m. when told it was that or nothing.

The following morning, William picked out his best suit to wear, a solid gray wool one, with a muted blue-striped tie to go with it. He made sure his shoes were well polished and he stopped enroute to the hotel to pick up a nice floral arrangement in a pottery vase. When William was sober, he was an excellent operations officer. He thought the whole assignment was a pointless one at best, but if he was to play the Ambassador's special assistant, he would play it well.

The Hotel Henry the Navigator sat on a quiet, cobblestoned street in an older and upper-class part of the city. The three-story building had a turn-of-the-century look, with lots of elegant wrought iron decorative work around the windows and balconies. It had obviously been a top of the line establishment in its day, but now it probably appealed mostly to travelers "of a certain age," like Braganza. He stopped at the front desk to confirm the room number of Sra. Braganza. It also allowed him to tactfully confirm that the name the woman gave over the phone to the Embassy was the one in which the room was truly booked.

He skipped the elevator and walked up the long, curving stairway, thickly carpeted and its railing made of mahogany. He could easily picture ladies in long gowns gliding down those stairs back in the 1920s and 1930s while an orchestra played softly in the dining room. Braganza's suite was at the far end of the second floor hallway.

Within only a few seconds of knocking, the door opened. Braganza had obviously been sitting in a small chair right by the door awaiting his arrival.

"Senhora Braganza?" he asked in Portuguese.

She replied, "Yes" and gestured gracefully with her left arm for him to enter. He crossed the threshold and immediately presented the floral arrangement.

"With the compliments of Ambassador Brown," he said. "I am his special assistant, William Wythe."

She nodded demurely and pointed at a nearby table where he could place them. It quickly crossed his mind from her behavior that she had been presented with flowers hundreds of times during her lifetime and knew just how to respond. She truly was of an indeterminate age, but certainly eighty or more he guessed, judging from the many lines on her face. She wore just a touch of makeup, but not so much that she was trying to disguise her age. She had beautiful white hair. Her dress was fairly simple, but clearly quite expensive and in a style of decades gone by. She wore only a few pieces of jewelry on her wrists and fingers, but the sparkle off them was definitely from real diamonds.

She extended her hand to shake his, while saying, "I am Gabrielle Braganza." She pointed to two chairs facing each other at an angle next to a coffee table upon which sat an elegant silver tea service, with some sort of family crest on the pot. "I took the liberty of ordering us some tea to drink while we chat. I do hope you like tea."

"I do indeed. That was very kind of you."

After she "played mother" and served both of them tea and they'd exchanged a few mandatory observations about the weather, William got down to business.

"I understand that you wish to meet privately with Ambassador Brown to discuss something confidential with him. And that it was Colonel North who had recommended this course of action to you. I am here upon instructions of the Ambassador to get a few more details as to the nature of the conversation you wish to have with him. As you can imagine, there are many people who would like to meet with Ambassador Brown, but he is a very busy man. I am here to ascertain the importance of the matter you wish to discuss with him."

"Of course, I understand perfectly that many people seek to meet with him. May I call you William?"

"Certainly."

"By the way, William, you speak Portuguese beautifully. Do you have Portuguese ancestry?"

"Thank you for the compliment. I don't believe I have any Portuguese heritage. I simply had an excellent language instructor back in Washington."

They both smiled and sipped a little tea.

William wanted to get directly to the key point. "So, when did you meet with Colonel North?"

"I will get to him shortly, but first I wish to explain to you who I am, so that everything is in context." She then began quite literally with her birth in 1910. She had a thick photo album laying on the coffee table in front of them and she had many aging photos and documents to accompany her story. When she'd gotten to about age ten in her story, William again tried to get to her to explain her meeting with Colonel North and again failed. At this point, he settled back in his chair and enjoyed his tea as there would clearly be no rushing of this grande dame and her story. "Oh well," he thought to himself, "someday, I'll be in my eighties and I'll appreciate it if someone sits and listens to my life's story."

William came back to attention when Braganza stated, "I had just turned eighteen in 1928 when I was told that my father was Dom Manuel II, the last King of Portugal." She then reached over into an attaché case and pulled out an elaborate legal document in English, attesting by Manuel II that while Gabrielle had been born out of wedlock, she was his daughter.

Not that William was a lawyer, but it certainly looked quite official and could presumably be checked in some courthouse in Middlesex, England where the original had supposedly been filed. As the clock ticked past twelve o'clock, she continued to show him old black and white photos of herself in England over the years. She came to be treated by other royal families of Europe as Princess Gabrielle through the 1930s. He found fascinating the pictures of her in England with Princesses Elizabeth and Margaret of the House of Windsor during WWII. Almost fifty years had passed since those photos had been taken, but it was easy to see that the wrinkled and refined lady sitting before him was the woman in those photos with the young English royals.

"Did you grow up in Portugal?" asked William, who'd become intrigued with her story.

"I was born in Portugal, but after the revolution, I spent most of my years in England and France. I of course visited Portugal many times during the 1930s and after the war."

"But you have maintained your Portuguese language very well."

Braganza smiled. "All of my nannies when I was a child were Portuguese and thus I grew up speaking my native tongue."

Braganza then picked up her life's story after the war. She explained that she did finally marry, but she spent little time speaking about her husband, an ex-pat Portuguese from a banking family. There'd been no children and he'd been dead for more than twenty years. Apparently, he'd left her with a fair amount of money, so while she was not terribly wealthy, she could live "comfortably" as she phrased it. She explained that though she had married and used the prefix "Mrs.", she had kept her maiden name of Gabrielle Braganza.

The topic of money finally brought her to the topic of why she wanted to speak with the Ambassador. "I've been reading in newspapers in recent months that with the collapse of those horrible Communist regimes in Eastern Europe, a number of those royal families that had been forced to flee right after the war were thinking of returning. Hungary and Romania are supposedly contemplating creating some political system with a royal family like the United Kingdom has. There has even been talk of those families getting back their properties in those countries. My father had been overthrown by a Socialist revolution and I want back from the current Portuguese Government the properties of the Braganza family, which were confiscated in 1912. I was discussing with Colonel North a few weeks ago about whether I might be able to get the American Government's support on this matter and he suggested that I bring the matter up directly with Ambassador Brown."

"Where and when did you meet with Ollie North?" asked an amazed William.

"No, I don't believe his Christian name was Ollie. I think it was Mark. I have his card over in that desk somewhere if it really matters. He's temporarily assigned at NATO command here in Portugal. He's a very nice gentleman. Have you met him?"

"No, I don't get out to the NATO Headquarters very often." William tried not to blatantly breathe a large sigh of relief from learning that it was a different Colonel North entirely!

"I'm not interested in all the properties, but I definitely want back what is now the Presidential Palace, the Foreign Ministry and the Justice Ministry. I have a detailed list here in my case."

"Very well. I think I have a complete picture of the issue so that I can explain it to the Ambassador and I'll let you know within 24 hours as to whether he will want to meet with you." William didn't have the heart to tell her in person that the Ambassador wouldn't give a damn about her claim on Portuguese Government property – that he'd only sent William because everyone feared she'd been in touch with the infamous Ollie North. He'd at least let her live in hope for a day before he phoned her and explained that while Ambassador Brown was sympathetic with her situation, she would have to negotiate this domestic matter directly with the Portuguese Government.

As he prepared to leave, she forced upon him the attaché case which contained all of her photos and documents. "You will need these to fully present my case to Ambassador Brown."

"Of course, thank you. I'll get these safely back to you in just a day or two." He then made a hasty exit.

As he was getting into his car parked in front of the hotel, two northern European-looking gentlemen sitting in a non-descript Ford across the street from the Hotel entrance caught his attention. They looked like two Hollywood, Grade-B movie thugs and they seemed to be watching the hotel. Their car didn't move when he left so he doubted that he'd been the focus of their attention. There were probably twenty guests staying in the small hotel, so that made for twenty possibilities of who they were interested in at that residence. Or, it could be that William was just being a little paranoid and the two were sitting in that car for one of a dozen other plausible and innocent reasons.

As he started the engine, he laughed at what a wasted day he'd spent with Braganza, at least as far as the fear of an Ollie North connection was concerned. Still, all-in-all, he'd heard an interesting three-hour historical story of a fascinating life. He was curious as to who had been her mother. When he'd asked, she simply said that she was not allowed to get into that matter. She knew, but her father had told her that she was to never speak of her mother. William only knew that the "Queen-pretender to the throne" was named after her mother, and that her mother had left for America only a few months after Gabrielle's birth. When she'd met with her father in 1928, he told her that the reason her mother had not been around as she was growing up was because she'd been a very busy woman who'd died in 1920. What more Gabrielle actually knew of her mother, she'd refused to share.

As he pulled away from the hotel, he remembered that the Algerian Embassy was hosting a National Day reception that afternoon. He checked his watch. It began in twenty minutes, as he recalled. He didn't actually have an invitation. As a mere second-secretary, generally he didn't merit receiving invitations to diplomatic functions being hosted around Lisbon. However, he'd learned over the years that as long as one was well-dressed, rarely did any junior flunky at the front door actually ask you to produce an invitation. Sometimes, William would simply carry in one hand an empty white envelope, the size of which usually contained such formal invitation cards. He'd express salutations in English and a broad smile for whatever celebration it was that day. He'd also try to strike up a conversation with whomever else was going up the sidewalk to the front door of the event. His theory was, if he looked like a diplomat and seemed to know another diplomat or two, surely he was supposed to be there.

Aside from wanting to attend the reception in the ever wishful hope of any case officer that he'd meet some worthwhile target, his experience over the years had been that Algerian embassies always served very good food at their national day receptions. Dozens of people were flowing through the Embassy's grand front entrance and nobody was checking for invitation cards. Strictly speaking, they did not serve alcohol at Algerian receptions, and indeed they did not in the main room of the affair. However, they had a small bar in a side room, where bottles of wine and liquor were kept down out of sight. In this discreet fashion one could get something better than the fruit juices being served elsewhere. William headed straight for this hidden bar and ordered a Scotch on the rocks. It wasn't 18-year-old Oban, but it was drinkable.

Another gentleman of about fifty, also by himself and speaking Portuguese also ordered a Scotch. The stranger, probably a European, was dressed in a nice suit, but not an expensive one. He had black hair, thick bushy eyebrows, a swarthy complexion and what William vaguely considered "Mediterranean" facial features. Somewhere down in the Balkans, or even Turkish, was William's first guess. He was suffering from a bit of middle-age, mid-waist expansion, but nothing too serious. Once they both had their drinks and had stepped away from the bar, William greeted him, in Portuguese, and offered a toast, "To the people of Algeria."

The stranger smiled, repeated the toast and took a good-sized swallow of his drink.

Continuing in Portuguese, he said, "I'm William Wythe of the American Embassy," and extended his hand.

"I'm First Secretary Yordan Stambolov, from the Bulgarian Embassy."

"A pleasure. Have you been in Portugal long?"

"Almost four years, and you?"

"I only arrived about eight months ago, so I'm still learning my way around the city, and determining where the decent bars are."

They both laughed. "Well, Mr. Wythe, give up now about learning the streets. Once you're in the old part of Lisbon, you'll never know where you are and you'll find that every one-way street is always going in the opposite direction than you wish to travel."

Again, they laughed. Both gentlemen had drained their glasses. William raised his empty glass, looked at it and said, "I guess since we are right here by the bar, we might as well get another round."

Yordan smiled. "An excellent suggestion. I think the Ambassador can afford two more glasses of Scotch for his thirsty guests."

Once they had new drinks, the two then moved off to a semi-quiet spot by some potted palms and continued their conversation, covering the usual get-acquainted topics of family, previous postings, have you ever visited my country, etc.

After about ten minutes, William had decided that Yordan was a Bulgarian intelligence officer and it was time to end their first encounter. He didn't want to look like some pushy CIA officer, trying to learn too much about the Bulgarian at their first meeting. His suspicion that Yordan was intel was because of the way he conducted their conversation. He made no inquiry as to what "portfolio" William handled in which section at the American Embassy – that was practically the first question out of any real diplomat's mouth after an introduction. The opposite number quickly wanted to learn if the other man was worth knowing. Could he elicit any good rumors from him on whatever issues he was covering for his embassy? Yordan simply asked personal questions, so he'd know enough to be able to request a name trace from his Headquarters about his new "friend." The same was true for William's behavior.

William proffered his calling card and stated, "I hope that we meet again in the future." Yordan did the same and then the two men moved on around the reception hall. William never suggested with "hard targets" at a first encounter a specific plan for having a lunch or coffee or anything else in the future. He calculated that such behavior made you look like an overeager CIA guy. Lots of diplomats from the Commie countries would overlook the fact that you might be a CIA officer; they just didn't like pushy ones. He'd keep an eye out for Yordan on the diplomatic circuit for future opportunities to chat. In the meantime, he'd send into Headquarters a request for information about his new Bulgarian friend. William was certain that the response would come back positive that he was an officer of the DS, the Bulgarian External Intelligence Service. William grabbed several nice shrimps being offered by the tuxedoed waiters, shook a few more hands and then headed for the door. He'd met one interesting person – that was enough for one afternoon.

CHAPTER 4

WWII

Late July 1944; Budapest, Hungary

After the Allies had successfully landed at Normandy on June 6, 1944 and were steadily pushing forward through France that summer, Admiral Miklos Horthy, the leader of Hungary, was beginning to have doubts about his alliance with Hitler and the Nazis. The Russian Red Army was also rapidly moving westward through Romania and Bulgaria. A Hungarian official near Horthy, secretly working for the British, passed word of Horthy's concerns and his contemplation of withdrawing from the war to a British Special Operations Executive officer working in Hungary. SOE officer Nigel Brooks managed through this intermediary to arrange a secret meeting with Horthy one Saturday afternoon at the Admiral's hunting lodge on the outskirts of Budapest. Brooks wished to discuss with Horthy the possibility of Hungary unilaterally announcing a ceasefire before the Red Army entered Hungarian territory. Admiral Horthy was a realist and could see the handwriting on the wall as to how the war was going to end. His goal was to negotiate the best deal for his country that he could. He'd already been considering seeking such an armistice with the Red Army, so he was happy to meet with a representative of the British Government and discuss options. Aside from the big picture issues, he had one personal demand of Brooks and the SOE.

After arriving at the back door of the lodge, Brooks was relieved to see that he had not been led into a trap, but was quietly ushered into the main room and introduced to the Admiral. He'd seen a few pre-war pictures of Horthy, but the man who stood before him looked very exhausted and many years older than he had in 1938. Using German as their common language for discussion, the two politely discussed the progress of the war to date for the initial fifteen minutes.

"Admiral, it seems that you've been the 'Acting' Head of State of Hungary for many years. How is it that you came to this position?"

Horthy laughed. "Through no desire of my own I can assure you. A bit of Hungarian history for you Mr. Brooks. Charles IV, the last king of Hungary, was dethroned in November 1918, with all the chaos that came with the end of the Great War. The King said that he would play no role in the administration of the country in the future, but he did not abdicate his throne. There was then a brief Communist government of about four months, but then Bela Kun was overthrown in a popular uprising. The National Assembly that was formed voted to remain as the Kingdom of Hungary, but did not invite the last king back to rule – thus it needed a regent. That was me. I was elected Regent on March 1, 1920 and still am till this day." Horthy laughed.

"Well, let us turn to the proposal that I bring you today. And I am speaking on behalf of Prime Minister Churchill." This would have been news to Mr. Churchill, but Brooks figured he'd be forgiven that exaggeration if Horthy did agree to an armistice. "Given the direction of the war, particularly the rapid advance of the Red Army, I'm suggesting that you unilaterally announce an armistice with the Allies and remove Hungary from the war." Nigel may not have spoken with Churchill, but he knew the P.M. would be very happy if he could somehow keep the Russians from occupying Hungary.

"It's an interesting proposal, but I must give it some thought as there will be repercussions from the other direction. Herr Hitler will not take kindly to such an announcement. And I would also need one personal favor granted me by your Government. I want a small package containing my personal wealth safely transferred to Portugal and secretly stored there for me until after the war."

Brooks responded that it unlikely that London would agree to such a transfer, as the British could not know from where that wealth came from. And even physically doing it would be very tricky. However, this personal favor seemed to be the only sticking point to an agreement, so Brooks claimed that he would consult London via wireless and return the following Saturday with an answer.

Admiral Horthy stood and stated, "Until next Saturday." He then simply turned and left the room.

Brooks knew what London's answer would be to such a proposal so he didn't even bother asking SOE Headquarters. Instead, he sent a coded message directly to his SOE colleague and friend in Lisbon, Tristan Trafalgar Nelson. They'd spent six months together during their paramilitary training and had become very close. Nigel also had the feeling that Tristan had very flexible scruples, if there was something in it for himself.

While waiting for Brooks to supposedly check with London, Horthy directly approached the Portuguese Chargé in Budapest, Carlos de Liz-Texiera Branquinho, and sought personal assistance with transferring his "wealth." Horthy had had a good relationship for several years with the last Ambassador, Carlos Sampaio Garrido, who'd been recalled a few months earlier. Horthy had turned a blind eye while the Portuguese Embassy had helped thousands of Jews avoid being sent to concentration camps in Germany by issuing very questionable Portuguese identity documents to them. Horthy offered Branquinho continued recognition of such Portuguese documents, if he helped Horthy get a personal box to Portugal for safe keeping until the end of the war. The Chargé was at first optimistic, but a few days later told Horthy it couldn't be done. Sending any diplomatic pouch in wartime would be difficult and expensive. It would require Portuguese Prime Minister Salazar's personal approval and he would want to know exactly what was going on. The Chargé also discreetly speculated that Salazar would probably want a sizeable percentage of whatever was being shipped. Horthy had no interest in sharing and thus decided to wait to see if the British would agree to his request concerning his treasure.

Horthy waited at his hunting lodge the following Saturday, hopeful that Brooks would have positive news from London. After the opening minutes of polite conversation, Nigel began by saying that he would need to know precisely what would be in the box Horthy wanted taken to Portugal.

Horthy remained silent for several seconds, but saw that he had no other option. "Very well. Another lesson in Hungarian history for you. Shortly after I took over as the Regent, the royal jewel maker in Budapest discreetly came to me and asked what he should do with the safe full of the diamonds, rubies and sapphires that belonged to the King. The "jeweler" said that he had kept the jewels hidden during Bela Kun's reign of 133 days and the general chaos after the armistice of November 11, 1918. I quietly took control of the jewels, to wait and see what became of Charles IV and just sat on them."

"You were certainly in a most peculiar situation," replied Nigel.

"After the King died on the island of Madeira on April 1, 1922, I didn't know who exactly owned the jewels, but they were in my possession. The jeweler had also died in 1921, so nobody other than myself even knew of the treasure's existence. If the monarchy was ever restored, they would be at the ready for the next king. If there never was another king, well, I had a nice rainy-day fund." Horthy and Brooks both smiled. "I had no intention of turning them over to the chaotic fools running the country in those years. At this point, I believe the treasure is as much mine as anyone else's."

"I agree that they are as much yours as anybody's and once the war is over, you will of course need personal funds to get by on — as will we all." The two then sat there in silence for several long seconds, staring at each other, before Nigel again spoke. "I can personally arrange through a colleague of mine in Portugal to transport your box of personal items for safe storage in Lisbon."

Horthy smiled with pleasure, until he heard the next sentence.

"However, my friend and I will both want ten thousand American dollars for making this happen."

After a long silence and seeing no other option, Horthy leaned forward in his chair and shook Nigel's hand. "Very well. We have an agreement."

Over the next several minutes, they worked out a mechanism whereby the "friend" would hide the jewels in Portugal, then return to Budapest to tell only Horthy the secret location of the treasure. The discussion ended with Horthy saying, "I remind both you and your friend that if either of you try to trick me, I still have a very long arm and both of you would come to regret it." There was no smile on his face.

"Understood. Your payment in cash to both of us is quite sufficient."

All went as planned, except that by the time Tristan Nelson returned to Budapest in late October to personally tell Admiral Horthy where he had hidden the jewels in Portugal, Horthy had been kidnapped by the Nazis and taken to Schloss Hirschberg in Bavaria. They'd taken his son, Miklos Jr., a prisoner as well and put him into a concentration camp. To save his son's life, Horthy had revoked the armistice with the Red Army, but it didn't really matter, the Nazis had already taken direct military command of Hungary. It also made no difference as the Red Army kept moving forward and eventually had complete control of the country in any case. Horthy would be treated quite well at the castle in Germany, but he was a prisoner. As the U.S. Army advanced through Bavaria in spring 1945 and neared the castle, the Nazi guards fled and the Americans took him into custody. He was questioned about numerous Nazi leaders, but never charged himself with war crimes.

Back in Budapest in October 1944 when first taken away by the Nazis, it wasn't clear if Horthy would ever be returning, would be shot, or just what would be his fate. Tristan learned of Horthy's disappearance only when he returned to Budapest. He went ahead and gave Nigel a cryptic message for Horthy, just in case Horthy did ever return, that only the Admiral would understand as to where the jewels were hidden. On Tristan's secret travel back out of Hungary, he simply disappeared. Reports filtered back to Nigel that Tristan had run into a group of the pro-Fascist Arrow Cross Party, and had been shot. That was the last that the SOE heard of him, even back in Portugal, and he was presumed dead.

In December 1944, Nigel was wounded in fighting in Hungary and was medevacked first to southern Italy and finally back to England. He had no idea whether Horthy was alive or dead. The Regent simply had never returned to Budapest. Nigel's best guess was that he was dead. SOE HQS had gotten wind of Tristan's travels out of Portugal, even though his trips had not been officially authorized, but London had no idea of exactly where he'd gone or why. For a while the British Army even had him listed as a deserter, but with the end of the war, it was a lot easier to clean up awkward administrative details by simply listing people as M.I.A. He had no spouse listed, so there wasn't any question of owing anybody any money. His parents had been killed in the blitz back in the 1940, so it was easiest to just let matters rest.

Nigel was finally demobilized in late 1945 and was hanging around London with friends he'd made while in the SOE – a number of them from very upper-class families. MI6 and the SOE had attracted a lot of such men and women, because many of them had had the benefit of travel around Europe in their school years and had learned foreign languages – exactly the people those agencies had been seeking during the war. It was through such contacts that Nigel came into social contact in late 1945 with Gabrielle Braganza. She was a bit vague with Nigel about her background, but he judged from her behavior and circle of acquaintances that she was clearly from a wealthy, royal family. Apparently, she'd spent most of the war years at one royal estate or the other in England and knew Princesses Elizabeth and Margaret well. She was also quite attractive and charming.

CHAPTER 5

Lisbon, 1990

*A*fter the Algerian National Day reception, William simply headed for home that dreary and overcast Tuesday afternoon. Rain would begin at any moment. It never snowed in Lisbon, but William was discovering that in late fall that it certainly did experience cold rain with some frequency. It was only three o'clock and he could have gone back to the Embassy to report the results of his meeting with Senhora Braganza. However, since it had turned out to be a Mark, not Ollie, North with whom she'd met, there was nothing significant to report to the Embassy. Besides, he figured he'd just let the Ambassador and the other great minds who'd come up with the plan of making him the potential fall guy await the results until Wednesday morning. When he arrived home, his first task was to make himself a decent drink! He'd had enough of mint tea that day to last a month and the quality of Scotch being offered at the reception had left much to be desired. He filled a cut crystal whiskey glass with a generous portion of Oban single malt over lots of ice and headed over to the couch in his living room. He liked the tinkling sound ice made as it bounced against the glass. Some people found wind chimes soothing. William found the faint sound of tinkling ice equally so.

He settled down on the comfy couch in his den and sat the old lady's large attaché case of memories on the coffee table in front of him. After several long sips of his single malt, he turned his attention to the case. He opened it and started going through her souvenirs of a lifetime. After a quick perusal of everything, he randomly decided to explore Volume III of a dozen small, leather-bound personal diaries. This one covered from the end of WW II in May 1945 till January 1948. He propped up his feet on the coffee table and began to read the entries of a woman who was then in her mid-thirties. As she'd been educated in England from an early age, she wrote in English. She had a delicate and steady hand and she made very intelligent observations about the people she encountered.

She recorded in her diary that in October 1945 she'd met British Army Captain Nigel Brooks at a party in London. She described him as tall, with dark brown hair and delicate features in his late twenties. He'd been in the Special Operations Executive. This was the secretive, behind-enemy-lines group created by Prime Minister Churchill to "set Europe ablaze." She'd found it quite interesting that he'd spent most of 1944 within Hungary. She was also clearly quite taken by the fact that he was very handsome and charming. He'd been wounded in his right leg in early 1945 and had been brought home to England, where he'd spent the rest of the war. He still walked with a slight limp because of that wartime injury.

There were several other short entries about Brooks throughout that fall. She noted that he was from a simple, working-class background, but he had many upper-class friends because of the war. William decided from her entries that she seemed to be genuinely fond of Nigel. Her comments starting in mid-December about their relationship got quite interesting. He refreshed his drink and then read on:

"December 13, Friday — Nigel invited me to go spend this coming weekend with him out at Aylesbury. He said there was a lovely inn there, where we could relax and enjoy the countryside. I suspect he has more on his mind than 'enjoying' just the countryside. A 'goal' I am not totally against myself. We've been getting more and more intimate, but there is only so much one can do in the back of a taxi. He shares a small flat with two other former soldiers, which affords us no privacy.

December 16, Monday — We arrived by train late last Friday afternoon and took a nice stroll around the small village before dinner. The buildings were all at least two hundred years old and there was a lovely, old stone church, St. Mary's, at the end of the main street. The food at the inn was quite good and we were starting on our third bottle of wine. Nigel began telling me about one important operation he'd undertaken in Hungary in October 1944. He was clearly trying to impress me, so as to get me to go to his bedroom after dinner instead of back to mine. I was more than ready after the first bottle, but I didn't wish to interrupt his well-thought-out strategy to achieve that goal.

He told me over dessert that he'd been conducting secret negotiations in early fall 1944 with Admiral Horthy, the Regent of Hungary, about pulling his country out of the war. If he did that, Horthy first wanted a favor from the SOE – the smuggling of his personal wealth to Portugal and to have it stored there, until he could retrieve it after the war. Nigel finally agreed, but he had to do it 'unofficially' with the help of his SOE colleague and friend Tristan in Lisbon.

Tristan came to Budapest, took a case of jewels to Portugal and then returned several weeks later to Budapest in order tell only Horthy directly where he'd hidden the jewels. Unfortunately, the Nazis had arrested Horthy and his family and taken them to Germany before Tristan returned to Hungary. In case Horthy ever did return, Tristan left a message with Nigel that only Horthy would understand. 'Go sleep in the main bedroom where your mistress spent her 21st birthday. The treasure is in the obvious place. Your son will know the combination.'

Nigel told me that Tristan was killed by Hungarian fascists while leaving Hungary that second time and Nigel had heard nothing more about Horthy by late-1945. He presumed he was dead too. Nigel joked that now only he knew where Horthy's treasure was hidden – and someday he'd just go get it for himself and me. Not sure I believe Nigel's story, but we did have a wonderful weekend in Aylesbury, what little we saw of it!

January 1st, Wednesday — Plans for New Year's Eve with Nigel never happened. I just learned this morning that sadly a bus had hit and killed him crossing the street yesterday. I now feel terrible for having cursed his name last evening when he never showed up to take me to the party. The leg wound he suffered in January 1945 had left him with a limp and he couldn't move quickly, which is what might have caused his accident. How ironic to have survived five years of war and then be killed by a London bus. That was the last I ever heard about the treasure, assuming that his fanciful story was even true. Both Brits who knew where the treasure had been hidden are dead and probably Horthy himself is as well"

William was fascinated by the diary entry, though like Braganza herself had been, he was skeptical of the tale. Nigel might well have simply invented the whole story as a way to try to get Gabrielle in bed. He'd seen several photos of her during the war and she was certainly worthy of lying to in order to seduce her. He swung his legs up onto the sofa and stretched out. He laid there on his floral print couch for almost an hour without moving. The first ten minutes were spent thinking about the missing wealth of Admiral Horthy.

He then began comparing his life to Gabrielle's. They were different in many ways of course, but there were similarities as well. She'd certainly led a very interesting life that had crossed paths with many important people of the twentieth century. He'd also met during his career a number of government leaders and many diplomats from a variety of countries. And he'd met many American congressmen and senators when they were on "fact finding" trips to embassies where he'd been posted.

As for his Agency record, a smile actually came to his face when he thought about that. The last decade hadn't been much, but he recalled a number of good recruitments during his first two decades in the espionage business. William recalled that one of his instructors early in his training had called him a "natural." By that, he meant that people felt comfortable talking to him and he had a talent for getting them to reveal to him fairly soon in their relationship what was truly important to them. William could then decide whether there might be something he could offer to them – should something be lacking in their lives – and all they had to do in return was provide him secrets of their governments. It was all the same game regardless of the different cultures of his targets. Some might take longer to reach a decision, the Chinese being the slowest, but the motivations were universal.

The Soviet diplomat he'd recruited on his second tour abroad did it for ideological reasons. He'd actually believed that giving the American Government secrets would somehow eventually lead to a new system of government in the U.S.S.R. with civil liberties and democracy for all. William was himself skeptical that the CIA obtaining such secrets was what had finally brought down the Communist regimes of Russia and Eastern Europe in 1989 and 1990, but who knew – perhaps the cumulative effect of all the intelligence gathered had led to an American foreign policy that had at least helped kick the Commies to collapse.

The Chinese diplomat he'd recruited years earlier had said "yes" for the goal of a better life for his family, for the future of his young daughter in particular. He had no delusions that he was bringing change to the lives of a billion people. He just wanted to help his daughter and that required money to pay the needed bribes. As he lay there on his couch, for the first time in his life he wondered what had become of some of the people he'd recruited ten or fifteen years earlier. Unfortunately, for reasons of compartmentation, once a case officer moved on after the initial recruitment, that officer generally never had anything else to do with the case. William thus really didn't know what had happened to those men in subsequent years. Had they in fact eventually made it to America, or had they wound up in prison cells, or worse?

The cynical ones who'd agreed to cooperate simply because they wanted more money in their lives probably did wind up happier – presuming they'd never been caught. A Bulgarian from twelve years earlier came to mind. He'd simply wanted more money to give him and his wife a better life and also to fund his chasing women on the side. Plus, he'd liked to gamble, but was not good at it. He'd stolen money from his Embassy with which to gamble to try to make up for his initial losses — and of course he'd then lost that money as well. Unfortunately for him, but fortunate for William, auditors were coming soon from Sofia and the man needed a quick "loan" from a friend. William and the CIA were happy to make him that loan. He'd never read of any Bulgarian spy scandal over the subsequent years with that fellow's name mentioned, so perhaps he had survived and was still enjoying his married life, his chasing other women and his gambling.

As for the three recruitments of his who'd had ideological motivations and had wanted to eventually move to America – the shining land of the free – well, concerning those, he was doubtful if in the end they'd found life in America all they'd hoped it would be. Not that America didn't have freedoms and opportunities unknown in much of the world. However, the real America could never have lived up to the high expectations those three individuals had held in their minds when they'd agreed to spy for that mythical land in their minds called America. William had never lied to any of his recruits, but on the other hand, he'd never considered it his duty to shatter illusions that targets of his had held as to how much their lives would improve with that extra money or that home in America. Yes, lots of diplomats around the world had dreams and delusions of what the future held, including himself. With such thoughts, he fell asleep.

When he awoke an hour later, it was because his stomach was growling. He realized that he'd never had lunch and he staggered, still half asleep and half-drunk into the kitchen. After a can of soup and a peanut butter and jelly sandwich, he phoned for a taxi and headed for the jazz club. Having spoken in Portuguese for almost three hours that day, his brain was tired. His command of the language was quite good, but spending hours thinking and speaking in a language not your mother tongue wore out a person, at least it did William. He was glad that there were few customers there that evening, as he wasn't really in the mood to be sociable and charming. His Brazilian friend, Olivia, was there and he did chat with her during his breaks. She too had had a long, hard work day and had come that night to the club to take her mind off her job. So, neither were exactly at their best that evening.

She did have a proposal for him. "There's a new film that just opened at the cinema in Cascais, called *The Thief*. It's actually a Portuguese production about a jewel thief in Lisbon. As you probably know, many films shown here are made in Brazil, but this is actually a Portuguese movie, which is supposed to be quite good. Could I interest you in going with me tomorrow evening to see it?" While they'd been chatting at the club for several months, this was the first time there'd be any discussion of "going out."

In general, William avoided mixing his social life with his piano gig, but he had quite enjoyed conversing with her over the past few months and she certainly was attractive. After a few seconds of awkward silence, he managed to get out of his mouth, "Yes, that would be lovely." He thought about suggesting they have an early dinner before the movie, but he decided that that sounded too much like a "date." "Would you like for me to pick you up or shall we just meet at the cinema?"

Him picking her up and then returning her to her apartment later in the evening sounded to her too much like a "date" and so she replied, "I'll be running around on several errands late tomorrow afternoon. I'll just meet you there at the entrance at say 7:00 p.m. The film starts at 7:15."

He gave her a big smile. "Excellent, I'll meet you there tomorrow evening." He checked his watch. "We'll I better get back to the piano."

Tuesday had been a long and busy day and he slept hard that night.

When he awoke the next morning, he was still in the exact same position as when he'd crawled into bed. He rose early and had a long, hot shower. He remembered how he and his dead wife used to enjoy showering together. He had a small mirror fastened in the shower and used an old-fashioned straight razor with a pearl handle to shave close. Some mornings his hands were a little shaky from the previous night's drinking and he had to settle for an electric razor, but he preferred the ritual and results of a blade.

He arrived promptly at 8:30 a.m. Wednesday morning at the Embassy. That was the official starting time for work and William tried to always be at his desk precisely on time. It would be hard to prove if William was "hung over" in the morning, but "arriving late" was quantifiable and he didn't want to give the COS any easy grounds for requesting his recall.

A quick check of the phone directory for staff out at the nearby NATO base confirmed that there was indeed a recently arrived U.S. Marine Colonel Mark North assigned there. His first step was to report the "good" news to the COS that it was a Mark North, not Ollie North, who'd been in touch with Braganza. As soon as Elliot heard that fact, he had no further interest in anything else that William had learned from his lengthy chat with the charming old lady.

Elliot then met alone with the Ambassador and passed along the good news that the unknown caller had been recommended to seek an appointment with him by Marine Colonel Mark North, not the infamous one. The COS never allowed anyone from the Station other than himself to meet with the Ambassador. Both the COS and the Ambassador found it amusing that the woman wanted back the major government buildings of Lisbon, and were relieved that there was no connection to Ollie North. End of story as far as both of them were concerned and certainly no need for the Ambassador to meet with her.

After his meeting with Ambassador Brown, the COS instructed William to simply phone the woman back that day and tell her the

Ambassador had no time to meet with her. William did quickly write up a one-page memo for the record about the meeting with Senhora Braganza. Fortunately, as a last-minute thought, he also briefly mentioned his noticing two gentlemen, who looked like gangsters from a 1930s movie, sitting in a car outside of her hotel. He wrote that they appeared to be watching the hotel and had not followed him when he left. Those last few sentences would soon come to be quite important.

In fact, for almost a week, William had had a feeling that he was under surveillance as he came to work or went about the city. He'd not been able to confirm this gut feeling by seeing repeat license plate numbers or anything as firm as that. It was simply an impression he had when he'd noticed for example that a car had stayed in his side mirror's blind spot for several blocks, but then it would turn off at an intersection as he continued on straight. Or, he'd see a car with two passengers that always stayed sixty or seventy yards behind him – never getting closer despite William speeding up or slowing down in the traffic. Each Friday, all case officers were to file an electronic report on any incidences of suspected or confirmed surveillance. No one had actually reported "confirmed" surveillance since he'd arrived in Lisbon eight months earlier. A few officers had occasionally noted something suspicious, but William suspected that some if not all of those reports were put in there just to show the COS that they were taking his instructions seriously. After some hesitation, he did write up his suspicions of surveillance in the weekly report. He downplayed it as just "gut feelings" as he didn't want his colleagues to think he was being paranoid and getting surveillance when no one else at the Station was seeing any coverage. This report was also about to play a very important role in his life.

His "suspicions" were in fact true. The Agency's special CI team of ten surveillants with five vehicles had had him under surveillance for the past six days, but they were very good and they were keeping a very loose circle around him. They also changed rental cars every second or third day, so he would not see "repeats" of car color or plate numbers of any vehicle he might have even suspected.

William had brought into the Embassy that morning the old gal's attaché case of memories. Given his quick dismissal from the COS' office, he figured there was no point in even bothering to mention to him what he'd read the previous night in her diary about the Hungarian jewels hidden somewhere in Portugal. It was probably all fantasy anyway, but he might personally look into the story himself – even if only for amusement. On the other hand, should he be able to stumble across a "bag of treasure", well, that might make a nice retirement plan. He knew of many senior Agency officers who'd retired on a Friday and by Monday had been hired by various beltway consulting firms at two or three times their previous week's government salary and were back doing practically the same job. If they could feather their retirement nests in that way, why shouldn't he benefit from finding some missing WW II loot? "Treasure" of some kind for which there probably wasn't any documented ownership. The Kingdom of Hungary no longer existed. And even if Horthy had any descendants, he doubted if any court would be inclined to return anything to a WW II dictator and ally of Hitler. He hadn't a clue where to begin his search for the alleged jewels, but figured he should start with learning more about Horthy and the others mentioned in the diary. Had Horthy actually been killed by the Germans in October 1944? Could he somehow learn more about Nigel Brooks and this Tristan of the British SOE in Portugal, who'd supposedly actually hidden the jewels? Both had been dead for some 45 years, but still it would be good to at least confirm that such men had existed. In the decades since the end of WW II, many books had been written about the exploits of the SOE. William was acquainted with the British Military Attaché in Lisbon who was a bit of a history buff. He'd arrange to meet soon with Colonel Clarke and inquire of him the names of any good books on the wartime SOE. He might even have some handy in his personal library.

William waited until after lunch before calling Senhora Braganza. He wanted it to appear that the Ambassador had at least taken some time before making his decision about her request. He would inform her, as gently as he could, that the Ambassador had declined to meet with her. William was prepared to lie to her that he'd fought like a lion on her behalf, but that Ambassador Brown felt strongly that it would be inappropriate for him to get involved in such a domestic Portuguese issue. However, when he phoned, the hotel desk clerk informed him that Mrs. Braganza was no longer staying at the hotel, and refused to provide any further details. William thought that very strange – she hadn't said a word about planning to check out from the hotel just twenty-four hours earlier. He was debating what step to take next when two other officers came into his office to speak with him and he became distracted. He'd try again later when perhaps someone else would be on duty at the front desk. He'd given her his calling card at their meeting. If she had changed hotels, perhaps she would take the initiative and phone him yet that afternoon.

William made sure he was at the entrance to the Cascais cinema five minutes before the agreed-upon time with Olivia Wednesday evening and had the tickets in hand. Upon arrival, Olivia looked lovely, as she always did. This evening in a cream cashmere sweater and a dark wool skirt with faint stripes to it. His impression was that she must get an excellent discount at her dress store, given the wide range of wardrobe he'd seen her wearing over the past months at the club.

"Good evening," he said as she approached and he leaned in to give her a kiss on each cheek, Brazilian style. If she'd still been single, she would have gotten three. Every Brazilian woman got two. The third kiss for singles was to wish them luck in finding a good husband.

"Good evening. Ah, I see you already have our tickets. There probably won't be a big crowd on a weeknight, but it's hard to tell since this movie has gotten very good reviews. They found two seats away from the other twenty or so moviegoers present – that way they could whisper to each other without disturbing anyone else. It was actually a joint French-Portuguese production, but in the Portuguese language, and very well done. The story was basically of a middle-aged jewel thief named Diego, who was ready to retire, but he needed one more major heist so that he and his much younger and beautiful girlfriend could go live happily and comfortably ever after somewhere along the Mediterranean Sea.

The robbery of a very wealthy German family, living for some reason in Lisbon, was brilliantly planned and executed. William found it interesting that the director had Diego rob a rich German, rather than a rich Portuguese family. Presumably the Portuguese audiences would find that less of an offensive crime and clearly the film was trying to make Diego a sympathetic and likeable character. The slightly inept police lieutenant who was in charge of the investigation was getting nowhere. It appeared as though Diego was going to get away safely. He had only one more step to execute – to pass the jewels to the fence and take the money. The policeman was sitting at a café one night, having drinks with his retired father and complaining of all his problems, when he saw a known fence enter the restaurant and sit down in a quiet corner. He placed a Fodor's travel book of Spain in the center of the table. A few minutes later, a handsome, middle-aged man came over and joined him. They seemed to be having a business discussion and then about ten minutes later, the second man who'd arrived took off his hat and laid it on the table. Shortly thereafter, an attractive, well-dressed woman in her early thirties walked over to them, sat a small briefcase down on the floor between the two men and then walked off without saying a word. The fence picked it up, laid it on his lap and opened it so that only he could see inside it. He smiled and then started taking several thickly-packed envelopes from his inside coat pockets and slid them across the table.

The policeman then went over with his service revolver drawn and arrested both men. End of movie.

William turned his head slowly from side-to-side a few times. "Poor bastard – caught by blind, bad luck," thought William. "He'd executed a brilliant robbery and was only caught at the last moment through sheer bad luck. Two million residents in Lisbon and our likeable criminal chose to meet his fence at a restaurant where the primary policeman chasing him was having a drink."

As the lights came up, Olivia spoke, "So, did you like it?"

"Yes, very much. The film is very well done and Diego is made to appear a likeable character. I think the audience was rooting for him to get away with his girlfriend and live happily ever after."

"Oh, absolutely. From the moment I saw that he had robbed a German, I guessed that he was going to get away safely. Nobody likes rich Germans, so robbing him was acceptable, but then the director tricked us and Diego does get caught. However, I found the finish a little unbelievable. Diego has brilliantly planned his robbery, but then is caught by the fairly hapless policeman simply by bad luck."

"Oh, I suppose such things do happen that way," replied William.

"Perhaps, but after being so clever in the robbery, why would he meet this fence out in a public place?"

"Ah, I see what you mean. Well, I guess the director had to have some way to explain why Diego is caught at the last minute and that crime does not pay – even if it was only a German who'd been robbed!" They both laughed.

William walked her to her car and gave her a brief kiss, American style, before opening her car door. She blew him another kiss as she pulled away. William realized his fondness for Olivia was growing. Too bad, he thought, he was not a successful international jewel thief and he couldn't just go live comfortably on a sundrenched coastline after one last, big score! A wishful smile came to his face as he walked back to his car – but that only happened in the movies.

Chapter 6

*J*ust after lunch on Thursday, Lizzie Lee phoned the COS and asked in her sweet southern drawl that he immediately come to the Ambassador's office. The pace of her speech and the urgency of the request for his presence contradicted each other. When Elliot arrived he found the Embassy's Chief of Security and the DCM already there. Ambassador Brown handed the COS a letter, which had been placed in a plastic sleeve, to keep fingerprints off of it. The letter had arrived that morning at the Embassy through the regular Portuguese postal system, addressed to the Ambassador. As the COS read it silently, the smile disappeared from his face. The Ambassador then requested that Elliot read it aloud for the group. The COS wet his lips and began to read the hand-printed letter.

"I am part of group sent to Lisbon to kill Bill, the CIA man. It will be car bomb. This for what he did in Greece against the fighters of Libya. I soon be father. I want go away with my wife and new child and live peaceful life. I give you facts on assassination team. You give me US$100,000. Why did you not respond to my first letter? If you interested, place ad for used, red Cadillac for $30,000 for sale by US Embassy in this Saturday issue of Correio da Manha and I mail another letter to Ambassador with specifics how to contact me for meet. Be careful with this information. I do not wish to die.

A."

Ambassador Brown spoke first, in his usual slow, monotone voice. "Neither I nor Lizzie Lee remember seeing this 'first letter' that is referenced in this letter. I understand we get dozens of crackpot letters every week, addressed to me or the Embassy in general. Lizzie has told me that the local employees down in the mail room screen everything addressed to me via the public mail service and they simply throw away the crazy or obscene letters. I presume they did so with this fellow's first letter. My initial opinion is that he's some crack pot, but I wanted to hear thoughts from all of you." The Ambassador clearly didn't want any blame for anything being thrown away placed on the local-hire ladies who worked down in the mail room.

The Embassy's Deputy Chief of Mission, Stephan Chesterbrook of the Connecticut Chesterbrooks, endorsed what the Ambassador had just said. He was well known for always agreeing with whatever Ambassador Brown said, wrote or thought. His father and grandfather before him had been ambassadors and he knew well that the fastest path for himself becoming an ambassador was to keep one's current Ambassador happy.

Alex Wilson, the Embassy's Chief of Security then spoke. "I'm paid to be cautious and protect all Embassy personnel and I don't think we can just immediately dismiss this as written by some crack pot. I think we should place the ad in Saturday's paper as requested and see what happens."

The CIA Chief of Station spoke last and smoothed his red striped tie as he began. "Well, as you all know I do have a William on my staff and Bill is of course the familiar of William. And William wrote a memo this very morning concerning his call on Mrs. Braganza at her hotel yesterday, in which he noted that two men in a car appeared to be 'watching' the hotel when he came out. He had not spotted anyone following him from the Embassy to the hotel. Nor did the two appear to follow him when he left there, but it could have been another car that followed him after he left the hotel." He smoothed his tie again and continued, "Perhaps most alarming is that William did serve in Greece about a decade back. Soon as we're done here, I will send an IMMEDIATE precedence cable back to my Headquarters to get their thoughts on this. I'll get back to you Mr. Ambassador before the day is out."

"That's good. We will need to report this threat in State channels as well, but Alex can wait to do that until after you hear back from your people. We'll meet again this afternoon." Ambassador Brown then reached over to a different document laying on his desk and started to read it. His usual indicator that a meeting was over.

However, Alex spoke up before anyone could start rising from their chairs. "Until we have a better idea of what we're facing, perhaps for the safety of William, I will assign a couple of my locally hired security people to escort William home this evening, watch his house all night long and then escort him back to the Embassy in the morning."

The COS started to reject that offer. He didn't want there to be any impression that the Agency had to depend on the State Department for help, but the Ambassador spoke first. "Wouldn't be a bad idea, just to be on the safe side, if the CIA Headquarters doesn't order some other course of action by the end of today. Let's at least cover William till tomorrow morning. And I think it might be prudent to also place a security car tonight at your home, Elliot, and of your deputy."

"An excellent suggestion," quickly responded DCM Chesterbrook, with a serious look upon his face as he nodded in agreement with the Ambassador.

The COS didn't really like the idea, but it wasn't worth arguing with Ambassador about it.

When the COS returned to the Station office space, he quickly called for an all-hands meeting in his office. He read aloud to everyone the letter and solicited their opinions. Thoughts ranged from it being clearly a crank letter to a genuine threat tied somehow with the current Iraq problem. William said nothing. After fifteen minutes, the COS dismissed everyone except William. The COS saw this as a golden opportunity to get rid of him. He indicated for William to close his office door and then retake his seat. Elliot's face was taut and he spoke in very measured tones.

"William, your safety is the first and foremost concern of all of us. I think that for your security that you should go home to Washington D.C., until we can sort this issue out – at least for a week or so. Be a nice vacation for you at government expense. I'll include that recommendation in the cable I'm about to send to Headquarters."

William's eyes narrowed and he spoke very slowly. "I don't concur with that plan at all. That letter refers to 'Bill' and as you and everyone else at this Embassy knows, I always go by 'William.' As for the reference to

Greece, there was a terrorist incident in Athens in which I'd been involved, but that was eight years ago. Who waits eight years to seek revenge, when I've been available for such targeting at other overseas assignments?"

"What actually occurred in Athens?" asked the COS. His brown eyebrows rose dramatically whenever he asked a question. "I saw nothing in your personnel records sent out here to Station about a terrorist incident when you were in Greece." Elliot's fingers of his left hand started to tap on his desk top. An unconscious habit of his when he was irritated.

"There's not much to tell. It was over in less than a minute. Two terrorists, affiliation unknown, charged one evening into a local restaurant which was frequented by US military personnel posted at the NATO offices at Athens. I happened to be there having dinner with a military friend and I was lucky enough to get the AK-47 from one terrorist and then killed him and his colleague. A couple of customers in the restaurant were slightly wounded, but otherwise all ended well."

The COS was amazed at this action by William, the underachieving alcoholic, and even asked him why wasn't that event mentioned in the copy of his personnel records that had been sent out to Station when William had arrived at post?

"That was a long time ago. They gave me the Distinguished Intelligence Cross, but I requested in later years that that not be advertised at future postings. I didn't want to seem to be living on my past performance." William crossed one leg over the other and folded his large hands together across his waistline. His green eyes narrowed.

"And were those two terrorists Libyans?" Elliot's eyebrows again arched as he spoke.

"We never learned anything about them. They had no identification on them and no group ever claimed credit for the attack."

"Hmm, if they had been Libyans, then this letter to the Ambassador would make more sense."

William repeated his point on timing. "If this letter is related to that incident, why have they waited all these years for a revenge attack?"

"I have no immediate answer to that, but I still think it prudent that you temporarily leave the country. You just reported in the weekly surveillance report that you 'felt' you'd recently started getting very discreet surveillance. That could be this Libyan team preparing its strike."

William knew immediately he shouldn't have ever written up that report, given that he'd never been able to confirm the coverage. And now it was being used by the COS against him. "Maybe I had surveillance, but I will still fight the idea of my leaving the country, up to and including to Chief Europe Division – since it is such an unsubstantiated threat."

The COS knew that William and the Chief were longtime friends. And since he'd so resisted William's assignment in the first place, the Chief would probably correctly interpret his recommendation as just a ploy to get rid of William. He knew it would seem a little ridiculous that an officer who'd previously won the highest decoration the Agency awarded for valor under fire in saving others' lives couldn't now take care of himself in these vague circumstances.

"Alright, I'll leave it up to Headquarters. You will, however, take the protective coverage offered by Alex Wilson whether you like it or not."

William reluctantly agreed to the latter and also agreed to start carrying a Browning 9mm sidearm, but insisted that he continue his Agency work and his personal life. He would have been even more dismissive of the alleged threat, had it not been for his recent "feeling" that he was in fact being followed about the city.

As soon as the COS had finished with William, Wilson, the Security officer, asked to see him. The two of them were fairly good friends.

"Just thought you might want to know that soon as you left the meeting with the Ambassador, the DCM suggested to the Ambassador that this anonymous threat might be the perfect occasion to get rid of your entire Station. Or at least, perhaps everyone, but yourself."

"You've got to be joking. What did the Ambassador say?"

"He said he'd give it some thought. As you probably already know, neither of them are big fans of the Agency, especially the DCM. He thinks that the Agency causes more problems than it ever contributes to US foreign policy. That the Agency detracts from the conduct of true diplomacy, blah, blah, blah." Wilson made a gesture with his right hand as if jerking off. They both laughed. "His argument is that with a threat against an Agency officer, we can't know for sure which of you might really be the target and so you all should leave – for your safety. His twisted logic is that he doesn't really care if someone shoots a CIA officer, but he's worried that one of his real Foreign Service employees might be shot by mistake."

"Thanks for telling me. And let me know if you hear anything more on this topic"

After Wilson left, the COS ruminated further on the situation. He was trapped. If he argued that the threat was serious enough to have William withdrawn, the Ambassador could then argue that the entire Station should be sent home for its safety. He'd have to think more about requesting William's "temporary" recall to Washington.

In the end, the COS simply reported the threat to HQS and asked that several security/bodyguard officers travel immediately to Lisbon to aid in providing 24/7 protection of William while this threat was investigated further. In closing, the COS wrote that at some point, the Agency might want to temporarily take William back to Washington for his own safety, but did not insist upon that action at the present time. Before hitting the send key, Elliot again read the message and again smoothed his tie down his chest and stomach. He was very conscious of his recent five pound weight gain and almost subconsciously began doing isometric toning flexes of his abdominal muscles.

His mind then turned to the question of whether this terrorist threat might hurt or help his chance for promotion in the coming year — his primary, personal goal for 1991. The threatening letter would definitely bring a lot of 7th floor attention to Lisbon Station in the coming weeks. In the end, he concluded that this might work out very well for him. Even if William did get killed, he'd still be OK as long as it appeared that he had taken all appropriate steps possible to protect him. With that in mind, he upgraded the precedence of his cable from IMMEDIATE to FLASH. That was the highest precedence there was and was to be used only in cases of an imminent nuclear or terrorist attack, or threat of death of a senior U.S. Government official. The communication computers were programmed so that a cable so marked went to the head of the electronic queue of all other cables as it moved along the encrypted digital highway to reach its intended recipients. A copy would also automatically go the Deputy Director of Operations, the fellow in charge of all CIA clandestine operations.

At times, Headquarters could move as slowly as the U.S. Postal Service, depending on the issue at hand. Safety of its personnel at any post in the world however, was always a top priority concern. Money was never an issue when it came to physical security for its officers in the field. Within five minutes of its arrival at CIA Headquarters that morning, the desk officer for Portugal interrupted a closed-door meeting chaired by Chief Europe Division to hand him a paper copy of the cable. Just so no one could possibly miss the importance of such a cable, the word FLASH was printed in inch-high, red letters across the top and bottom of the cable.

"Shit!" was the Chief's one word response as he rose and left the meeting he was chairing without any explanation to the others around the conference table. A minute later he was on an internal secure phone line to the Deputy Director of Operations. The Agency took threats against the lives of its officers very seriously. There were too many stars already on a wall down in the main lobby to honor those who had died in the line of duty. Below the dozens of stars carved into the marble wall, there was a glass case with a large ledger listing by year the names of the officers who'd made the ultimate sacrifice for their country. Except, that most of the line entries were left blank. If the officer had been serving overseas undercover, only a gold star appeared in lieu of a name. If someone had worked in the shadows, they remained so even in death. Nobody in the Agency, from the DCI down to the lowest cafeteria worker, ever wanted for there to be another star added to the Honor Wall.

The FLASH response back to Lisbon informed them that a five-man security team would be arriving via private jet at 0600 hours Friday morning. It asked that the Station secure whatever formal agreement was necessary from local authorities for these five men to carry weapons. This was actually just a formality. They would be landing with weapons and would carry them whether any local official gave them permission or not. Deputy Chief Europe was currently in Paris and would divert his travel plans to come immediately to Lisbon to assess the situation. His arrival time on Friday would be sent to Lisbon Station as soon as it was confirmed. An Arabic translator, an analyst who specialized on Libyan terrorist groups and a bomb specialist would also arrive along with the security detail, just in case they might be needed to help in the investigation of this threat. A decision on whether to pull William out for his own safety would be made once Deputy Chief Europe arrived and had had a chance to speak with all concerned. Headquarters concurred with the idea of William staying at his own house that night, but suggested that William go home in a car belonging to the Embassy security team, and return on Friday morning in the same manner. Since a bomb was allegedly in the attack plan, he should no longer use his own car for any travel.

The cable ended with the sentence: "Everybody watch your six in these coming days." An old Army phrase referring to the hour markings on a clock and meaning to watch your back. Elliot could be a first-class prick, but he certainly knew how to write a good cable that got everybody's attention back at Headquarters.

After receiving the Headquarters response, the COS went and briefed the Ambassador, DCM and Chief of Security. The Ambassador was very impressed with the speed of the response and the major resources being committed to this alleged threat.

"It sounds as if your Agency is taking this letter very seriously. Do they have any other information to support this threat being genuine?" asked Ambassador Brown.

"If they do, they've not shared it with me. I think their position is simply that until proven otherwise, we have to act as if it is a genuine threat. I'll bring Deputy Chief Europe Division around to meet with you tomorrow once he's arrived from Paris."

"Absolutely. Tell Lizzie to postpone any meetings I have tomorrow out of the Embassy and to interrupt me at any time you need to see me during the day."

"Thank you, Mr. Ambassador." The COS then turned to Alex Wilson. "Alex, if I give you the names of the security detail arriving in the morning, can you take care of any niceties with the Portuguese Judicial Police about our men carrying weapons while in town?"

"I'll do that. They won't like it, but they'll agree."

The Ambassador interjected, "If you get any resistance Alex, tell me and I'll personally call the Minister of Justice!"

"Thank you, sir. I'll call on you if needed. I've already spoken with the Chief of the Lisbon District of the Judicial Police about our 'situation' and he'll have a marked JP vehicle circling around all night long in the area of Estoril where William lives — just to dissuade anybody who might be planning something from doing it this night. There have been a few house burglaries in the neighborhood recently, so residents seeing more of a police presence won't see it as out of the ordinary. In fact, the neighbors have been demanding more patrols anyway."

"What exactly did you tell the JP Commandant was going on?" asked the COS.

"I simply told him that we'd had a threat against an Embassy officer, which we're taking seriously while we investigate it further. He didn't ask for any particulars."

"Well, I think we've done all that can be done today," said the Ambassador, bringing the meeting to an end. He didn't particularly like the CIA, but he took it as a personal affront that some group might be planning on killing anybody on his staff!

CHAPTER 7

*A*t four o'clock, two black, four-door Ford sedans drove out through the big, iron front gates of the Embassy compound. They had regular Portuguese license plates, so nothing linked them to the American Embassy. In the first vehicle were two locally-hired security guards. William sat in the back seat of the second car, and he was accompanied by three more security officers. All of them carried side arms and even William had been issued a 9mm Browning from the Station supply. Personally, he thought it was rather overkill, but he realized that it was the most exciting thing to have ever happened for the Lisbon Embassy security detail and they were going all out to provide William safety.

Enroute to his home, they first made a brief stop at the Hotel Henry the Navigator to return an attaché case to its owner. Chief of Embassy Security, Alex Wilson, had reluctantly agreed to that request and only because no one knew in advance that William would be making such a stop. William had tried phoning Senhora Braganza again around 3:00 p.m., but had again simply gotten the story that she'd checked out of the hotel. So, he decided that with a personal visit to the hotel's front desk, he might be able to learn more. Upon arrival, William had the cars pull over to the curb well before arriving at the main entrance, so as not to draw attention to himself. One guard insisted on accompanying him into the hotel. William asked him to at least wait by the front doors, again so as to keep a low profile. However, as the Portuguese generally were rather short people, at six foot two, asking João to be "low profile" was rather wishful thinking on William's part.

The desk clerk was a man in his early forties, with thick glasses and thinning hair. He'd also been behind the elegant marble front desk two days earlier when Wythe had first called upon Senhora Braganza. As on Tuesday, the man was trying to appear interested in his job, but with as little success today as previously.

"Good afternoon," said William in English, as he approached the desk.

"Good afternoon, sir," replied the clerk in excellent English. "Welcome to the Henry the Navigator. How may I help you?"

"You may recall that I was here two days ago and met with Mrs. Gabrielle Braganza."

"Yes, sir, I remember you," he replied, but William noticed that he reacted a little nervously upon hearing Braganza's name.

"When I phoned earlier today, someone told me that she had checked out. Did she leave a forwarding address or phone number? I need to get back in touch with her."

After first looking to his left and right to confirm that no one was within hearing range, the clerk leaned slightly forward over the counter and lowered his voice. "I'm afraid there was a terrible accident and Mrs. Braganza is dead. She was coming down the grand stairway on Tuesday evening, presumably on her way to dinner, and tripped. An ambulance came, but she was already dead. Truly a tragedy."

William slowly shook his head from side-to-side. "Yes, a tragedy. She was such a charming lady. Have her next of kin been notified?"

"It didn't appear that she had any living relatives, but perhaps the police would know for certain. You might want to check with them."

"Yes, of course, I'll do that." William had Braganza's attaché case in his left hand, but decided not to simply leave it with the clerk. Perhaps if he ever learned of a relative, he'd pass it along to him, or at least to the police. "I'd like to attend any funeral service that will be arranged." He sat down the case and reached for a blank piece of paper on the counter and a pen, upon which to write his name and home telephone number. "I'd greatly appreciate it if you could notify me if you hear of any such service being held, or if any relative comes to the hotel." William took from his wallet an American one hundred dollar note and slowly slid it across the cold marble to the clerk, along with his name and number. William smiled. The clerk removed the sheet and monetary note from the counter without even looking down and placed them in his jacket side pocket all in the same smooth motion. He nodded in agreement and smiled.

"Certainly sir." After receiving the money, the clerk leaned forward again and said, "I heard the police say that it looked as if someone had searched her room. Many things had been pulled out of drawers and thrown on the floor, but our Manager has told all of us to keep that detail strictly to ourselves."

William nodded his understanding for discretion and departed. His large shadow in the lobby to protect him exited the doorway a few seconds after William. As he reached the lead security car, he stopped to tell the driver that he was ready to go home. Once seated in the back seat of his car, he pondered the situation. He realized that elderly people such as Braganza did have accidents, but it was an interesting alignment of coincidences. He called on her, then he saw two "heavies" straight out of an old B-grade gangster movie sitting outside of her hotel, her diary suddenly in his possession talked about a hidden WW II-era treasure and within a day she was dead. William didn't believe in that many "coincidences" occurring naturally.

A half hour later, the two cars pulled up to his modest home in the upper-class suburban neighborhood of Cascais. The security man seated next to him asked for his door key. "Please wait in the car until we have a quick look inside your house."

William handed over the key and told him the five digit security code to turn off the alarm. Five minutes later he was given the OK to go into his house. As he entered, the man who'd just checked out his house said, "Perhaps you just have a very incompetent housekeeper Mr. Wythe, but it appears as though someone has gone through your possessions, looking for something."

William followed the man through all the rooms in silence before speaking. "Yes, indeed. Someone has certainly done a thorough job of searching every drawer and cupboard. Was the security alarm on when you first entered the house?"

"No sir, it was already turned off. Are you sure you set it this morning?"

"Absolutely, I'm always very careful to do so."

"I know you'll need to go back and thoroughly check around the house, but does it appear if anything in particular is missing? Do you have a safe of any kind here in the house?"

"No, no safe. I'll have to go back through the house more carefully, but nothing obvious is missing."

"I need to call Mr. Wilson and let him know what has happened. I'm sure that he'll want to come personally and have a look around the house. In the meantime, we'll wait here with you, if you don't mind?"

"Of course. I'll go ahead and take a more careful look around the house." He carefully shifted Braganza's attaché case from one hand to another. He couldn't imagine what the thieves might have been looking for in the house, but he was glad that he'd taken the case with him to the Embassy that morning.

Actually, his first act was to walk over to the liqueur cabinet and get some ice out of the small fridge built into the cabinet. After placing the ice in a glass, he poured himself a generous portion of single malt whiskey. He drank as he strolled through the house a second time. Nothing seemed to be missing. He took a seat in a comfortable reading chair in his living room. Mr. "six foot two" had taken up a position just inside the front door.

Alex Wilson arrived twenty minutes later. After looking quickly around himself, and discovering a broken pane of glass in the back door, he rejoined William in the living room.

"You told my man that you were certain that you'd set the alarm this morning when you left the house?"

"Absolutely."

"I'm sure you did. This was a first-class job. They put a bypass wire on the backdoor, after they broke the window pane, so it never registered with the alarm box when the door was opened. Then they managed somehow to completely turn off the alarm system. These weren't a couple of misguided teenagers who entered your house."

William smiled. "Glad to hear I merited top-of-the-line burglars."

Alex took William out of hearing range of his locals and lowered his voice. "Were you keeping anything 'job-related' here in the house of special value?"

"No. And so far, I haven't found anything of value that is even missing. The stereo, color TV, all the electronics are still here. They didn't even take the brand new twelve-bottle case of Oban whiskey in my kitchen cupboard, which cost more than the TV!"

Alex shrugged his shoulders. "Maybe they thought there was something here that wasn't. Or maybe someone drove up in front of your house and they panicked. Who knows?"

At that moment, three Judicial Police vehicles pulled up in front of the house. Alex looked out the window. "Oh, I phoned Captain Machado just before I left my house. He said he would be coming over with a few of his men, in case there was anything they could do to help."

"Well, that should give my neighbors something to talk about in the coming days, now that we have six cars parked out front."

"Excuse me a minute. I'll go out and talk to the JP fellows."

William continued to look around the house, but could find absolutely nothing missing. Given the mess made, the thief had clearly wanted him to know they'd been searching for something. He'd have the technical officer from the Station come out tomorrow to do an electronic sweep – just in case the burglary was simply a cover for someone having come in and planted a few microphones around the house.

Alex returned and introduced JP Captain Machado, who immediately went to examine the back door and then wandered around the rest of the house. Fifteen minutes later, he rejoined Alex and William in the living room.

The thirty-something Machado looked good in his perfect-fitting uniform. He'd obviously had it custom-made, which meant he had family money, or he was especially corrupt. The Captain spoke decent English, but he knew that both Americans spoke Portuguese very well, so he began in Portuguese. "I agree with Mr. Wilson. This break-in was conducted by a very professional burglar – not some amateur thief. As for why nothing appears to have been taken – who knows?" He then shrugged his shoulders and turned his two palms up to the sky. "Perhaps someone came and knocked at your door, which scared the thief. Perhaps, you didn't have what the thief was looking for in your house. Not to offend you, but perhaps the thief was looking for expensive jewelry or top-of-the line electronics."

"Well, thank you, Captain, for coming so promptly and checking."

"That is our job Mr. Wythe. Mr. Wilson also told me that there has been some sort of anonymous threat against your life received through the mail. Whether this break-in today is related to that threat or not, I'm going to leave a marked JP car with two of my officers out in front of your house for the rest of the night. We can discuss tomorrow what measures we may introduce permanently in the coming days."

Alex Wilson doubted that was really necessary, but knew it would be insulting if he turned down Machado's offer of protection. "Thank you, Captain, for your kind offer of assistance. I will also be leaving one of our cars here with two men in it and one man inside the house until morning. As you said, we can all discuss tomorrow what further steps we wish to implement in the coming days."

William finally got rid of all his "guests" and was down to just one Embassy security guard in his living room. He phoned Nick at the club and claimed that flu-like symptoms had befallen him and so he wouldn't be playing at the club that night. He retired upstairs to read for a while and went to bed at ten. With Embassy guards and JP officers around and inside his house, he certainly felt secure, but still couldn't immediately fall asleep. He continued to think about just what the burglars had been searching for in his house and his mind kept coming back to Senhora Braganza's attaché case. Around two, he finally fell asleep.

For the drive to the Embassy in the morning, he had the two Embassy security cars and a JP vehicle leading and one ending the procession, so they didn't even have to stop for red lights. William thought it amusing that he had more security than Ambassador Brown normally had when he traveled about in the city.

The unmarked CIA private plane arrived as scheduled at 0600 hours and by the time William and his entourage arrived at the Chancery at 0830, there was quite a team assembled in the Ambassador's personal conference room. Elliot had been at the Embassy since 0600. He wanted all of the visitors from Washington to report back later that he was taking the threat seriously and was on top of all matters, including being in his office at the crack of dawn.

The COS introduced William to the five security/paramilitary officers, the Arabic translator, the Libyan analyst and the bomb expert. The only name Wythe remembered afterwards was Adam Corya, who was in charge of the security officers. All five had short, military-style haircuts, broad shoulders and probably had body fat percentages well below ten percent. All five had in fact previously been in the U.S. Army or Marines. The Agency had discovered that it was easier and cheaper to let the American military train and give experience to such men for 6 or 7 years and then the CIA would simply hire them away for better salaries. William had actually run into Corya somewhere in years past, but couldn't remember exactly where. He appeared to be maybe five years older than the rest of his team, but with equally broad shoulders and a trim waist. William guessed that all five men of the security detail were wearing custom-made sport coats. No department store would normally carry coats in the needed measurements to correctly fit men with their builds.

While being respectful to the COS, Corya quickly took charge of the planning meeting. William found it amusing to watch Adam politely, but firmly make it clear to Elliot it was he who would be making the decisions regarding the security of William or any other Agency officer in Lisbon in relation to this anonymous letter threat. The team had brought light-weight bullet-proof vests for William, the COS and the DCOS, for whom wearing them was not optional. He also had extras for any other Station personnel who wished one as well. Within an hour, Corya had worked out a schedule for who would cover William and when. Since it was allegedly a bomb being planned against William, he would no longer use his own vehicle. When he travelled to and from his home, or anywhere else, he would be in an Embassy general carpool vehicle, which was watched 24/7. One of his men would drive and a second man would sit in the backseat with William. A third man would always be at William's house. Corya accepted having a trail car with a couple of the Embassy local-hire security guards, but rejected having a marked police car. He explained that it simply drew too much attention to the other two cars. A JP car and men permanently outside William's house was fine, as the "bad guys" would probably already know where he lived.

The COS had been in a slow burn for the past hour, but just before the group meeting broke up, he again took control.

"I'm sure there is nothing I can tell any of you gentlemen about how to best carry out a protective mission, but there are some subtle political ramifications that I might have to take care of under certain circumstances."

Corya knew from experience that as soon as some senior official used the phrase, "nothing I can tell any of you gentlemen," that was a sign that he was about to tell them how to do their job.

"A shooting incident on the streets of Lisbon, particularly if any civilians are hurt, would put the Agency and me in a very awkward position. So, before you go pulling your weapons, be absolutely positive that there is an armed terrorist on the scene. Enjoy your stay in Portugal."

As they were walking out of the room, one of the security guards commented softly to another, "Would it be OK if we just accidentally shot that arrogant twit?"

Unfortunately for him, team leader Corya overheard the comment and gave him an unpleasant look. At a private team meeting a few minutes later, Corya addressed his men on the upcoming assignment. He finished on the subject of the COS. "I know that the COS can be a little brusque, but I asked around at Headquarters about him before we left. He has a good rep – a by the book sort of guy. Hallway rumor has it that he's a real 'climber' so just accept that he wants to guarantee nothing screws up his future promotions and live with it." A "climber" was an informal, derogatory term for an Agency officer who saw his main task as getting promoted, not making recruitments or advancing US foreign policy goals. The danger to those around such people was that they didn't mind on whose backs they stepped on to rise up the promotion ladder. Corya was sure that if anything untoward happened during their assignment of guarding William Wythe, the COS would clearly lay the blame on him and his men.

An hour later, the Ambassador asked the COS and Mr. Corya to come to his office to discuss the security arrangements for William. After Corya finished explaining the plans he'd made, Ambassador Brown raised one small problem, as he called it.

"I was just on the phone with the Portuguese Minister of Justice, under whom the Judicial Police fall bureaucratically. The head of the JP had complained to the Minister that they were being excluded from security measures on William."

"I don't want a marked police car as part of our travel package. It just puts a red flag on our convoy," commented Corya.

"Understandable, so he and I reached a compromise that they can have one unmarked police vehicle in the convoy, which will carry four of their counterterrorist squad men. If some sort of fire fight takes place on the streets of Lisbon, the Minister wants to have Portuguese police officers there."

Corya had had enough losing battle conversations with ambassadors to know that he was not going to win this argument. He gave a look to the COS to see if he wished to enter the discussion. He did not.

"As you wish Mr. Ambassador," was Corya's one sentence reply before he stood to depart the chancery.

The car carrying William would also always have in it a jamming device to interfere with nearby radio wave signals, in case the bad guys had placed a radio-signal detonated bomb somewhere along his usual path and planned to detonate it as William's car passed by. That device was actually loaned to the Americans by the Judicial Police for the duration of the security detail on William, so there was a hidden silver lining to letting them be part of the vehicular convoy. The JP normally used it whenever they had a foreign VIP visiting Lisbon.

After studying Lisbon street maps for an hour, Corya, his team, plus two of the local security men went out to examine in person different potential paths for traveling between Wythe's home and the Embassy. From that evening forward, William's entourage would vary its routes and departure times each day. In which of the three-car entourage William sat would also vary each day. And only Corya and the other Americans would know prior to an actual departure what those details were for each trip. All these steps were designed to make a possible assassination attack harder for the bad guys to execute. However, it was next to impossible to protect someone if the assassin was willing to give up his own life in carrying out an attack.

Charles Earle, the European Deputy Division Chief, arrived at the Embassy at two and immediately met with the COS, then the Ambassador and finally with William. Elliot didn't like to be excluded from the meeting between Wythe and Earle, but when the Deputy Chief said he'd like to meet alone with William, there was little the COS could do, but respond, "Of course. I'll send William right in."

"William, how are you?" asked Charles, as he gave him a firm handshake.

"Well, other than this silly letter business, I'm fine."

"Elliot's pretty concerned about you."

William grinned. "I'm sure he is."

"He thinks you should come back to Washington for your own safety until we have a better idea of what's going on here."

"I'm sure he does."

"Yes, of course he didn't want you here in the first place, did he?" Earle gave him a big smile. "That's why I wanted to talk to you alone. What's your opinion on this threat?"

"Well, it could be real, but so far all we have is this one letter. Could just be some crackpot. I now have more bodyguards than the Prime Minister of Portugal, so until we get something firmer, I think I'm fine right here. If, repeat if, we ever get more intelligence that supports there being a real threat, then we can reevaluate the situation. But for the moment, I see no reason for me to go anywhere."

"Fair enough. I figured that would be your attitude. OK, go out and find Elliot and ask him to come see me please. I'll inform him of my decision."

"Thank you," replied William with some relief in his voice. He started to get up to leave, but then sat back down. "By the way, just between you, me and the Chinese listening devices in the wall, what is Elliot's background? He seems rather young to be a GS-15."

Charles grinned. "I don't really know that much about him. He's home based in Latin America division. Rumors are that he made some spectacular recruitment a few years back at his last assignment down in South America. Immediately, he went from being rated just your average case officer who'd just made GS-14 to being considered a super star and instantly promoted to 15. Then he was offered the Lisbon job." Charles shrugged his shoulders in befuddlement. "Case of just being in the right place at the right time I guess."

"OK, thanks. I was just curious. I'll go fetch him."

William returned to his office. There was little else to be done until the newspaper ad appeared in Saturday's newspaper. William rejected Corya's "suggestion" that he cancel all activities other than traveling between his home and the Embassy. He agreed to minimize his appointments around the city, but he had no intention of becoming a hermit because of this threat, which he still regarded as quite unproven. He would still play piano on his regular two nights at his Club, though he didn't bother mentioning that to the COS.

Within the Station there was a discussion of whether this apparent break-in might have been part of a botched terrorist threat. Some were thinking of the recent warning letter received by the Ambassador, but no conclusion was possible.

Just in case the break-in was linked in some strange way to his calling on Braganza and having her briefcase, William decided that from now on he would leave it at night under his desk in the secure area of the Embassy.

As word spread around the Embassy of the strange burglary attempt, a few quick wits joked that the fact that nothing was stolen was rather an insult as to what William had in his house.

When he and all his bodyguards reached his home that evening, they found an unmarked JP car containing four members of the JP's Hostage Rescue Team already there. An officer who simply introduced himself as Rodrigo was in charge of this team. The Portuguese officer was nearly as tall as Adam, with equally broad shoulders and a weathered face. When he came into the house, he and William recognized each other from somewhere.

"We know each other, I believe," began William in Portuguese.

"Yes, we've met. Earlier this year at a counterterrorism session that your Embassy organized," he replied in excellent English.

"Ah, yes, I remember you now. So, you and Mr. Corya have worked out a mutually agreeable plan?"

"I believe so. My men will simply stay around your house, 24/7, but not accompany you when you travel. This will give a few of your American security detail a chance to rest during the hours you're at home."

William glanced over at Corya, who nodded his agreement with this plan, not that he actually liked it. He then went outside to check on guard points, leaving William and Rodrigo alone. William then switched back into Portuguese.

"When we first met, I recall that you were the Deputy in charge of the entire JP Counterterrorism unit, weren't you?"

Rodrigo gave a mild grunt. "Yes, and when my boss retired a few months later I had been slated to become the chief. Unfortunately, at just about that time, the Minister of Justice started his program of "diversity" within the JP. He brought in some 'preto' who was originally from Angola and who'd been a traffic cop down in Faro to be the next chief of Counterterrorism. I was asked to stay on as his Deputy, so that somebody knew how to run the place. I told the Chief of the Judicial Police to go have sex with a goat, and to just move be back down to the HRT. So, here I am."

William suppressed a smile. He doubted if the "preto" had actually been a traffic policeman in Faro, but he could certainly understand Rodrigo's anger at assignments being made for political reasons and not merit. William had sadly seen a similar growing tendency at the Agency in recent years. He thought he should give Rodrigo a compliment.

"Well, I'll certainly feel more secure here at my home now that you and your team will be guarding me."

"You can sleep soundly Senhor Wythe." He then gave William a quick salute and said, "Now, I should get back outside and make position assignments for my men. Até logo."

"Até logo," replied William.

The following afternoon, William was passing down a hallway on the second floor of the Chancery when he saw a number of high-ranking military officers from several NATO countries coming out of the Embassy's conference room. He hadn't heard anything officially or unofficially about there being such a meeting of senior officers that day, but then the COS shared little with his underlings. He stood back along one wall to let all the gold braid pass. He'd been looking to his left when suddenly from his right, he heard a deep voice, calling his name. "William, how the hell are you?"

It was an American two-star Admiral named Mike Young that William had known years before in Athens.

William grinned. "Mike, what brings you to a backwater like Lisbon?"

"I was just giving a briefing to a few of our Allies. Are you assigned here now?"

"Yes, been here almost a year. Shouldn't you be off somewhere preparing for a war?"

"Naw, the big boys are planning the war. I'm just an errand boy, sent out to brief some of our so-called friends."

The Ambassador had stopped very near to the Admiral, had heard their exchange and was appalled that one of his Embassy's junior officers, even if with the CIA, dared call an Admiral by his first name. Nor did he like William referring to Lisbon as a "backwater post."

"How long are you in Lisbon? Will you have time to chat at some point?"

"Probably not. We've got meetings the rest of the afternoon, then this evening your Ambassador is hosting a small dinner at his residence for me, and I leave in the morning at 0600. Are you free to come to the dinner tonight? We could catch up then."

"I'm free tonight, but I suspect that the seating chart is already pretty well set." William had been around long enough to know that the guest list at the Ambassador's residence for a VIP like Admiral Young had been worked out days or even weeks in advance.

"The hell with the seating chart. I'm sure the Ambassador can figure out where to put one more chair next to mine." He turned to the Ambassador. "Couldn't you, Mr. Ambassador?"

The Ambassador put on his best fake smile. "No problem whatsoever, Admiral."

He turned back to William. "See, I told you there would be no problem to add one more plate to the table. Or do we need two places? Have you remarried or have some significant other in your life these days?"

"I'm still single, though there is a Brazilian woman I'm seeing currently. I'm sure she would enjoy meeting you."

"Perfect. Mark, my aide, will work out the arrangements and get the details to you. I'll see you tonight."

The Admiral and the Ambassador then moved on down the hallway. A few minutes later, the Admiral's Aide, a "mere" Naval Commander, spoke with the DCM about including William and his date to the dinner that night.

Mr. Chesterbrook wrinkled his face and tilted his head slightly. "Well, it's not as easy as simply pulling two more chairs up to a table. The guest list was carefully worked out days ago. I'm afraid that there simply isn't any room for two more guests."

Commander Emmert smiled slightly. "That's a shame about the space limitation. Well, I'll leave it to you to figure out who will be cut from the dinner so as to make room for William and his dinner guest."

"I'm not sure if that's possible at this last minute."

The Commander's smile disappeared. "Oh, I'm sure a bright fellow like yourself can figure something out. William and his date will be arriving with the Admiral and it's going to be rather embarrassing if there aren't chairs for the three of them. They might just have to leave and go somewhere else for dinner." The Aide then walked on in order to catch up with the Admiral.

The lowest ranking person coming to the dinner that night was the DCM and his wife, so it was himself he would have to cut from the dinner. He was not a happy man and swore William would pay someday for this insult – even if it hadn't been William's idea of coming to the dinner.

William immediately went to his office and phoned Olivia at the dress shop. He told her of the last minute invitation for dinner at the Ambassador's residence, in honor of Admiral Young. Olivia was quite thrilled and as any women would have, immediately inquired as to what sort of dress she should wear.

"Well, I will be wearing my tuxedo, as will all of the civilians and the military officers will be in their dress uniforms, complete with all their medals and ribbons." William had a sudden thought of wondering if perhaps Olivia didn't have an appropriate dress with her in Lisbon. "If you don't have the right attire here with you, perhaps the manager of your store would let you borrow something from the shop, just for the night."

William couldn't see her smile through the phone line, but she replied, "What an excellent idea. She likes me and I think she might let me borrow something. At what time will you pick me up?"

"I'll be there at 6:30 sharp, but I won't be in my car. It will be a black Embassy sedan, a couple of them actually." He laughed. "I'll explain when I get there."

His four-car security convoy pulled up in front of her three-story apartment building promptly at 1830 hours. It was in an older, but elegant neighborhood, populated mostly by businessmen at least half way up the corporate ladder. William and one of his Agency bodyguards went up and rang her doorbell. Fortunately, she had a ground floor apartment. A few seconds later, Olivia opened the door. She was wearing a beautiful floor-length, strapless blue gown. She had a matching silk shawl over her shoulders. She'd also managed a visit that afternoon to the beautician, so her hair looked perfect as well.

"Good evening. My, you look gorgeous. Did you just happen to have that old thing hanging in your closet, or did you borrow it from the shop?"

Olivia laughed. "I borrowed it from the shop and two of the seamstresses worked several hours to fit me into it this afternoon."

"Someday I'll have to meet this Simone and thank her. Perhaps I should just go ahead and buy it for you since it's already been adjusted to your size."

"No, no, that's not necessary. It's so rare that I need such a dress these days." She didn't want to tell him that it cost over $4,000!

They started down the five steps to the street and she noticed that there was a total of four black sedans blocking her narrow, cobblestoned street.

"My, you must be quite an important man at your Embassy to merit such security!" she teased and then waited for the security man to open her car door.

Once they were seated and the motorcade had started moving, William began to explain. "Someone wrote a letter to the Ambassador, claiming that there is a plot underway to kill someone at the Embassy. It didn't name me specifically, but the clues slightly pointed at me. Therefore, Ambassador Brown is taking no chances."

"Well," she replied, "you certainly know how to make an impression when you pick up a woman for a dinner date and I'm sure my neighbors were impressed as well." They both laughed. The two guards in the front seat silently smiled. Corya liked her already. William briefly explained how the guest of honor that night, Admiral Young, and he had been friends years earlier in Greece.

"Well, it will be nice to meet your old friend and some of your Embassy colleagues. I hope I am appropriately dressed?" she asked with a thin smile.

"I'm sure all the men will appreciate your attire immensely. And as for the women who will be there, I suspect there will be inquiries as to who made your gorgeous dress."

"Ah, so you're suggesting that I may be able to send a little business in the direction of Casa de Simone?"

"Perhaps. And then your boss will believe that it was a wise decision to loan you that gown for this evening." William was too tactful to ask, but the diamond earrings and necklace Olivia wore sparkled like the real things. He wondered if current day faux diamonds were that good, or perhaps Simone had thrown in a little jewelry to go with the gown.

The convoy of four cars did attract some attention as it pulled up to the entrance of Ambassador Brown's residence. The two-hundred year old mansion had belonged to the American Embassy ever since WWII. Before then, it had belonged to the family of a wealthy merchant who'd first had it built. He'd owned a fleet of ships that brought exotic products back from the Orient to Europe.

The mansion had a large dining hall and a small one, for more intimate gatherings. Tonight's dinner for twenty was in the "small" hall, which was sixty feet long and only had three crystal chandeliers hanging from the ceiling. Electricity had replaced the one hundred and fifty-two candles that had originally burned in each chandelier. However, they were turned off and tall lighted candles stood on the linen-covered dining table to provide illumination. The walls had a Chinese theme and were covered with ancient silk scrolls painted with various sailing scenes.

Many of the guests were the same generals and admirals of European countries who'd been at the afternoon conference. William had been correct. Olivia attracted the attention of many at the dinner. She found Admiral Young to be quite charming and humorous. She could understand why the two men had enjoyed each other's company back in Athens. She was seated at the dinner table in between Admiral Young and William. Ambassador Brown sat on the other side of the Admiral.

After an excellent fare of grilled swordfish, freshly caught that morning, and numerous toasts, Ambassador Brown turned to Admiral Young with a question.

"Tell me Admiral, how did you and William meet back in Greece?"

William found it slightly amusing that the Ambassador for the first time ever referred to him by his first name, as if they were old friends. Commander Emmert had briefed the Admiral earlier in the evening that William was not the Chief of Station, so he made no embarrassing comments as to his old friend's current position.

"Hasn't William told you why we became such close friends in Athens?"

"We simply knew each other back in Athens, years ago – nothing to really tell," quickly interjected William.

"What do you mean 'nothing'? You saved my life as well as dozens of others." That certainly caught the attention of the Ambassador and many others at that end of the table, including Olivia.

"I'm afraid William has been too modest to talk about that event, but please do, Admiral," requested the Ambassador.

"Well, William and I were having dinner one evening at this restaurant in Athens that was popular with NATO military personnel, when in came these two terrorists with AK-47 assault rifles. They were wearing balaclavas over their faces and had hand grenades on their belts, just like in some Hollywood movie."

By this point, conversation had stopped up and down the table so that they could hear the Admiral. William sat staring down at his plate.

"William here was just coming back from the Men's Room and came out behind one of the terrorists, who didn't see or hear him. William put his hands on the sides of the man's head and in one swift motion snapped his neck. Before he fell to the floor, William had his arms around him and grabbed the AK-47. While holding up the dead man's body as a shield, he used the gun to shoot to death the second terrorist. A few customers wound up with minor wounds, but the only dead people were the two terrorists."

"My god, William, that's extraordinary," exclaimed the Ambassador. "A genuine hero, and a modest one at that. He's never said a word about that action in Athens."

"As I said, that was many years ago. I simply got lucky that night."

The Admiral raised his glass to propose a toast and the rest of the table followed suit. "To the man who saved my life."

As the dinner ended and guests began to leave the Ambassador's residence, Admiral Young pulled William aside for a brief and private discussion.

"I don't know how your Agency works, but how in the hell are you not the Chief of Station here in Lisbon instead of that weasel Loken?"

William laughed. "You always were a quick judge of character. As for why I'm not the chief, well, let's just say that various things have happened over the years. It doesn't really matter. I just need to get in a couple more years abroad so as to pay for my daughters' college educations, then I can hang it up and go home and relax. It's a long story that you needn't worry about."

"If you say so, but with this military build-up, I can have about anything or anybody I want. You say the word and I'll personally request that you be detached to my staff as a special advisor. We can come up with a proper title if you want to move."

"Listen, Mike, I really do appreciate your offer, but I think just staying here and keeping my head down is best for me at this point in my career. I'm not looking for promotions or glory. I just need a steady paycheck for two more years. After that, you can come visit me on my front porch somewhere back in America."

Young patted him firmly on the shoulder. "Alright, if that's want you want to do. By the way that Olivia is a great gal. You might want to work at hanging on to her."

"I'll do that. Say, before you go, any prediction on how this upcoming fight's going to go? I'm not asking when it will start – that's none of my business, but what's your personal prediction on how it will go? The American public doesn't like wars that drag on and on with no clear end, like Vietnam. Saddam's been spending all that oil money of his on weapons for years. He might actually have a decent military force."

The Admiral laughed, then leaned close to William's ear. "We're going to go through Saddam's Army like crap through a goose, to quote General Patton. This war will be over before CNN even has a chance to leak any secrets to the public." William laughed so hard that others on the other side of the room turned to look at them.

"We could have invaded a month ago, but President Bush wants every country in the world to be part of his coalition for appearance's sake, which is good I guess." He then leaned even closer to William and lowered his voice. "Even the Russians are quietly behind us. Gorbachev told President Bush two months back that Russia had cut off all overhead photography or any other kind of intelligence support. That Iraqi bastard's blind and won't even know from what direction the main attack is coming."

"Couldn't happen to a nicer dictator. I trust no one has orders to try to capture him alive?"

"Well, American forces always respect the right of an enemy combatant to surrender, but well, you know, shit happens in wartime." Young grinned and said goodnight.

During the drive back to Olivia's apartment after the dinner, she sat very close to William and they held hands. He felt like a teenager on a first date.

"I like very much your friend Mike. He has an excellent sense of humor, particularly for a career military officer."

"Yeah, he's a great guy. It's a shame we rarely see each other as the years have passed."

"That fellow named Loken that I met for a few minutes. He clearly has no humor does he?"

"No, he's a very serious man."

"Does he not have a wife, or did she just not come tonight to the dinner?"

"I believe he was married, but I heard that they divorced after their last overseas assignment somewhere down in South America."

"Ah, that is too bad." She pondered silently to herself if the man seemed so unpleasant in part because of the lack of a woman in his life, or if his being so unpleasant was why his wife left him.

A minute later, William's security detail arrived back at Olivia's apartment. He wanted to pull her to him and kiss her, but having two armed men in the front seat killed that inclination. He simply said goodnight and gave her a quick kiss on her cheek. "I'll be in touch. Boa noite!"

By the third day of the special security protection on William, it was clear to the CI surveillance team that his enhanced security escort was there to stay for the foreseeable future. It would be impossible for them to conduct discreet surveillance of William. The team used their laptop to send an encrypted message back to Headquarters, informing Committee XII of their problem and asking for instructions. "Given the impossibility of conducting discreet surveillance on Wythe, should we depart the country or just sit quietly and wait?"

Paul, head of Committee XII, checked with the Security officer for Europe Division and learned of the anonymous letter telling of a planned assassination attempt on someone at Lisbon Station, possibly Wythe. Nobody knew how long the special protective detail would stay in Lisbon.

Headquarters advised the team two days later that most all of its members should return to Scandinavia, while Jane should stay in Lisbon and simply confirm daily that Wythe still had his protective detail.

There had still been no sign of the arrival of the alleged KGB mole handler at either Portugal or Spain. A week later GOLDFISH reported via a pre-arranged dead drop that Parshenko's trip had been postponed till early January, with no reason known for the delay. Paul and the others speculated on whether perhaps Wythe had somehow signaled to Moscow about having the protective security detail on him and thus not currently available to meet. Perhaps Wythe had indeed mailed something that night on the shopping street near his home. Harry stuck with his minority position that GOLDFISH was providing nothing but, pure, one-hundred percent bullshit.

CHAPTER 8

*T*he Embassy placed the car advertisement in the Lisbon newspaper as requested by the "volunteer" in his latest letter. By three days later it had still produced no response, so a decision about what to do next about the alleged assassination plot was left hanging in the air. However, support for the argument that the threat was real did show up that Saturday courtesy of the National Security Agency. They had been tasked with checking back on any intercepts it might have of any intercepted classified Libyan embassy traffic in or out of Lisbon in recent weeks that might be even remotely linked to an assassination attempt. They found one small tidbit. It was such a short and unclear telegram that initially the NSA hadn't even bothered distributing the intercept to the rest of the U.S. Intelligence Community. It was addressed to the one-man Libyan Intelligence Service representative in Lisbon and simply read: "Be prepared to provide support as needed to the three-man team entering Portugal this week."

There was debate over what exactly that sentence meant. The CIA went back to the NSA and asked for the intercept in the original Arabic. One CIA analyst who specialized on Libya thought much depended on the verb translated as "entering" Portugal. Could it have actually been the Arabic verb usually translated as "arriving?" After much reluctance and only after the intercession of the DCI personally to the Director of the NSA, was the original Arabic version handed over. The NSA never liked to provide the original intercepts because they felt that to do so lessened their claim that they too did "analysis" of intercepted material and they were not simply a code-breaking organization. Once the CIA analyst had seen the original Arabic intercept, he agreed that the verb had indeed been correctly translated as "entered" and not "arrived." His intellectual point was that if a two or three-man team was legally coming to the Libyan Embassy, the sentence should have used a different verb, i.e. to arrive. To his mind, "entering" Portugal much more likely implied that it was an illegal, or certainly a non-official, entry. His linguistic interpretation of the sentence sent to the Libyan intelligence officer in Lisbon thus supported the view that an assassination team had been sent to Portugal, as the "volunteer" claimed.

This esoteric linguistic fine point was discussed at a meeting called by Ambassador Brown on Monday morning. At the end of an hour, everyone finally agreed to simply continue the 24/7 protection around William until something further was learned. The security team leader from Washington, Corya, hated attending such group meetings – where somebody would come down in favor of every possible option. His snide comment towards the end of the meeting was, "I guess if a bomb goes off and kills William, then we can conclude with a high probability that the threat was genuine."

The Portuguese Judicial Police began checking on all known Libyans that had legally entered the country in the past month. The Portuguese Security Intelligence Service put full-time surveillance on all four diplomats of the Libyan People's Bureau in Lisbon. The latter step was to cover the possibility that an official at their embassy was in contact with and providing support to an assassination team in the country.

The other focus of the Embassy in early January was the impending war over the Iraqi occupation of Kuwait. No firm date had been announced for an attack, but everyone down to and including the cafeteria staff knew that something would happen soon.

Spending most of his evenings at home, except for his two nights per week at the Club playing the piano, William had plenty of time to think about Mrs. Braganza's diary. Could there really be a treasure trove of Hungarian jewels hidden somewhere in Portugal, as Nigel had proclaimed to her in 1945? Being a trained intelligence officer, he concluded that the proper initial step for reaching a conclusion was to first gather more information about the players in the alleged transfer of "wealth" from Hungary to Portugal back in 1944.

Fortunately, there was a decent library at the American Embassy and the Portuguese woman who ran it liked William and was quite happy to assist him in his research. She didn't even ask him why he was researching such arcane historical topics. Within a few days, he'd learned that Regent Miklos Horthy had been the legal leader of Hungary from 1920 until October 1944. After having announced in early October 1944 Hungary's withdrawal from its alliance with Nazi Germany and an armistice with the Red Army, the Germans overthrew him and took direct control of the country.

To his surprise, William also learned that the Nazis didn't just shoot him in October 1944, but rather took him and his wife to a castle in Bavaria, the Schloss Hirschberg. He remained a VIP prisoner there of the SS until the American Army got close on May 1, 1945, and all the German soldiers simply fled. Then the Americans kept him a prisoner and found him a willing participant in questioning about various Nazi leaders in pending war crime prosecutions. Horthy himself, however, was never put on trial.

In 1950, the Americans were willing to release Horthy, but the question was, to where? The Communists were running Hungary, so that wasn't really an option. To most people's surprise, Horthy requested permission for himself, his wife and his son, Miklos Jr. to resettle in Portugal. That permission was given, as long as there was no publicity about his move and Horthy stayed entirely out of politics once he arrived in Portugal. He and his family moved to the upper-class neighborhood of Estoril, on the outskirts of Lisbon. There he lived comfortably and quietly until his death in 1957 and his wife died a few years later.

Asking to resettle in Portugal seemed to support the story that Horthy had indeed managed to secretly transfer wealth to that country. William also thought that as Horthy had managed to live well in such an upper-class neighborhood for seven years that he'd had access to the "treasure" that the two SOE officers had smuggled out of Hungary for him. Perhaps Senhora Braganza's diary had it wrong about when Nigel and Tristan had died and Horthy had in fact somehow gotten the coded message Tristan had left for him as to where Tristan had hidden the treasure in Portugal.

Perhaps, there was another player in the game that Braganza had not known about? There were simply too many unknowns for William to confidently reach a conclusion.

As for research on Braganza was concerned, he learned that she'd spent most of the post-war years in England. She'd been married for a few years, but then her wealthy husband had died in an automobile accident. There were no children. Over the years, she'd also written many letters to the Portuguese Government demanding "her property" back. They considered her an annoying, but harmless and probably senile old lady. The Government no longer even bothered to reply to her letters. She had been to Portugal many times in the fifties and William wondered if her path had ever crossed with Horthy's. William could find no indication that that happened, but if she had, perhaps that would explain how Horthy had learned of the location of his treasure and thus had the money needed to live well in Portugal.

At home that evening, he took advantage of Rodrigo's presence to ask him if he knew of anyone still alive in Estoril who might have known Admiral Horthy back in the 1950s.

Rodrigo laughed. "I was only born in 1950, nor did I live in Estoril. Why are you interested in such a person?"

"I just recently learned that the ruler of Hungary during WW II, Miklos Horthy, had been allowed by Salazar to quietly move to Portugal in 1950. He lived here in Estoril until his death in 1957. I was curious if there was still anyone alive who might have known him with whom I could speak."

Rodrigo rubbed his chin in thought for several seconds. "The only person still alive who comes to mind who might have known Horthy is Duke Wilhelm. He is a distant and elderly relative of Queen Beatrix of Holland who has lived for many years in Estoril. Duke Wilhelm has been a gathering point for various minor royals and claimants to various titles in Eastern Europe that don't exist anymore, except on paper. He apparently is himself comfortably wealthy and involved with fund raising for many charitable organizations. He's lived for some reason in Portugal since the early fifties – perhaps he simply finds the weather superior to that of the Netherlands. Given the circles he ran in, he just might have come across Horthy here in Estoril back in the 1950s."

William found that a promising lead. He thought he'd also try his luck with Rodrigo on Braganza. "And have you ever heard about an elderly Portuguese woman named Gabrielle Braganza, who claims to be the daughter of the last king of Portugal?"

"What was her name again?"

"Braganza," replied William.

"No, that name doesn't ring any bells with me. If she's a daughter of Dom Manuel II, she must be as old as dirt!"

William laughed. "Well, she's at least eighty."

"My, you're interested in a lofty set of people – a former dictator and the illegitimate daughter of the King of Portugal! Are they connected?"

"Oh, I doubt it, but I did meet the sweet old lady last week. She was telling me her story of supposedly being of royal blood. I was just curious if she's totally crazy, or if there's anything to her claims."

"Well, I've never heard of her, but that doesn't mean much. She might well be an illegitimate daughter of old Manuel. The rumors we heard in school were that he was quite the dashing, romantic figure in his younger days, especially after he'd been overthrown and had nothing else to do with his free time – which was all day long."

"OK, thanks for chatting with me. I'll see if I can track down this Duke Wilhelm fellow."

The following day was the bi-monthly diplomatic association luncheon, which met in the ball room of Le Meridien Hotel. Each gathering featured someone from the Portuguese Government, speaking on a topic hopefully of interest to the foreign diplomats. That month the guest speaker was the Minister of Finance, who was to address the topic of Portuguese economic prospects in the coming year. This was a popular topic and almost one hundred diplomats had turned out for the luncheon. Most were there to hear the guest speaker, but the event was also popular with intelligence officers under diplomatic cover from many countries as it provided a good opportunity to mingle with prospective targets.

William was there in hopes of "accidentally bumping" into his new Bulgarian acquaintance. The Headquarters traces William had requested on First Secretary Yordan Stambolov had come back positive that he was indeed a DS officer. They also advised that he came from a very distinguished background of Bulgarian politicians and military personnel going back almost a century. Headquarters noted that several Agency case officers had met him in previous years. None had ever found him terribly friendly, but they encouraged William to pursue him as time permitted.

William figured his best chance of finding Yordan in the large crowd of people was to wait by the bar, which proved successful. Yordan seemed as happy at encountering William as William was at seeing the Bulgarian. They again used Portuguese to communicate. When the audience was encouraged to take a seat at any of the luncheon tables, the two of them mutually agreed to sit together. This gave William thirty minutes to elicit further information about the Bulgarian and to enhance rapport with his target, in the parlance of the CIA. Yordan was obviously doing the same with William. Both men had been at the game long enough that they knew well how to tactfully make inquiries about the other's background, family connections and basic views on the world's situation.

"Bone-throwing" was a favorite technique of William's. When he wanted to know some aspect of his target's past or family, he first mentioned something about himself in that regard. Most people would then tell him something similar about themselves. But even if not, at least it then wouldn't seem inappropriate for him to then ask the person about their family, education, or whatever.

William started his agenda that afternoon by mentioning that despite being a widower for almost ten years, at times he still missed his wife and felt rather lonely. He claimed that his wife had died in a car accident, which was sort of the truth.

Yordan responded in a melancholy way. "I know what you mean. I lost my Elena to cancer five years ago, after twenty-three years of marriage. After so many years together, I doubt if one ever really gets accustomed again to living alone. Do you have children?"

"Yes, two daughters, who are finishing university back in America, but I'm afraid we've grown apart in recent years. They've reached an age where they have their own lives to live." William gave out a small sigh, indicating such is life. "How about you?"

A smile came to Yordan's face. "Yes, I also have a daughter back in Sofia. She too is busy with her own life, but she was just diagnosed with breast cancer, so everything is on hold for her right now. I wish I could be back home with her, to lend her moral support, but my job is here." He shrugged his shoulders and gave a small sigh similar to William's."

"I've never followed such things. Is there pretty good medical care for cancer-related problems back in Bulgaria?"

"Fortunately, yes, there is excellent care available in Sofia." What he didn't say to William was that while there were a few excellent doctors and hospitals, you had to be part of the governmental or military elite to merit access to such treatment – or have enough money to buy the needed access. In the past, Yordan being a colonel of the DS could have gotten her the right doctors and care, but in the currrent days of chaos and civil unrest, who knew. And he didn't have enough money to simply bribe the needed hospital administrators to get her the needed treatment.

"Funny how once you reach our ages, you realize how fast time has passed and think that perhaps you should have focused more on one's family," commented William.

"Oh, you're still a young man, William," replied Yordan with a smile.

William laughed. "That isn't what my back and my knees tell me when I get up in the morning!"

Yordan raised his glass of Scotch and proposed a toast. "To our old knees!"

"And to our old backs!" They both drained their glasses.

"So what do you do to enjoy life in your free time here in Lisbon?" asked William.

"I'm a fisherman. I'm not a very good one, but it relaxes me. And you?"

"Oh, I like listening to old jazz music, reading a good book while enjoying a good single malt whiskey. I lead a pretty quiet life." He never told other diplomats about the nightclub where he played piano. That small world he kept a secret only to himself.

The two continued chatting and subtly asking personal questions for another fifteen minutes and then turned their attention to the other six luncheon guests at their round table. Once the speaker began his talk on the prospects for the economy in the coming year, they both pretended that they cared, but took no notes as many others were doing. Forty minutes later, there was a polite round of applause and everyone headed back to their own embassies.

"It was nice seeing you again, Yordan. Até logo!"

"Até logo!"

Upon returning to his Embassy, William sat down at his computer and typed up a short summary of his conversation with Yordan. He didn't make it sound too interesting. He saw no reason to get Headquarters all excited – that would only encourage someone sitting three thousand miles away from offering him advice on what to do next with the Bulgarian. He was also leery that if the COS thought the lead sounded too promising, he'd come up with one of his annoying suggestions that William turn the developmental over to another Station officer. He had no early gut feeling that Yordan was recruitable, but he did enjoy his company.

Over at the Bulgarian Embassy, Stambolov was writing his version of the same luncheon conversation to send to his DS Headquarters back in Sofia. He held no delusion that one could recruit an American these days. Communism was collapsing in the Soviet Union and throughout Eastern Europe so there would be no more ideological recruitments. Nor did Bulgaria even have enough money to simply buy an American. His time with William was strictly for show. Should his Government soon start closing some of its DS offices abroad, or even entire embassies around the world, in order to save money, he wanted on the record at least a few reasons as to why Lisbon should stay open. Besides, he actually enjoyed William's company.

William learned the following day that Duke Wilhelm was hosting a charity event at his home that coming Saturday evening to promote musical education in the schools. For a mere $500, William too could have a ticket. Why not? William wanted to learn if the Duke had known Braganza or Horthy. Such questions could only be answered if he could meet the man.

At the charity event, William did finally catch the Duke standing alone and approached him. He could think of no subtle way to build up to his questions, so he simply went for the direct approach, after introducing himself.

"By the way, I recently met Gabrielle Braganza. Did you by chance know her?"

The Duke smiled. "Of course, I've known her for many years. So sad her falling down those stairs at her hotel."

"Very sad, I'd just been talking with her at her hotel the day before. What a charming woman."

"Was she asking for your assistance in getting back all the buildings in Lisbon that used to belong to the last King of Portugal?"

William laughed. "As a matter of fact, she did, but she also told me much about her own fascinating life."

"Indeed, it was. She was always so pleasant."

"And on the topic of former famous people, I also recently learned that the former Regent of Hungary, Miklos Horthy, had also lived here in Estoril for many years after the war. Did you by chance know him, since you were practically neighbors?"

"As a matter of fact, I did. He was a very learned man."

"I see that someone is waving for you from the bandstand, so I shan't detain you any longer. But perhaps we could have dinner some evening soon and discuss your own interesting life here in Portugal."

"Gladly, give me a call one day and we can set a date." He handed William his card. "But now you must excuse me. I have to go and award the trophy for this year's winner of best musical student of all the area high school students." They shook hands and the Duke headed to the bandstand. William had achieved as much as he had hoped for, and made his way to the front door. His security detail escorted him home and then they settled in for the night. The men outside would be relieved at 0400 hours. The man staying inside the house would normally change at 2300 hours, but since it was almost that when the group reached William's house, the new man came on duty at 2200 hours. All of the security detail would be awake on duty all night long while William slept.

Four nights later, William and the Duke met for dinner at the luxurious Clube dos Empresarios in downtown Lisbon. During the phone conversation to arrange a meeting, the Duke asked if the American had ever eaten at that establishment. Upon hearing that he had not, he suggested that they dine there, so William could get acquainted with it.

Upon arriving, they were ushered into a very plush lounge full of comfortable leather chairs and couches. On the walls hung very high quality oil paintings. This was clearly a restaurant where the shakers and makers of Portugal dined. From the smiles and greetings the Duke received from various waiters in tuxedos, it was obvious that he was a regular. Once seated, they were handed a drinks menu. William was pleased to see that they had a wide choice of single malt whiskeys. Over drinks, they studied the extensive food menu and remained in the comfortable lounge area until told that their food was ready. They then moved out to a table in the dining room and their food was immediately served. It was an equally well-appointed area, with tables far apart to ensure privacy for the customers' conversations.

William finally got to the topic of Miklos Horthy. "So, had you known the Admiral prior to the war, or only after he was allowed to quietly immigrate to Portugal in 1950?"

"I met him in the early 1950s in Estoril. He stayed very much at home the first few years, but eventually he began to socialize with a few others in our neighborhood." I met him through John Clarke, a former American Ambassador to Hungary before the war."

"Estoril is a very upper-class neighborhood. Horthy must have managed to arrive from Germany with money," suggested William with a slight tilt of his head as if it was a question."

The Duke smiled. "You'll be astounded by the truth of where his money came from," responded the Duke. He then took a drink of wine to let the suspense build, before he continued with the answer. "Rich Jews donated money to help support Horthy and his family."

"You're right, I'm astounded. Didn't Horthy order the shipment of hundreds of thousands of Jews from Hungary to detention camps in Germany during the war?"

"No doubt he did, but then he didn't exactly have a free hand in such questions. What he also did, under the table so to speak, was to prevent even worse steps to be taken in Hungary. The Portuguese Ambassador in Budapest before and during the war, Sanpayo Garrido, assisted many Hungarian Jews, as did a Swiss diplomat, and eventually the famous Swede, Raoul Wallenberg. They often did that by issuing very questionable identity documents proclaiming the bearer to be a citizen of Portugal, Switzerland or Sweden. Horthy ordered the local authorities to honor these so-called 'Schutz-pass' that were being issued to Jews. He also recognized many buildings around Budapest run by Wallenberg as Swedish diplomatic territory – and in those buildings hundreds of Jews were being kept safe."

"Not a well-known story," replied William.

"Anyway, it was this former American Ambassador John Clarke who organized the raising of funds among Jews for Horthy's welfare in Portugal."

"Truly an amazing story. So, he was a war criminal, but he got a break because he could have been an even worse war criminal? I'm not sure how an old ethics professor of mine from my college days would interpret that."

"Yes, well, for a purist of ethics, Horthy was an evil man, but it's easy to sit in a classroom and say, Horthy should have stood up to Hitler. However, Horthy lived in the real world of the war-years. Saying every Nazi was as evil and guilty of everything that happened as every other Nazi is a pretty simplistic approach to life. Maybe saving a few thousand Jews counts for something. Look what happened in October 1944 when Horthy tried to pull Hungary out of the war. Hitler simply had him arrested and taken to Bavaria. He was lucky he and his family weren't shot."

"What did Horthy do with those seven years in Portugal?" asked William as he enjoyed an after-dinner Scotch.

"He wrote an autobiography and he chatted with friends, old and new, but always in private. The condition of his permission to live in Portugal was that he stayed completely out of politics."

"And did he totally obey that restriction?" asked William.

"Yes, I believe he did. Although, there were rumors that Horthy's death in 1957 was not entirely natural, even though he was 88 years old."

"How so?" inquired William.

"Well, he was in fact very healthy late in life. I'd attended his 88th birthday party just a few months earlier. When he suddenly died of a heart attack, one rumor around Lisbon was that the KGB had administered a drug to make it look like a heart attack. There had been the Hungarian uprising the previous year and the story was that the Soviets didn't want Horthy around as any sort of rallying point to bring back the pre-Communist days in Hungary."

"You think there is any chance that rumor was true?"

The Duke laughed. "I've seen enough of international politics in my seven decades to know that nothing can be dismissed. I don't think he would have been much of a rallying point for the average Hungarian citizen, but what was reality and what was feared in Moscow are two different things. The KGB was certainly going around Europe and assassinating a number of emigres in the 1950s, so who can say for sure about Horthy."

"No, I guess you can't rule out hardly anything in the post-WW II era of politics," replied William.

Having learned about where Horthy had gotten his money to live on back in the 1950s, William returned to believing that the "treasure" might actually still be hidden somewhere in Portugal. If so, he thought that it must have driven Horthy half mad, believing that his wealth was hidden somewhere in Portugal, but he had no idea as to where.

Over dessert, William turned to the slightly more delicate subject as to who might have been Horthy's mistress or mistresses in the mid-to-late thirties. The Duke found that question rather amusing, but did reply.

"One afternoon towards the end of Horthy's life, the two of us at the end of lunch at his home had turned to discussing beautiful women we had known in our younger days. This came about because of a photo of Zsa Zsa Gabor on the cover of a local Lisboan magazine laying nearby on a coffee table. She'd been visiting Lisbon for a few days. Horthy smiled and said that her older sister, Magda, was actually much prettier. He went on to claim that he'd had an "arrangement" with her back around 1936 or 37, but then she'd moved on to being the mistress of Portuguese Ambassador Garrido for several years. That became very important when the war began because the Ambassador helped save Magda's family, who were Jewish."

William smiled. "They say that in diplomacy timing is everything, but I guess with whom you're sleeping at times is equally important!"

"Indeed it is!" replied the Duke. "If you'd like, I could introduce you to Horthy's son, Miklos Jr. I'm sure he could tell you more about his father's girlfriends!"

William declined and both men again laughed. The Duke was too polite to ask why William was interested in such an odd topic.

"Do you think Horthy and Senhora Braganza ever met back in the 1950s here in Lisbon?"

The Duke closed his eyes for several long seconds and thought. "Not that I'm aware of. I don't recall either of them ever commenting anything about the other. I think Gabrielle stayed in England through most of the 1950s. Her husband was still alive at that time. Why do you ask?"

"Oh, nothing really. Having met her recently, I was simply curious whether two people who had lost everything, so to speak, and had that in common might have become acquainted."

"Well, it's true that many families which had once had titles and estates prior to WWII gathered together at times for mutual support – or simply to talk about the good old days."

"And just out of curiosity, why have you chosen to spend most of your life down here in Portugal rather than back in the Netherlands, where I presume you are still the Duke of something or someplace?"

The Duke smiled. "The weather here is better, the wine excellent and my niece, the Queen, and I can't stand one another. A visit of about two days a year back to Holland, preferably when the Queen is traveling abroad, is quite sufficient."

"Ah, I understand perfectly. I once had such a relationship with a sister-in-law!"

The Duke raised his glass, "To undesirable relatives!"

William raised his drink as well and the two gentlemen clinked glasses.

"And now, I must be getting off to home. I'm to be presenting some artistic award or the other tomorrow morning at the absurd hour of 9.00 a.m.! So, I must go and get enough sleep so that I can be witty and charming so early in the day. A task that's getting harder every year, regardless of the time of day!"

When William arrived home at 11:00 p.m., he was not feeling sleepy and headed into the living room. He poured himself a generous portion of single malt, sat down in his comfortable, brown leather chair and began thinking about some of the things the Duke had told him. If Magda Gabor had in fact been Horthy's mistress in the mid-1930s, he now needed to learn in what year she turned twenty-one years old and whether she'd ever visited Portugal. He also debated the ethical point with himself on whether Horthy had merited special treatment by the Allies because he hadn't been as evil a dictator as he might have been during the war.

The JP team chief Rodrigo walked in, bringing to an end such philosophical thoughts by William.

"Did you have a good dinner at the Clube dos Empresarios?" asked Rodrigo.

"Outstanding, thank you."

"And did you enjoy talking with Duke Wilhelm?"

"A very delightful man. Have you ever met him?"

"I've briefly spoken with him a few times when he was holding some charity event at his home and various high-level governmental figures were in attendance, so we were providing security. He always seemed a well-educated and pleasant man," commented Rodrigo.

"Indeed he is." William looked at this watch and decided it was bedtime. "I'll see you in the morning, Rodrigo. Boa noite!"

"Boa noite!"

CHAPTER 9

The following morning, William was sitting in his Embassy office, staring at a photograph of Mount Rushmore. The General Services Administration of the Federal Government had probably bought a thousand copies of it, placed them in a cheap frame and shipped them out to American embassies around the world, so there would be a touch of Americana in those buildings. The GSA also probably paid three times the price for each print that anyone could have walked into a K-Mart and bought the same photograph, but never mind, it was a nice picture. His mind soon tired however, of thinking about the four heroic presidents who'd helped make America the amazing country that it had become and he turned to thinking about Braganza's diary.

William tried making an assessment of what progress he'd made with his investigation into the intriguing story he'd found in her diary. In truth, it wasn't much. The only real conclusion he reached was that he needed assistance in researching all the different angles. He was busy with activities related to preparing for the upcoming Iraq war – or at least they were activities creating the impression that the American Embassy Lisbon was contributing to the war effort. And there was still the issue of the anonymous warning about an assassination plan against a Station officer, possibly himself.

There were only two Iraqi diplomats in the city, but there were a few dozen Iraqi businessmen sprinkled around the country at that time as well.

International cargo ships also arrived almost daily at the port of Lisbon; ships which might have a few Iraqi nationals on board as seamen. One concern was possible terrorist acts by any of those Iraqi citizens once a shooting war started down in the Gulf, so one task for the Station officers was checking on all such persons.

As for getting assistance on researching the Braganza story of hidden wealth in Portugal, he decided to turn to Olivia. They'd become quite close over the past month. They'd still not slept together, but at his age, sex was not really a high priority in a relationship. Not that the thought of her in his bed hadn't crossed his mind; he was old, not dead.

He invited her to come to his house for lunch on the coming Sunday. For some odd reason, he'd invested in recent years in top-quality pots, pans and cutlery. Odd, because he rarely did any start-from-scratch cooking. However, his kitchen gave a visitor the false impression that a master chef resided in the home. In fact, he wasn't a great cook at all, but he did have a limited repertoire of five dishes that he could prepare reasonably well. The weather in Lisbon had turned chilly, overcast and damp, so he chose to serve Hungarian goulash for their upcoming luncheon, during which he planned to request her research assistance. How appropriate a meal, he thought, to go with his request to her.

When he went up to the cafeteria for lunch that day, he noticed a clear change in behavior by his colleagues. This was his first visit there since the Ambassador's dinner. Most everyone smiled and said hello and several invited him to join their table. At first, William was puzzled, but then he realized that the story had obviously spread since that dinner of his actions in Athens. He'd gone from being regarded as a pleasant, but generally useless drunk to being treated as a heroic figure who'd singlehandedly stopped a terrorist attack. This was exactly why he tried to keep that whole story a secret, but the cat was out of the bag now and he might as well be gracious. He mused over his soup that day how all it took to raise one's stature was to have killed two people.

When Sunday arrived, he alerted his security detail that he had a female guest in a blue Fiat arriving around noon, so she would receive only friendly nods when she pulled up in front of his house instead of questions. Once he'd prepared her a cocktail, they settled into comfortable chairs in the living room. It was her first visit to his home and she admired a number of the impressionist oil paintings on the walls. They were copies, but still, very good ones.

"I noticed two cars out on the street in front of your house with men in them and a fellow walking out in your side yard. You must be a very important American," she teased him with a wide smile.

"It's just more of the precautionary steps related to that anonymous letter I told you about before the dinner with Admiral Young. I still think the letter was just some sort of prank, but the Embassy is being cautious."

Olivia stopped drinking. "So all of those men out there are Americans?"

"Some are Americans, some are from the Judicial Police."

"And they stay out there all day and night?"

"Yes, and when I'm not entertaining a guest, one of them stays inside the house all night as well." He smiled.

She smiled back, but then her face turned serious. "With that many men assigned to you, I don't think that the Ambassador believes that letter was just a joke."

William shrugged his shoulders. "Who knows? In any case, they won't interfere with our lunch."

"Perhaps that letter was from someone who has heard you play the piano and is simply a harsh critic?" She giggled slightly.

He gave her a faux dirty look. "Perhaps, but now a different subject. Tell me about your childhood. Where was home for you in Brazil?"

"Well, I was born in 1948 on a fazenda, out in the countryside, near Porto Alegra, in the south of Brazil – an only child. My father managed a large cattle ranch, though he died when I was fairly young. I am partially of German ancestry. My maiden name was Berger. However, my mother is a Brazileira, as you can tell from my coloring." She laughed and pointed at her arms and her permanent sun tan. "In the south of the country, particularly around Sao Paulo, there are many people of German and Italian ancestry. I was studying at a fashion design studio in Rio de Janeiro when I met Paulo and we were married in 1970. I've kept working over the years in the clothing world and Paulo became a successful business man. We never had children. I've greatly enjoyed the world of arts and music over the years in Rio. Have you ever been to Rio?"

"Yes, I've been there a couple of times, but unfortunately for only a few days. I enjoyed the food, the jazz and the beautiful beaches."

She stared rather wistfully into her glass. "It really is a magical city, if you have enough money to enjoy that good life."

"Well, that's true of most of the large cosmopolitan cities of the world."

They continued chatting about Rio for a while. She then asked of his childhood. He explained that he'd been born in Indiana, but had grown up around the world as an Army brat. He then talked about where his two daughters were studying in America.

Finally, he looked at his watch and informed her that it was time to move to the dining room. She was glad that he'd asked no questions of her father.

She was impressed with his goulash and the mixed salad, served European style, at the end of the meal, which was light and fresh. He cheated a bit on the dessert – it was simply vanilla ice cream, but with chocolate syrup, ground up walnuts and several cherries. He called it an American sundae.

Over espresso after the meal when they'd returned to the living room, he brought up the story of having chatted with the late Mrs. Braganza and her desire for assistance in making the Portuguese Government give back to her her father's properties. Olivia found that quite amusing.

"She also gave me to read the night I'd met her an attaché case full of her documents, including her diaries. There were several interesting entries for late December 1945." He then told her the story of Horthy's "treasure" and how it had supposedly been smuggled and hidden in Portugal in late 1944. She found that quite intriguing.

"You think there's any truth to her diary comments?"

His eyebrows raised and his head tilted. "Hard to say. I don't doubt that she accurately wrote in her diary what Nigel, the SOE officer who'd served in Hungary, had told her. The question is whether what Nigel told her was the truth, or perhaps he was just trying to get her into his bed and thus he might have indulged in a little hyperbole in trying to impress her."

"What is hyperbole?"

William smiled. "Hyperbole is a polite word for lying, for exaggeration." Her English was so good, at times he forgot that it was not her native tongue.

She laughed. "Oh, you mean it was bullshit?"

"Yes, well, that's one synonym for the word."

She smiled. "Well, young men have been known to lie to women to get them into bed."

William wasn't sure how to safely respond to that comment, so he simply ignored it and moved on. He told her of his research to date, including his conversation with Duke Wilhelm, all of which seemed to indicate that there was a reasonable chance that the story was true. William explained that he was going to soon visit the British Military Attaché Clarke in Lisbon in hopes of getting the names of books from him that told the story of the British SOE back during WWII. "Clarke supposedly has a large, personal library of military topic books and he might even have a few such books on hand that he could loan me."

"Do you think he'd be willing to do so?"

"I think he might, if I give him an interesting story as to why I'm interested in the old SOE. It would help a lot if I had the full names for the two SOE officers who supposedly had been players in the smuggling scheme. Beyond that idea, I wanted to ask if you would be interested in helping me with this research? Even if we never find the treasure, it will be fun searching. And if we find it, well, we could share the find. You presumably enjoy your work, but you probably don't want to work in a dress shop the rest of your life."

She smiled broadly. "No, not for the rest of my life. So, yes, I would enjoy working with you on this treasure hunt." Upon getting a positive response, he assigned her to visit in the coming week any local newspapers and magazines from the 1930s that were still in business in 1990 and check their archives.

"According to the Duke, Horthy's mistress in the mid-1930s had been Magda Gabor, the older sister of the well-known Zsa Zsa Gabor. Magda turned 21 in June 1936. You need to look for historical proof in old newspapers as to whether Magda had celebrated her 21st birthday in Portugal, and if so, exactly where? It would be great if we could confirm that she'd been in Portugal in June 1936."

"I can easily do that, but wait, supposedly the one British SOE officer didn't hide the treasure until October 1944, when he was in Portugal because of the war. How would he have known what happened in 1936?"

"That's why I need to know more about those two SOE officers mentioned in her diary. Maybe one of them had lived in Portugal for years before the war."

"I understand. OK, I'll ask a couple of the older ladies at the dress shop what newspapers and magazines from the mid-1930s are still in business today. If there are any, I can then make up a story as to why I want to check their archives. The other possibility is that the national library might have on file such old newspapers."

"Excellent. You can work that angle and I'll try to learn more about the two SOE officers."

"When you were talking about your dinner with the Duke, you said you turned down his joking suggestion that you could go chat with Horthy's son, but maybe that wouldn't be such a bad idea."

William smiled. "You really think I should inquire of him about his father's mistresses back in the 1930s?"

"No, not that in particular, but if you could find an excuse to meet with him, perhaps you might learn something useful about Admiral Horthy's life once the family had moved to Portugal back in 1950."

"Ah, I see what you mean." He pursed his lips and tilted his head to one side. A habit of his when he was contemplating something. "Let me give that some thought and see if I can think of some justification for asking for an appointment with the president of a pharmaceutical company."

"Just a thought," concluded Olivia. She then reminded him of his promise at the recent dinner to explain at a later date why he drank so much.

He'd hoped she'd just let that promise slide, but he had indeed promised her at the Ambassador's dinner that he would do so and so he would. He poured each of them a high-quality brandy and began to speak slowly as he swirled the golden liquor in his snifter.

"It's a long and complicated story," he began as he stared down at the table, "but here is the short version and for it to make sense, you also need to know that I really work for the CIA, not the Department of State. Obviously, I'd appreciate you keeping that little fact to yourself."

Olivia nodded her agreement. Then she smiled and asked, "Do you have any other little secrets?"

He returned her smile. "Well, we all have a few secrets that we like to keep to ourselves, but perhaps I should save any others for another day."

She would have loved to have asked more about those "other" secrets, but didn't want to interrupt his story about his drinking, so she remained silent.

"When we were serving in Malta about a decade back, my wife, Mary Beth, and I had two cars. Normally, I drove our small Mercedes and she would use the Toyota. She taught at the local American School. Our two young daughters were spending the summer back in America with her parents. She'd been telling me that there was engine trouble with her car for over a week and I'd simply been too lazy to do anything about it. One morning, she went out and it wouldn't start at all, so she took my Mercedes. She was only four blocks from our house when the ambush with an RPG and then machine gun fire occurred. We learned later, a Palestinian terrorist group had been watching my patterns for many weeks and planning the attack. They had a rough idea of when I left the house and that I always drove the silver-colored Mercedes Benz. Regrettably, my wife was actually in the car the morning they carried out the attack.

"Oh my god, that's horrible. Did they ever catch the men who did it?"

"That's a whole other story. Within a few months, my Agency had tracked down the three men principally involved in the attack and knew where they were staying at a particular terrorist training camp in Libya."

"And?"

"And President Carter was trying to broker a peace deal between the P.L.O. and the Israelis at the time and the White House put a freeze on any sort of retaliatory strike. My Headquarters said we would get them another day. After several months of waiting patiently, of course there was no peace treaty reached and by then the three men had vanished. Thank you Mr. Carter and the U.S. Government!"

"That's terrible."

"Everyone told me that her death wasn't my fault, but I knew it was. If I'd just gotten something done days earlier when she first told me about her car trouble, she wouldn't have been in the Mercedes when it was attacked. That's when I started drinking heavily – to forget my guilt and my pain."

"Understandable. That's quite a psychological load to carry around in your head. Don't they have psychiatrists to help people with such problems?"

"I suppose they do, but I thought I was too much of a real man to seek help. I prefer the comfort of my Scotch to ease my mental guilt that I caused her death. If I ever come to have some real purpose in life again, maybe that pain will ease and I will drink less."

Olivia couldn't think of anything appropriate to say, so just remained silent.

"Anyway, I've kept my job, because of my past record and because of the sympathy over how Mary Beth had died. I haven't been worth much for many years. I only got this Lisbon posting out of friendship and explaining that I only needed three more years of serving abroad. I get an educational allowance for my two children when posted overseas and I need that extra money to pay for the last of their college educations. I promised my friend, the Chief of Europe Division, that after this tour, I'd turn in my papers to retire and would no longer be an embarrassment to the Agency."

"And on that promise, they gave you this Lisbon assignment?"

"Yes. It's not much of an assignment, but it keeps me overseas. My Chief of Station hates having me here and gives me nothing but shit tasks. That's how I wound up meeting with Braganza." William laughed. "He thinks he can make my life so miserable here that I will ask to leave, but that will never happen. I just say 'yes sir' and do whatever ordered."

"How awful. Doesn't he understand about your wife and the need for the educational allowance money?"

"Maybe he knows. Maybe he doesn't, but he doesn't really care. He's simply a self-centered, first-class prick."

Olivia smiled, as she thought of her husband. "Yes, I've known a few such men myself in my life."

She wanted to change the topic to something more positive. "Well, everyone was certainly impressed with Admiral Young's story about you stopping those terrorists in Athens. Perhaps that will change your image with your Embassy colleagues. I must say I was very impressed with your heroic actions in Athens."

William laughed. "You want to know the truth of that night? I didn't hesitate to attack that first terrorist with my bare hands because I was so drunk I didn't care if he killed me or not. And how I hit the second terrorist with one shot, I'll never know." He shrugged his shoulders. "They say God watches out for fools and drunks. He was certainly working overtime that night, but enough about the past."

As William was being very forthright with her, Olivia decided to share with him more of her own background.

"If you've wondered why I came to Lisbon, it has to do with my marriage of almost twenty years."

William remained silent, so she continued. "In February of this past year, my husband started seeing a gorgeous twenty-three-year old Carioca, a girl from Rio. He'd met her at a Carnival party. By June, I'd had enough and told him I was going to Lisbon for a while and that he had six months to get over his little fling or I'd be getting a divorce and taking at least half of his money. He's been a successful businessman for many years and has a good amount of money hidden away. That is what most Brazilian men do, so as not to pay taxes or to someday possibly have to give any of it away in a divorce settlement. Unfortunately for him, I know where it's hidden and his money is what he really cares about in life."

"I'm sorry to hear that. Is there that much money on the table that he might have to give up?"

She lied. "Not that much by American standards, but for him even a hundred dollars is more than he'd care to lose to me."

Olivia didn't care to tell William that she was in fact a very wealthy woman. So, she didn't want to say that she'd taken out seven million dollars from his hidden accounts just before giving him the six-month ultimatum. She only informed Paulo of that fact via a letter after arriving in Lisbon. He could hardly go to the police about it since he'd never declared in his tax statements to having that money.

"Nothing has changed with his mistress over the last six months, so on December 1st, my lawyer back in Brazil filed for divorce."

"Not to be pessimistic, but Brazil has always been a very male-dominated society. Will his having a mistress really be considered much of grounds for divorce – or at least one where he has to share his wealth with you?" asked William.

Olivia smiled. "The legal documents given to the judge included lots of photos of him with the bimbo, particularly out in public places in Rio. You see, in Brazil, it's fairly standard practice for men of wealth to have mistresses, but husbands are not supposed to embarrass their wives by taking the mistress out in public in their home city. My husband knows the judge will force him to give me much of his money."

"Ah, a subtle aspect of society I was not aware of in Brazil."

"My husband reacted negatively to my filing for divorce and sent word that he didn't want a divorce." Olivia kept to herself that a divorce might cost her husband another forty million dollars, in addition to the seven she'd already physically taken for safe keeping.

"He flew over here in late December to plead with me, but I think he simply doesn't want to part with any of his wealth, not so much as to lose me. I also suspect that he's hired private investigators here in Lisbon to see what I've been doing in Portugal and to try to dig up any "dirt" on me – just in case my divorce request did eventually go to trial back in Brazil." William still just thought that she was a mid-level employee at the Lisbon dress shop. He had no idea she actually owned the exclusive dress chain and was a woman of wealth.

William didn't have the courage to ask her if their growing relationship had anything to do with her decision to go ahead with a divorce.

Just before three, he sent Olivia on her way and he indulged in an afternoon nap. He had scheduled a dinner with Yordan for 7:00 p.m. at a seafood restaurant down at the water's edge in Cascais. He was feeling a bit tired from all the conversation with Olivia and he needed some sleep if he was going to have a productive session later that evening with the Bulgarian.

First Secretary Yordan Stambolov had an apartment in downtown Lisbon, away from where the other Bulgarian officials resided. Most of the staff lived in the four-story building that served as both the chancery and apartments for the Bulgarians. That made it easier for the security man at the Embassy to keep an eye on all of them and also saved the Bulgarian government money. The fact that Yordan was allowed to live off on his own was another indicator that he was a DS officer. He needed privacy away from inquisitive eyes for his own developmental work against targets. Plus, as a senior intelligence officer of the State, he had "earned" the privilege of a degree of privacy that most citizens of his police state did not. Access to better food and products were perks that came with being part of the elite, but being allowed privacy was perhaps the most appreciated privilege that came with being an officer of the DS.

William gave instructions to his security detail as they neared the restaurant that night. All but one Agency officer who drove the sedan William was in shifted to another car a few blocks before they reached the parking lot. William having a driver, Yordan could understand. William showing up in a three-car convoy would have raised a lot of questions to the Bulgarian which William did not want to have to answer. When the American arrived, Yordan was already inside and had secured a nice table off to one side and far away from most other customers. This location would afford them a good deal of privacy in their conversation.

"Good evening, William."

"Good evening, Yordan. Did you have any trouble finding the restaurant?"

"No, it was quite easy, though it's funny. I've probably driven by here a hundred times over the years and never once noticed it. You've been here six months and already know of such out-of-the-way places!"

William leaned forward and lowered his voice. "I'll share with you my secret – Fodor's Travel Guide!"

William had selected this place for their dinner because he knew from a previous meal there that besides having good seafood that they stocked Oban's 18-year old Single Malt Whiskey.

"If you're in the mood for Scotch, I'd like to recommend to you that you try a particular brand of single malt."

"Why not?" was his simple reply.

William saw that Yordan was scanning the price list of drinks on the menu, so he immediately issued an edict. "It was my suggestion that we come here, so the dinner is on me. Or I guess I should say that it will be covered by my representational allowance at the Embassy." Since it was fairly obvious to both men that the other was an intelligence officer, William saw no reason to make any pretense that Uncle Sam wasn't picking up the tab that evening.

"Why not? It is clear that the American Government has more money than the Bulgarian Government has, especially these days with all the disturbances going on back in Bulgaria."

William saw that as the perfect opening and launched directly into the topic of, "So, what's really going on in Eastern Europe these days? Are we going to see real changes come, or will the Soviet Army eventually step in everywhere and restore the Communist regimes as it did in 1956 and 1968?"

"Oh, who can say for sure? I'm just a tired, old Bulgarian, waiting to retire. In years past, the General Secretary of the Soviet Communist Party in Moscow would have stepped in and restored Communist Party rule in all of Eastern Europe. But I personally suspect those days are gone. The "disease" isn't just in Hungary or Czechoslovakia. In fact, Comrade Gorbachev has already said that the Warsaw Pact members of Eastern Europe are on their own."

"And what about Bulgaria? I don't pay much attention to your country, but it seems I've seen a few news stories recently that the days of Communist Party total control are coming to an end."

"Well, Zhivkov has been out of power for almost a year now and the Bulgarian Communist Party has formally given up the right to be the sole political party, so for all practical purposes, Communism is dead in my country. People are now just fighting over exactly what will be the new system. Various organizations are being put out of business." Yordan smiled. "You understand what I mean?"

"Yes, I do." Neither man wanted to openly say the DS, but it was clear what Yordan was referring to in his comment. "And what might become of you?"

"I had planned on retiring this coming summer when I return to Bulgaria, but who knows if I will still have a pension by next summer." He shrugged his shoulders.

"Bulgaria is clearly headed into a period of change and lots of people are no doubt wondering what their future will be," observed William.

"Well, don't expect to see a whole lot of new faces. The top three or four hundred, who as dedicated Communists, have been running the country for many years will suddenly discover they have been "closet capitalists" and believers in democracy, and find ways to still be running Bulgaria as the country changes."

William nodded in sad agreement with Yordan's cynical opinion of politicians. A few top personalities will have to go, but probably all the next tier down of leaders will find a way to maintain their privileged lives.

William was tempted to make him an offer right then and there. It seemed as if Yordan was practically inviting William to pitch him, but he had no Headquarters approval yet to make any offer. He'd just have to wait, but he certainly had a perfect opening to return to if Headquarters did want him to pitch the man. Instead, William turned the topic of retirement to himself.

"I too am nearing the date when I shall retire. Maybe it will be best for both of us. We've carried out our duties for our respective countries in the era of the Cold War, but it appears that those days are fast coming to an end. Perhaps we both should just move on and leave the troubles of this new world to younger men."

"Perhaps, but I think your future is more secure than mine." Then the Bulgarian laughed and raised his glass of Oban. "To the future!"

William raised his glass as well, clinked his class against that of his Cold War opponent and said, "To the future!"

The food arrived and they continued their conversation while eating their swordfish.

"I have a question, Yordan, if I may. There is a story I've heard for years, but have never known how much of it is true or not. If you'd rather not discuss it, fine, but I'm curious about the so-called umbrella murder back in the late 1970s in London of a Bulgarian defector – supposedly by the Bulgarian service. Any of that story true, partially true?"

Yordan smiled. "Ah, you mean Georgi Markov, in 1978. Yes, the DS killed him with the famous umbrella 'gun', which fired a tiny pellet of ricin into his leg. After his defection in 1968, if Markov had just gone on with his life as a writer, he would have been fine." Yordan raised his bushy eyebrows. "But he didn't. He started broadcasting on Radio Free Europe and the other Western propaganda radio stations against Bulgaria. Even that wouldn't have prompted executive action against him, but he kept getting more and more personal in his slanderous criticism of Leader Zhivkov and his inner circle."

"So it was General Secretary Zhivkov himself who ordered his assassination?"

"Of course. He told the head of the DS that he wanted him killed in a way so that Bulgaria couldn't be legally blamed, but so all the other dissidents would know Markov had been assassinated, as a lesson to them." "And your organization came up with the umbrella gun?"

Yordan laughed. "No, we didn't have such clever scientists in the DS. So, we went to the KGB in Moscow. We'd heard under-the-table about their umbrella device. At first, the KGB kept saying no and the issue kept being pushed higher and higher. I was told later by a good friend in the KGB that the matter finally wound up on General Secretary Brezhnev's desk. Zhivkov had made it a personal request from himself to the Soviet leader and so he couldn't say no. However, his final comment to the KGB director when he gave his permission was to make sure there was no way for this murder to come back to Moscow's doorstep. The Russians wouldn't even deliver it to the DS in Sofia. A DS officer had to fly to Moscow and unofficially be handed the umbrella, so there would be no record of any kind of its transfer from the KGB to the DS."

Now it was William's turn to laugh – at the fact that the KGB was so paranoid that it didn't want anyone in Bulgaria to know from where the umbrella had come. "And how did you learn all of these details."

"I was the man sent to Moscow to pick up the umbrella."

"Good thing it didn't rain during the trip and you might have had to open the umbrella," joked William.

"I was so scared of the poison supposedly inside, I never even opened the box to look at it. I might have been carrying a box of cucumbers for all I knew!"

William raised his glass of Scotch, "To cucumbers!"

The last half hour of conversation focused mostly on their respective daughters. Yordan's daughter, Tatyana, taught Spanish at a high school for the children of the privileged government, military and industrial directors of the country – or at least they used to be privileged. As for her breast cancer, the Bulgarian sounded a little less optimistic about getting her treatment started soon enough – the whole country was in such chaos.

Finally, they called it a night and both staggered out to the parking lot and bid each other goodnight.

When William arrived home, he made a half-page of notes to himself about their conversation, so that he wouldn't have forgotten the facts by morning when he would write up another short cable to Headquarters.

That Sunday night, William laid in his bed, staring at the far wall, his mind bouncing around to various topics. His oldest daughter had phoned him from Purdue University just as he arrived home from his seafood dinner. She was in her last year of studying aeronautical engineering. William always kidded her about having gotten her mother's genes for mathematics, as William found balancing his check book now and then a major mental challenge. He'd sent both his daughters pre-paid international calling cards as part of their Christmas packages he'd mailed to them – just a subtle hint that they could call him whenever the inclination struck them without worrying about their phone bills. They hadn't spoken about anything important, but it was nice to hear her voice. He still thought the anonymous threat letter to the Ambassador was likely just some prank, but the whole affair did remind one that you could never be sure if any conversation with a loved one might be the last one you'd ever have.

When he did write up the highlights of the dinner the following morning at the Embassy, he emphasized twice in the text that the openness of Yordan was because of the excellent personal relationship with William that had developed. A relationship based on both of them being "older", of having grown daughters, dead wives and other commonalities. He thought about listing their similar taste in Scotch, but decided that would be too much truth for Headquarters to handle. He hated being so self-promoting, but it was the best way he could think of to guarantee that the COS didn't try suggesting William turn the promising developmental over to another Station officer. In the last sentence, he also asked that Headquarters advise soon whether they in fact wanted William to try recruiting Yordan or not, as the right moment to do so with the Bulgarian was near.

When William saw the final version that had been signed off on and sent out by the COS, he noticed that the final sentence had been removed. He found an internal office email from Elliot shortly thereafter informing him that he had removed the final sentence as Headquarters would let him know what it wanted done when they felt they had enough information upon which to base a decision. They didn't need William telling them how to run Bulgarian operations. William shook his head in amazement. It was almost as if Elliot didn't want the op to move forward, at least not with William involved.

CHAPTER 10

*A*fter finishing his cable about the Stambolov dinner, William turned his attention to Embassy tasks related to determining the whereabouts of every non-official Iraqi citizen in Portugal. Such people were guesstimated at only about thirty to forty, but no one at the Embassy really knew. Such low-level businessmen or students would be rather long-shots as "sleepers", waiting to carry out terrorist attacks, but in time of war, every possibility had to be explored. The DCOS, who was twenty years younger than William, stuck his head into William's office just before lunch.

"You think it will actually be possible to figure out the location of every Iraqi in this country in a matter of just a few days?"

William smiled. "Yes, with the right amount of money, and the wrong kind of men, most anything is possible in Portugal."

The DCOS smiled back. "Well, I've got all the money in the world to give you, if you can come up with those wrong kind of men."

By "wrong kind", William meant Portuguese government bureaucrats, who were overworked and underpaid and for the right financial "incentive" would gladly provide confidential governmental data to the Americans. This was particularly true if the request for assistance was tied to the upcoming war.

No government agency back in Washington D.C. would officially share with any component of the American Embassy Lisbon when the war would start, but one didn't have to be an international relations expert to figure it would be in the next week or two. All the armchair military experts on evening news programs had been explaining for days to their viewers that temperatures started to rise all over the deserts of Kuwait and Iraq by early March. The American and allied forces wouldn't want to risk the danger of a war continuing on into the one hundred plus degree temperatures of summertime. Washington insiders had a different theory, not related to the upcoming weather. They calculated that by mid-January the Bush Administration would have decided that it had spent enough time going through the public motions of trying to "find a peaceful resolution" to satisfy world opinion — and could get on with kicking the hell out of Saddam Hussein and his army. An action that the realists had known from the beginning would eventually have to be taken.

Olivia started her background research on Monday in the archives of several major newspapers. She quickly learned that fifty-year-old newspapers had not only yellowed over those decades, but taken on an unpleasant smell as well. Of most value to her investigation, she learned from one old social column article that focused on the activities of the "rich and beautiful" back in the 1930s that indeed Magda Gabor had come to Portugal in June 1936 on holiday. She'd been accompanied by her mother, Jolie. The article reported that the beautiful young Hungarian had stayed at the famous Estoril Casino and Hotel, where she was photographed playing roulette with a handsome, young Portuguese polo player of the day. The reporter went into great detail about Magda's clothes and shoes she wore while gambling at the casino. She doubted if William cared much about the color of Magda's gown that night and skipped writing down those details. Per the article, the exotic international playgirl was headed next to the Busaco Forest Hotel, where she would celebrate her 21st birthday. William would be greatly interested in that detail of her visit.

Olivia reported all of this to William via phone Monday evening. These facts excited him. They seemed to fit with the details he'd found in the diary and also with what Duke Wilhelm had told him as to who had been Horthy's mistress in the mid-1930s. Perhaps Horthy's treasure was hidden at the Estoril Casino, but he thought it more likely that it was out at Busaco, as that was where she had been at on her actual birthday. He was really hoping that between the two locations that Horthy's jewels would be at Busaco, as it would certainly be a lot easier to steal something from a small hotel out in a forest than from the Estoril Casino!

Tuesday morning, William rose early. By 7:00 a.m., he was watching a local news program on a TV in the kitchen while he ate his bowl of Cheerios. His ears suddenly focused on a story reporting that the Dutch philanthropist Duke Wilhem had been killed during a street robbery Sunday night. He'd been stabbed around 9:00 p.m. while taking his dog for its evening walk. The Duke's wallet and watch were missing and the broadcast said the police suspected a mugging gone wrong. He also found an editorial in the morning paper calling for more neighborhood police patrols. The rich people of Estoril and Cascais didn't like hearing of a neighbor being killed in a petty street crime.

William didn't believe in coincidences and mentally noted that this was the second person who'd died within just a few days after meeting with him. What did the Duke and Braganza have in common other than him – and the fact they both were of an age that they'd personally experienced WW II? The matter of Admiral Horthy and the Hungarian jewels that had allegedly gone missing decades earlier obviously came to his mind. He'd learned of the jewels from Braganza's diary and had discussed Horthy with the Duke. Very likely there were other players to this story that he simply didn't know about yet and who might have had something to do with their deaths. It was very frustrating, akin to trying to solve a jigsaw puzzle, but without having all the pieces. Horthy's son popped into William's mind and he decided that a chat with him might be even more valuable now that the Duke was dead.

He concluded that there was no reason, nor time, to come up with a terribly clever plan. He'd simply phone the pharmaceutical firm as soon as he arrived at the Embassy, put on the usual bluff and bluster of an American diplomat, and ask for an appointment. He could always pin his request for an appointment to somehow being related to the upcoming war in Kuwait. William had long been a believer of the motto, "if you can't impress them with your knowledge, baffle them with your bullshit." Now was an occasion for the latter. His thinking then turned to Olivia. He contemplated whether she, as a close acquaintance and now research assistant, might be in any danger. He tried ringing her at her home, but without success. She shouldn't be of any interest to whomever killed Braganza and the Duke, but he'd prefer to be safe than sorry.

Promptly at 9:00 a.m., William phoned the Novo Pharmaceutical Company and explained his reason for calling. Once he'd been passed up the bureaucratic ladder several times and repeated the reasoning for wanting a meeting with President Horthy, he finally had an appointment for Wednesday morning. After listening to his own imaginative spiel about wanting to explore the impact of the upcoming war on Middle East pharmaceutical supplies, even William believed he had a legitimate reason for the meeting.

On Tuesday night, William went as usual to the club to play piano. He simply didn't tell the COS he was doing that. His security detail enjoyed the evening. Two of the CIA men who'd arrived from HQS came into the establishment with him, while two more stayed outside and watched the front door. Two of the JP's counterterrorism officers also came in with him. William wasn't sure what the reimbursement policy of the JP was for its officers while guarding someone in a night club, so he quietly told the waiter to tell those two gentlemen that their drinks were on him. It was a pretty good crowd for a Tuesday in January, as there was a group of twenty American tourists present as well as all the security guards!

An additional reason why William enjoyed playing piano at the club was that it gave him an opportunity to people watch. He knew most tunes well enough that he could play them while he scrutinized the customers seated at the tables. Being able to understand people was a needed skill for an intelligence officer. That analysis began before he'd ever even speak with a person – just from watching and "reading" their body language. At the club, he could learn some things if a person was seated alone, but it was easier if there were two, three or four together. It was an inexact science, if one could even call it a science, but William enjoyed the game. He could spot the couples really in love, the pairs in which one person wished they weren't there, or sometimes when neither person looked happy to be there.

Because of being on the verge of another major war, William reached back that night into his repertoire and played a number of the melancholy love songs from the first years of WW II, when the situation seemed bleakest for the Allies. The theme of lovers facing separation because of war still resonated well, regardless of when the war was. Such songs fit well in a candle-lit room, full of blue smoke. He could have been in a 1940s wartime bar in Paris, London or Berlin.

Several customers sent notes up to him with requested songs. Shortly into his second set, he received an odd missive. It read: "You have something of Gabrielle Braganza's that doesn't belong to you. Perhaps you should return it before any more 'accidents' occur." There was no name to the note. To signify that he'd gotten the note and understood the message, William announced that the next song, *We'll Meet Again,* was in memory of Senhora Braganza. He presumed that the note was in reference to her attaché case. William still hadn't decided what he would do with the case, but figured he might as well let whomever had sent the note to him know that he'd understood their message. He'd initially felt it rather overkill that he had four bodyguards in the club. Now he was glad they were there, although he couldn't tell them about the strange note, as he'd decided not to tell anyone at the Embassy about his private "treasure hunt." After his third and final set, several customers came up to briefly chat with him and then finally a single man who looked to be about fifty and had very Germanic features approached him. He had short-trimmed, brown hair and a face that appeared as though its owner had lived a very hard life. Contrary to the previous fans who'd spoken with him, there was no smile on his face.

He said in accented-English, "I enjoyed your playing *We'll Meet Again.*"

"I thought you might like it," replied William. "I have an attaché case with many old newspaper articles and photos that Mrs. Braganza gave me to study in regard to her desire to have several buildings that had once belonged to her father returned to her. I'll be happy to give the briefcase to whomever is her next of kin or rightful heir to her property. Would that be you? You know, there's nothing of real value in the case, so I'm surprised at your great interest in it."

"Don't pretend to be so naive. In the past few months, she has twice visited Bavaria where Herr Horthy lived after the war until he moved to Estoril in 1950. And in late 1989, once the Communist Regime in Hungary collapsed, she also traveled to Budapest with questions about Horthy. Perhaps you simply don't appreciate what is of value in the briefcase, but we do and for your own health and those around you, you should immediately give it to me." His face was hardening and his tone was getting harsher.

"And if your claim you have nothing to hide is true, why do you need so many bodyguards?" At that moment, Nick came quickly over to the piano. He hadn't heard the exchange between William and the stranger, but he didn't like the look on either of their faces. William had been smiling and happy while speaking with the first fans who'd come up to him after his final set. Not so much with this last fellow.

"Are you ready to go home, William?" asked Nick, who likewise had no smile on his face." He spoke to William, but was staring intently at the stranger. Despite Nick's age, he was still well-built and struck most people as a man you probably didn't want to start a fight with. Following his years with the Office of Strategic Services in WW II, Nick had been an enforcer for the Kansas City mob for several decades. He never liked to engage in a fight, but if one started, he knew how to quickly bring it to an end.

"Yes, just finishing up." He turned back to the stranger and said, "I'm glad you enjoyed the music."

The stranger nodded and said, "Yes, very much. I hope to hear you play again very soon." He then turned and quickly walked away.

"He didn't seem like a real friendly guy," remarked the owner.

"Oh, I get fellows like him from time to time. They all think they're music critics." William laughed. He didn't want to tell Nick or his security detail about the actual conversation he'd just had as he didn't want to tell anyone about the possible WWII treasure that he was searching for in Portugal.

One of the JP bodyguards had been watching the verbal exchange by the piano and followed the stranger out of the restaurant and noted down his license plate number before he could drive off. A quick radio check showed that it was a rental car. They'd follow up on that the next morning.

William didn't sleep well that night, even with his security detail surrounding his house. He was worried about Olivia's safety as he'd been unable to reach her all day. As he finally drifted off to sleep, he was thinking that the unpleasant visit at the club did seem to confirm that he was on to something concerning Horthy's missing jewels.

The following morning, when William came down for breakfast, one of the JP officers, accompanied by one of the CIA security officers, came in to speak with him.

"We checked on your unfriendly music fan from last night. His name is Jurgen Müller, a German national of Munich. According to Interpol, besides running a used car dealership, he's connected with an underground, neo-Nazi group. Such groups are illegal in Germany, so its members refer to it as a historical society and a survival skills club. That keeps them from being arrested, but it doesn't really fool anybody as to its real interests and goals. His father had been a colonel in the German Gestapo, who was killed in 1945."

"Did his dossier say anything about his being a piano player?" joked William.

"No, but we could check."

"He's a weird guy, but he doesn't seem like anybody who would be connected with a Libyan terrorist group." William cocked his head, shrugged his shoulders and raised his eyebrows. His typical gesture of "it's a mystery to me."

"Probably not, but we'll be getting some more information on Herr Müller and see if we can determine what he's doing here in Lisbon."

"We'll also run his name past CIA HQS and see if anything pops up," added the CIA man.

"Excellent," replied William. He turned back to the JP officer. "Are there really still neo-Nazi groups around? I would have thought that all that geriatric crowd would have died of old age by now."

"No, there's a whole new, younger generation come along. Some, like Müller, are children of old Nazis. Others are just thugs by inclination who find one right-wing group or the other a convenient place to hang their hats."

"Sad world. Well, shall we head for the Embassy?"

He phoned Olivia once he'd reached his office and learned that she'd been up in Porto the entire day before on business.

"Could you join me for lunch today here at the Embassy? We have several aspects of the research project to discuss."

"Certainly. What time do you want me to arrive?"

"Would twelve be convenient?"

"That will work fine for me. I'll see you in a few hours." She thought that it was a nice step in their relationship that he was willing to be seen with her again in front of his work colleagues.

William's security entourage arrived at the Novo pharmaceutical firm promptly at the appointed time of 1000 hours. From the look on the face of the rent-a-cop at the front gate to the grounds of the firm, William realized that the three cars did make a rather impressive entrance. Horthy Jr. happened to be looking out his office window on the top floor of the three-story administrative building of the firm. He too was impressed. Perhaps he'd underestimated the importance of a Second Secretary at the American Embassy. He immediately told his secretary to arrange for some coffee and pastries to be brought up from the cafeteria for the meeting. He'd originally only scheduled Mr. Wythe for a twenty-minute session, but along with the pastries order, he also told her to cancel anything on his schedule for the next hour and to hold all phone calls. One American bodyguard and one JP officer accompanied William up to the third-floor meeting. Horthy recognized security personnel when he saw them.

A pleasant smile came upon Horthy's face as William entered the president's outer office. "Good morning, Mr. Wythe," he stated in excellent English and extended his hand to shake that of his visitor. "Do come in."

The two bodyguards fell back, to wait outside as only Horthy, his secretary and William entered the inner suite. Maria was present to pour the coffee.

"Would you prefer to speak English or Portuguese?" asked Horthy as he pointed William in the direction of a comfortable chair around a circular coffee table, rather than at his massive desk of Brazilian mahogany wood.

William smiled pleasantly and lied like the perfect diplomat. "I do speak Portuguese, but not nearly as well as your excellent English, so let's continue in English if you don't mind."

The secretary poured both men coffee and placed pastries on beautiful hand-painted, china plates in front of them, then left the room. William had read that Miklos Jr. was eighty, but he was quite impressed with how youthful the man appeared. His hair was completely white, but he moved with no difficulties and looked more like a man in his mid-sixties. He obviously had good genes, or he was taking a lot of his own pharmaceuticals!

"Have you been serving long in Lisbon, Mr. Wythe?"

"Almost a year now – and a most pleasant year it has been. I understand that you've been living in Portugal for forty years, yes?" That statement served to let Horthy know that William had done his homework on his background. There then followed the typical, polite getting-acquainted chit-chat for several minutes, before Horthy stated, "So, Mr. Wythe, how is it I may be able to help you and the American Government today?"

"Well, as anybody who's been watching the news knows, there's about to be a major war in the Middle East involving Iraq."

"Of course."

"And there will be a number of ripple effects from that war. One will be in the field of the demand and availability of pharmaceuticals. Washington has tasked each American Embassy in countries that produce medicines to get an idea of who is currently supplying drugs to that region of the Middle East. I trust that such data for your company is not considered confidential."

"No, no, not confidential at all, though hopefully the data I will provide you will stay just with the United States Government. We actually sell more to African countries than the Middle East, and some products are sold here within Europe, but I will gladly make available to you the statistics on all of our external sales"

"That would be very kind of you," responded William with his perfected diplomatic smile.

Horthy went over to his desk and phoned to someone and told them to provide as quickly as possible all foreign sales data for the past two years. He then returned to his chair. "The data should be ready for you in about fifteen minutes."

"That will be wonderful. While we're waiting, I hope you won't mind if I ask you a personal question about your background."

"Not at all, what is your question?"

William took another sip of his coffee. "As I was doing my homework about you and your family, I came across the fascinating fact that your father was Admiral Horthy, the de facto leader of Hungary for many years."

"Yes, I am Miklos Jr. My father had indeed been the leader of Hungary from about 1921 till October 1944 when Hitler had him arrested and taken, along with my mother and myself to Germany."

"My question is, why did your father choose to move in 1950 to Portugal, or was he simply told that was his only option?"

Horthy laughed softly. "Well, there weren't that many countries interested in letting my father resettle in their country, but he did have a fondness for Portugal. He'd visited here a number of times back in the 1930s, both on official travels and vacation trips. My father and Antonio Salazar had become good friends before the war, which no doubt helped get him to accept the suggestion by the Americans that Portugal should agree to his request for settlement here in 1950. The West Germans didn't want to be permanently stuck with him."

"I see. Did Salazar put any conditions on your father being allowed to move to Portugal?"

"Nothing too strenuous. They were simply that my father was to lead a quiet life as a retiree and stay completely out of politics. Make no statements, nor give any interviews – that sort of thing, which seemed quite reasonable."

"Reasonable indeed, though it must have been difficult to adjust to a life totally in the shadows, after having been in the limelight as the leader of a country for more than twenty years."

A quick smile came to Horthy Jr.'s face. "You know that ban also applied to me, as I had been involved in my father's government – at least until I was kidnapped by the SS and put in Dachau prison."

"I hadn't known that," responded William with genuine surprise. "Then you were very lucky to survive the war."

"Yes, although I was kept at Dachau in a small VIP prisoners section, with some other gentlemen, so I had it slightly better than most people there. Very near the end of the war, I was transferred to Bavaria and joined my father."

"You've had quite a life. How did you get involved in the pharmaceutical business?"

"Quite by accident. In 1959, another Hungarian refugee living here in Portugal came to me and asked if I'd like to get involved with the founding of this company by two scientists."

"Ah, so they were looking for a capital investment from you?"

Horthy laughed. "I had no money, but the three others had no idea of how to organize and make a company function. I did."

"Well, it certainly appears as though you have done well with this company."

"At age eighty, I'd have to say that indeed I've done well, starting out in 1959 with almost nothing."

"If you don't wish to answer this question, I will understand, but having spent much of my life in the realm of international affairs, shall we call it, I'm curious as to who funded your family's early years here in Lisbon. The address of your family home in Estoril, where your father moved to in 1950, is in quite a nice neighborhood. If your father and you were to lead quiet lives of pensioners, did the Portuguese or American governments provide you financial support in those early years?"

"A very good question, Mr. Wythe. A number of people did give us money in those first few years, and I think Mr. Salazar perhaps did as well. Now, we didn't arrive with just the clothes on our backs, as many post-war refugees did, but we didn't arrive with suitcases of gold as several so-called historians and journalists have written over the years."

William gave him a sympathetic nod. "Yes, well there are still to this day many instances of when journalists never let facts get in the way of a good story!"

"Ha, I wish we had arrived with suitcases of gold! Actually, here's a funny story. In the last year or so of his life, at age 88, my father, like many old people, began suffering from dementia. Often, usually after drinking good Hungarian red wine, he would tell me in a confidential voice not to worry about money because he had a fortune in jewels hidden here in Portugal – that they would be arriving any day."

William smiled. "And did they?"

Horthy shrugged his shoulders and turned his palms upwards. "I'm still waiting."

William had two reasons to smile. The first was the one that Horthy understood; senile old man believes he has hidden treasure. The second was because it seemed to confirm the story in Braganza's diary of a plan for Horthy to use the British SOE officers to smuggle jewels to Portugal! Perhaps everyone was delusional, but several people believed in the same fantasy!

At that moment Horthy's secretary knocked on the office door and entered with the data that Mr. Horthy had promised to William.

Horthy stood up to take the envelope from Maria. William stood as well.

"Here is the data that you requested. Do let me know if there is anything else that my firm can do to help the American Government. The world will be much better off once it is rid of that evil dictator, Saddam Hussein."

William took the envelope. "Thank you very much for your time and your assistance." They shook hands and William departed. He tried not to smile too broadly, while walking out and thinking about Papa Horthy's "demented" dreams that he had a treasure hidden somewhere in Portugal!

William and his security entourage arrived back at the Embassy with plenty of time to spare before Olivia was to arrive for lunch at noon. He took the data he'd been given by Horthy down to the State Department's Economics Officer, who was quite pleased to receive the information. William couldn't see himself why anybody would care about such esoteric data, but each man had his own rice bowl to fill – and if he had made the Econ Officer happy, he was glad to have been of assistance.

Olivia arrived promptly on time, wearing a beautiful beige wool coat with shiny brass buttons down the front and up on the shoulders. Her purse was checked by security in the outer lobby and she walked through the metal detector to ensure that she was carrying no weapons. She handed over her Brazilian passport and was given a visitor's badge to wear while in the building. The local receptionist then phoned William and he came down to meet her. They went up a flight of stairs and exited the chancery on its backside. The building with the combined cafeteria, Marine barracks and bar sat about fifty meters away. They walked carefully across the square cobblestones to the cafeteria. The stones gave a nice "old world" look to the grounds, but had caused many a sprained ankle to people trying to negotiate them.

The Embassy cafeteria didn't serve the best food in the city, but it was adequate and certainly a safe venue, for both of them. She hung her coat on one of the hooks by the door. The spectacular internal décor of the antique building more than compensated for the average luncheon fare. The walls were covered with original, hand-painted ceramic tiles from the 19th century and the floor was of granite. They both opted for the baked chicken lunch special, which came with roasted potatoes and peas. Several of his male colleagues were discreetly eyeballing the two of them. No one could recall William ever having brought anyone to lunch over the past nine months, much less a very attractive woman. The other ladies in the cafeteria were admiring her stylish, beige jacket with a floral-print, silk scarf wrapped gracefully around her neck. The jacket and the cream-colored, wool skirt contrasted nicely. Being a typical male, William paid no notice, but her dark-brown hair lay precisely around her head and her facial make-up was perfectly applied. It should have been. She'd spent the last hour before coming to lunch with her beautician.

Once they were seated and had begun their lunch, William began to speak of his visit that morning to Horthy Jr. He told her of what the son had had to say about his father's late-in-life comments that he was expecting a treasure in jewels to arrive any day.

"Oh my, that is exciting. I would think that on top of all the other indicators, that that almost guarantees that the story of the SOE smuggling jewels to Portugal for Horthy in 1944 is true!"

"It certainly looks very promising."

A mischievous look came to her face. "And what did he have to say about who had been his father's mistress back in the 1930s?"

"I couldn't think of any way to tie that question in with a discussion of his pharmaceutical sales to the Middle East."

"Coward," she responded with a grin.

William turned to the topic of why he'd invited her to meet with him that day. He started by telling her of the news story about the murder of Duke Wilhelm on Sunday night, which the police were officially attributing to a mugging, but he had his doubts. He then got to the highlight of his briefing for her.

"I had an interesting visitor last night at the club. He sent a note via a waiter to me, as if it was a song request, but it was much more. He then came up at the end of the evening and we talked briefly. In sum, he told me that I should give him Braganza's attaché case before any more 'accidents' happen to people. I presumed he was referring to the deaths of Braganza herself and probably Duke Wilhelm as well. I told him I would gladly give the case to her relative or the legal inheritor of it, but as it contained nothing but old photos and press clippings, I didn't understand his great interest in it. He expressed skepticism of my statement and suggested that perhaps I just didn't appreciate what I had in my possession. At that point, the owner of the bar came over to us and the man left. This morning, I carefully went through all the contents of her attaché case once more and I still don't see anything that should be of particular interest to that fellow – other than perhaps those few lines in her diary about jewels."

"Goodness, that was a strange encounter. Had you ever seen this fellow before?"

"Never. The police later learned his identity from his rental car license plate number and told me this morning. His name is Jurgen Müller, a German national from Munich. He owns a large used car dealership there, but he's also involved with an underground, neo-Nazi group."

He noticed that her eyes quickly narrowed and she remained silent for several seconds at hearing of Müller.

"My, you do attract the nicest sort of people to your club," she finally managed to say with a slight smile. She didn't recognize the name Müller, but her mind flashed back to her own father. He'd been posted at the German Embassy in Buenos Aires, Argentina as the representative of the German Finance Ministry during the war. He'd also been the head of that Embassy's Nazi Party organization. As the war was coming to a close, he escaped into southern Brazil, with a new name and two large trunks full of Argentinian pesos that he'd managed to take from the Embassy.

"Anyway, I asked you to meet with me today to tell you that I'm concerned about your safety."

"I appreciate your concern, but what does Müller and those two deaths have to do with me? I have no connection to WWII or Horthy."

He realized how foolish it all sounded and tried to make a bit of a joke of it. "Well, you aren't secretly running a neo-Nazi organization like my friend Müller are you?" he asked with a smile. "I mean, you did tell me you were of German ancestry."

"Why do you Americans always think anyone in South America of German background is a Nazi?" Her own large smile hid her contemplation of the fact that his question wasn't that far off the mark, at least as her father was concerned. The German Ambassador in Buenos Aires had given him the money towards the end of the war to take to Brazil. He instructed him to set up a network to help resettle Nazi officials who would be fleeing from Europe in the coming months.

"OK, OK, so you're not a Nazi," he joked, "but you do have a connection with me, plus now your research work on the missing jewels. This Müller guy plays tough. He just might decide that threatening you was a way of putting pressure on me."

"Oh, I see. And just what am I supposed to do about this? Stop seeing you?" She grinned.

"That seems a little extreme. How about you simply start staying at my place, at least till this threat disappears. I have security guards to spare," he joked. "I don't want to tell them about our 'treasure hunt', but they'll probably think anyway that your staying with me is a matter of romance or sex."

"That's certainly an original ploy to get a woman into bed," she teased.

"You're welcome to sleep in whatever bedroom you like."

"I'll have to look around your house and see what my choices are before deciding," she replied with a small smile. "I assume you want me to move in tonight?"

"Yes, leave here after lunch in a taxi and go straight to your apartment and pack a few bags. Then go back to your shop till about six, when you can take another taxi to my place. Leave me your car keys and I'll see that your car is driven away later today and parked back at your apartment."

"You're taking this Müller fellow very seriously aren't you?"

"Dead serious. By the way, I'm stopping at the residence of the British Military Attaché on the way home to talk about the SOE of WWII. He has an extensive personal library at his home and he might even have a few books there he could loan me. I'd love to know more about this Tristan fellow who was supposedly with the SOE here in Portugal."

"How about I cook us dinner tonight? You might as well learn the worst about me."

William laughed. "I'm sure you cook just fine."

"Oh, and will I just be cooking for you and me, or do I have to feed your entire security detail?"

"I better try your food first before I subject those fellows to it. They carry guns you know!" He grinned.

Shortly thereafter she called for a taxi and headed to her home to pack some clothes. She couldn't decide if his invitation was purely out of concern for her safety, or perhaps it did have at least a partial romantic aspect to it.

William and his security entourage pulled up at Colonel Clarke's home promptly at 5:00 p.m. as scheduled. Clarke was a Sandhurst graduate and came from a family of career military officers going back several centuries. He expected punctuality. Unfortunately for the Colonel, he'd been just a little too young to have been a part of WW II and had been serving in the wrong part of the world when the Suez debacle or the withdrawal from Aden had taken place in subsequent decades. He was thus a warrior who'd never had a good war of his own in which to participate. He compensated for that by studying past wars and had a tremendous personal library. He'd even done a rotation at the Sandhurst Military Academy as a senior lecturer on military history. Despite his lack of time on a battlefield, he certainly looked like a career British officer should, tall with shoulders back, complete with neatly-trimmed mustache and a wind-weathered face.

Like William, he also appreciated a good single malt whiskey and William arrived with a gift bottle of 18-year old Oban.

After the initial greeting at the door, Connor commented about the heavy security detail. "Good God, even your Ambassador only has a one-car security escort and you have three cars full of people. Did you sleep with the wife of the wrong man here in Lisbon?"

"It's this crime-ridden neighborhood you live in. Anyone coming to this part of Cascais has to have a three-car detail." They both laughed. It was an inside joke. The British Military Attaches had all been living in this same glorious mansion in an exclusive part of Cascais for some forty years. Soon after WWII and while everyone in Portugal was still quite broke, the Military Attaché of the time secured a sixty-year lease of the mansion. The owner was a very pro-British member of a Portuguese aristocratic family, but who was broke at the time. Cascais had always been the upper class neighborhood of Lisbon, and had become even more elite over the last few decades. Fortunately, the British were still paying 1947 prices. Colonel Clarke's house was only exceeded in grandeur by the Ambassador's, which the British had owned for 150 years.

They went into the library where the Colonel had already placed a dozen selected books on the coffee table for William to examine.

"I already pulled out a few things that I thought might interest you. I do caution you however, take with a grain of salt some of what is written in these books, particularly the personal memoirs of old colonels written twenty or thirty years after the war – pretty questionable. If even half of what those old fellows wrote was true, we should have won the war in early 1944!" The Colonel laughed. "So what in particular are you interested in about the SOE during the war?" He'd opened the gift bottle of single malt and poured both of them a generous portion of the golden amber liquid.

"Well, I'd gotten talking recently with an old gentleman who was at the same dinner party as I was. We started conversing about WWII and he mentioned about how the SOE operated here in Portugal during the war. I'd always assumed that SOE men and women were operating up in Occupied France and the Low Countries. Why would there have been SOE officers here in Portugal?"

"You're correct that mostly the SOE was operating where the German Army was located, but I recall that there were a few chaps posted here. There would have been two reasons for that. One is that they staged out of Portugal for missions up into France or even to Italy and the Balkans. The second reason was to be ready in case Salazar threw in with the Nazis, or if the Germans simply invaded and took over both Portugal and Spain. I remember in particular that there were important wolframite mines here in Portugal. It's a mineral needed to make steel harder, be it for tanks or industrial drill bits. Had the German Army come into Portugal, the SOE was going to blow up and flood those mines."

"I never knew any of that. Any of those Portugal-based SOE chaps ever write their memoires?"

"None that come to mind, but I vaguely recall that one or two are mentioned in a few books that cover various operations and people. Let me thumb through the indexes of a few of these here."

"Check if you will for a fellow named Tristan in connection with Portugal – that was the first name of the SOE officer that the old gentleman was banging on about that night."

"Right." After several minutes of looking in different books, Connor spoke up. "Here we are, a Lt. Tristan Lewis. It says he was assigned to Portugal in June 1943 as a singleton. He disappeared in October 1944 while on a mission to Hungary, presumed dead at the age of twenty-five. His specialty was safe cracking."

"That must be the one. How many SOE officers named Tristan could there have been assigned to Portugal in WWII?"

"Well, Tristan was a fairly common first name back in those days. And one more thing, since it listed his specialty as safe cracking, there's a good chance he was a convicted criminal whom the SOE offered a deal of getting out of prison if he'd join the Army."

"Fascinating. If I encounter the elderly Portuguese fellow again, I'll have to ask him how and why he knew this Tristan."

"Do that. He just might have an interesting tale to pass along. My father always suspected that some of those fellows that SOE and MI6 picked up out of jails spent half their time in foreign countries committing crimes when not garroting Germans! And do let me know what you find out. Might make for an interesting article in one of our historical journals."

William made his farewell and then proceeded home. Olivia arrived about ten minutes later. He'd already told the security guards who had the nighttime shift that he was expecting a lady guest to arrive with suitcases that evening. Both the American and the Portuguese bodyguards grinned when told of William's expected female guest and that she would be staying for several days.

Upon seeing Olivia when she arrived in a taxi, one of the Portuguese guards discreetly gave William a big thumbs up and a grin of approval. The two American guards shared the Portuguese guard's opinion, but refrained from gesturing their thoughts to William.

In addition to two suitcases, Olivia had also brought a large bag full of spices and several kitchen utensils. She feared that a bachelor's kitchen shelves would be sorely lacking in needed items with which to cook a proper dinner. She'd also stopped at a butcher shop that day and had brought along the ingredients to make beef stroganoff.

Over dinner, William brought her up to date with what he'd learned from the British Military Attaché about Tristan Lewis, including about his safe cracking skills and possibly having been a criminal before the war.

"So it is plausible that the Tristan of Braganza's diary could have opened a hotel safe and reset the combination to something else," commented Olivia.

"Yes, but what safe could that have been that the hotel management wouldn't have then noticed that the official combo for it no longer worked? Surely, they would have done something about it and had it opened."

Neither had a good answer to that question.

"I suspect that we should make a visit soon to this Busaco Forest Hotel," suggested William.

"Just us, or will your own personal army be going with us?"

"Good point. I'll have to give a little thought as to how to get rid of my guards for the weekend. Also, with us probably being right on the verge of the invasion, this may not be the best time for me to be asking to take a few days' vacation!"

"Well, I can take some days off any time, so just let me know when you want to go," she stated with a sweet smile.

"You have the most understanding boss. When we do decide on a date to go out there, I'll have you make the reservations in your name and do it from the dress shop. We'll keep the trip as low profile as possible. I'll have to work on how to handle the security detail question."

They talked some more about her life in Brazil and he shared a few humorous stories of his previous postings. When the hands of the grandfather clock in the living room pointed to almost eleven, William brought up the slightly awkward issue of it being bedtime. She'd picked out one of the upstairs bedrooms shortly after her arrival as hers and had unpacked her clothes in there, but nothing said she actually had to sleep there. William's instincts told him that a suggestion to her of joining him in his bed would be gladly accepted, but given all that was going on around them, it just didn't seem the time to move their relationship to the next stage. He was under the threat of assassination, neo-Nazis were sniffing around him and he had a security guard sitting on the ground floor of the house.

He pointed at the clock. "I know that your dress shop doesn't open till eleven, but my slave-driving Ambassador expects me there promptly at eight-thirty in the mornings. I think it's bedtime."

"I'm feeling a little sleepy myself." She stood up, yawned and headed towards the stairs, and he followed behind her.

At her bedroom door, which they came to first, he started to ask her if she had everything she needed, but didn't get much said. Both of them simply leaned into one another and began a long embrace and kiss. His nose deeply inhaled the smell of her Quelques Fleurs perfume. He liked it a lot, almost as much as the delicate touch of her tongue wrapped around his.

He reconsidered his position on postponing the next step in their relationship, but showed some resolve and simply said, "Well, that will give me something very pleasant to think about while falling asleep tonight."

She gave him a sweet smile and softly replied, "Eu também."

He walked on down the hallway to his room without turning to look back. He wasn't sure he could resist changing his mind if she smiled at him once more that night.

The guards outside had watched carefully as lights went on in both bedrooms and a few minutes later went out, first in one room and a minute later, in the second room. One of the Portuguese guards then handed over a fifty escudo note to an American.

"I told you it wouldn't happen on the first night," said the American with a grin as he put the bank note in his pocket.

Both William and Olivia lay in their respective rooms thinking about the other. Debating in their minds whether they were truly falling in love with one another and why. He questioned whether it was actually "love" or was he simply looking for a new purpose in his life? Mary Beth had been dead almost ten years, his children nearly grown and his career coming to a close. No, he didn't think his feelings for her were based on such simplistic reasons. He felt good when around her and missed her when she wasn't. Some couples were good together while out and about doing things. With Olivia, he felt happy simply in her presence while they were doing nothing.

A similar stream of questions were going through Olivia's mind twenty feet away in the next bedroom. She began by thinking about Paulo. She'd loved him once, but she'd finally come to realize that he'd always been so independent, so self-reliant. She had always simply been an additional shiny ornament to his life. She wanted to be needed as well as loved and William did indeed need a partner in his life. He was handsome and funny and caring, but the winning factor was that he needed her. As she was finally falling asleep, she concluded that "love" couldn't be scientifically analyzed as she'd been trying to do so. Whatever the reasons, she did love William and that was all there was to it.

CHAPTER 11

I t was late Thursday night, January 17th. William turned off his bedside lamp and laid down in bed. Olivia was sleeping in the guest bedroom – mostly because neither of them had the courage to suggest otherwise to the other. A cold rain was hitting against William's bedroom window with a steady rhythm. He laid on his side in his bed, staring at the window which was covered with rain drops. Occasionally, one would lose its adhesion to the pane and gravity would bring it into contact with the next one and then they would start an uncontrolled slide downwards. All the droplets joining into one indistinguishable stream of water – sort of like all the years of his past decade of drinking — just an indistinguishable blur of time. But something had changed in the last few weeks and Olivia was now a part of his life, which seemed to have a renewed purpose. He was becoming very attached to her. He'd have to decide soon just how much of an attachment he would allow to develop. She deserved more than the man he'd been in recent years. He wondered if at this late date he could still change his life or was he now simply trying to sell himself a dream?

Dreams. That's what he'd fulfilled for many people he'd targeted over the decades. He hadn't just offered them money or a new life in America. He'd sold dreams to those people who were in need of them. His mind then turned to the upcoming war. Despite all the last minute, diplomatic phone calls around the world and secret, high-level negotiations that continued, most everyone had anticipated all that week that the shit was just about to hit the fan. It was like watching dark clouds gather on a hot, still summer's afternoon in the Midwest. Any farmer knew that rain would start pouring down in buckets any minute in that situation. And anybody who followed international politics knew that Saddam was never going to withdraw from Kuwait and that the multi-national force would be launching hell any day. The embedded American journalists with U.S. Army and Marine brigades on the land and out on the sea had stopped filing substantive reports. They were all now fluff pieces, like how a young Marine Sergeant was expecting news any day about whether his wife back at Twenty-Nine Palms, California had given him a son or a daughter. That was the only reporting that the military censors were allowing to be sent.

Just before midnight, the COS began phoning all his staff at their homes. His last call was to William.

"I just had a call from Headquarters. Attacks started thirty minutes ago – air, land and sea. Turn on CNN if you get it. Some idiot is broadcasting from his hotel rooftop in downtown Baghdad via a satellite link while we're bombing the hell out of the city."

"Thanks for the call. Anything we're supposed to immediately do?"

"Not tonight, but be at the Embassy at 0600 hours. You might also alert your security detail that the show has started – just in case this triggers an attack on you."

"I'll do that." The line went dead.

William went downstairs and found Corya reading a book and drinking a glass of cold milk. His 9mm was on the table, next to the milk – a rather incongruous picture that Norman Rockwell had never painted.

"Anything wrong?" calmly asked the head of the American security team.

"I just had a phone call from the COS. The attack started a half hour ago. You'd best let the team know."

"I'll do that."

"And we need to be at the Embassy at 0545 hours in the morning, for an all-hands meeting at 0600. You should probably come in and attend that as well."

"Will do." He put down the book and picked up his weapon. "I'll go advise the guys."

William felt sorry for the guards outside in the cold rain. He was impressed with the calmness of Adam. One would think that William had just informed him that he simply wanted to go into the Embassy early the next morning so that he could order pancakes for breakfast. Notification that the largest military invasion since D-Day had started had generated a three-word response of, "I'll do that." William then headed back upstairs to see if Olivia was still awake in her bedroom. If not, he'd just let her sleep till morning. He saw a crack of light from under her door, so he tapped softly on her door.

"Yes?"

"It's me. May I come in for a moment?"

"Of course." She pulled the covers up a little higher on her bare chest. He suspected she slept naked.

He pushed open the door and went over and sat down on the side of her bed. She'd been browsing through a magazine.

"I thought you might want to know that the war has started."

She reached over and took hold of his right hand. "Oh, I'm so sorry to hear that. I was so hoping that something would get worked out at the last minute. I know how it will end, but I hate to see all those young men on both sides die."

William thought of the famous George Patton line, "No bastard ever won a war by dying for his country. He won it by making the other poor dumb bastard die for his." He decided not to share that quote with her.

"I think it will be over pretty quickly. Saddam and his army have no idea of what state-of-the-art warfare by the U.S. military will be like."

"Stay with me please – just for a little while."

William kicked off his slippers, lifted the covers and slipped in beside her, confirming that she was naked. He put his arm behind her head. She turned and rested hers on his chest. He liked the feel of her body against his. He could tell by her slowed breathing that within just a few minutes she was sound asleep. A half hour later, he quietly left her and returned to his own room. He didn't get CNN on his local TV channels. He'd just have to wait till morning at the Embassy to learn how the invasion of Kuwait and Iraq was going. Surprisingly, he fell asleep within only a few minutes once back in his own bed. It was the tension of waiting for what he knew was coming that had been affecting his sleep the last few nights. Now that the war was on, he slept just fine.

Both the American and Portuguese guards outside the house were on high alert the rest of the night. The Judicial Police sent an additional car and four more men. They shared the COS' theory that the start of the war might be the trigger for the assassination plan on William. And if not, at least four more men earned some overtime pay.

The streets of Lisbon were completely deserted as William's ever-growing motorcade zoomed towards the Embassy at 0515 hours. There'd been rain through the night. The streets glistened as they sped along, totally ignoring the traffic lights.

The 0600 meeting called by the COS only took thirty minutes and was mostly an update of what Elliot had seen on CNN. All the faces around the table were very somber. They then reviewed what anybody knew about the whereabouts of any Iraqi in the country, or any "radical Islamist" types who might feel inclined to strike at an American citizen or the Embassy, in solidarity with Saddam. Personally, William thought the latter possible attacks very unlikely. Saddam had taken Iraq on a rather non-sectarian path and had put a number of mullahs in prison. Why would any fervent Muslim care to aid Saddam? But he kept his views to himself. He'd learned in his first month at post that Elliot had no interest in any opinions except his own. The COS constantly tapped his fingers on the conference table that morning. His usual sign that he was anxious or bored.

The COS touched briefly on his thought that the invasion might trigger the assassination attempt on William, but nothing had happened in the last six hours. William thought the COS almost sounded a bit disappointed that no one had tried to kill him.

"Please send me in the next five minutes any input you might have for my Sitrep to Headquarters that I'll be sending out at 0700 hours." Those were the COS' final words of the meeting. As they filed out of the room, William speculated whether any of the other officers might be having the same thought as his — what had been the point of coming in so early for that meeting – other than image building for the COS? When the Ambassador and the State Department officers showed up at their regular 0830, they'd learn how Elliot and his Agency team had been there since 0600. And by definition, if they'd come in so early, it must have been for some important reason.

William stopped to refill his coffee cup on the way back to his office.

Nobody had said anything directly to him, but for the past month, William had discreetly substituted top-quality Brazilian coffee courtesy of Olivia in place of the cheap stuff from the commissary. It definitely tasted better.

The Station's Sitrep, sent with IMMEDIATE precedence, would arrive at Headquarters within five minutes after leaving the Embassy. Given the time difference with Washington, he wondered who the COS thought would be there at 0205 hours to be informed that the Station basically had nothing to report, but was standing by to instantly launch into action — should Headquarters task it to do anything.

Discussion all day at the Embassy was about the war. William stopped by as usual at the Marine Happy Hour that Friday evening at the end of the work day. The bar was packed as everyone wanted to hear what anybody else knew, or just to exchange the latest rumors. William found the Gunny there as he was every Friday evening, drinking his tonic water with a lemon slice. William only ordered a beer.

"You look rather glum tonight, Gunny. Anything wrong?"

"No, I guess my wishing that I was down there in the sandbox is showing on my face."

William thought to himself that most men would be happy to not be in a hot war zone, if they had not been called upon, but he was sure that Aloysius Murphy was expressing his genuine desire – not just posturing for show. For true professional warriors like Gunny, if there was a war going on, he wanted to be involved.

As the two of them chatted about how the war was going so far in Kuwait, Gunny asked, "Anything further been learned about the supposed threat against you?"

"Not that I'm aware of," replied William. "I still have both the American and the Portuguese security detail, so I feel pretty safe," joked William.

"Anything else changed recently in your life?" inquired Aloysius in a slightly lowered voice.

"Nothing of any particular consequence," lied William. "Why do you ask?"

"Well, to be quite blunt, over the last two weeks, I've hardly seen you take a drink, and tonight it's been only one beer. It's like you've found a new purpose in life, or a new woman, maybe. None of my business exactly what's new, but whatever it is – keep on doing it."

William smiled. "Well, let's just say that I've been so busy, that I haven't had time to feel sorry for myself and to think so much about the past."

"That's good. Keep it up." Then he added, "Though I still think there's a woman involved here somehow," and laughed.

William laughed with him. "You jarheads always think there's a woman involved in everything!" William drank the last of his beer and stood to leave. "I gotta go make the world safe for democracy. Goodnight!"

"Goodnight William. Watch your six!"

Olivia arrived home on Monday a half hour after William. She'd stopped after work at a hole-in-the-wall carry-out chicken place just a few blocks from her dress shop and picked up a container of piri-piri chicken. She remembered that William had told her once that he quite enjoyed this style of chicken covered with the hot, African spice of piri-piri.

Over dinner, they spoke of how the war was going. Most of what William knew came from television news broadcasts and was as much rumor as actual fact. The first few days did seem to be going very well, with reports that American fighter planes were clearing the skies of all Iraqi planes that even dared to leave their bases. Russian-made fighters flown by Russian-trained Iraqis were simply no contest for the Americans. Over coffee after dinner, Olivia inquired about his two daughters and they spoke of them for a while. William then inquired of her, "Why have you and your husband never had children? Neither of you wanted children?"

Olivia laughed slightly and then her face turned quite serious. "We both wanted children, but nothing happened, for which he naturally blamed me. No Brazilian man could ever believe that he was incapable of fathering children."

"I suppose few men, of any nationality, like to believe that."

"Eventually, I saved some of his sperm after sex one night and secretly had it tested. It turned out that it was his problem."

William was curious how she did that, but didn't care to actually inquire. "And did you present that fact to him?"

Olivia looked shocked. "You've obviously never known any Brazilian men. Had I told him of the test and the results, he probably would have killed me on the spot with his bare hands."

The conversation then drifted through several mundane topics, before Olivia brought up a sensitive one. "What do you see in your future? I mean, you've said that in about two years you will retire. Then what will you do?"

"To be honest, I've never given it much thought. It always seemed a day so far off into the future that it was a topic I never considered really worth thinking about. I doubt if I'll continue to live around Washington D.C. Virginia never seemed like my home. It was always simply a place we'd lived in between overseas assignments. Besides, on just my retirement pension, I couldn't afford to live there. I'd have to take some contract job with one of the "beltway bandit" consulting firms – and wind up doing about the same type of work, except wearing a different colored badge hanging around my neck. No, I'd really prefer to move elsewhere for retirement, and really retire."

"Back to your home state of Indiana, maybe?"

He was surprised she'd remembered that small detail about him. He'd only ever mentioned it once and fleetingly. "Yes, I suspect I might just go home to Indiana – that would probably be the easiest choice." He then hesitated for a moment. "I suppose my decision might be affected by the question of whether it will still be just me, or if perhaps I might remarry someday." He then realized that was the first time in a decade he'd ever said out loud or even thought about the idea of remarrying.

Olivia blushed, but then said, "And do you think that might happen someday?"

William slid his hand across the table and gently took hold of hers. "Well, to be honest, until recently I didn't think I ever would, but recently I've been thinking that I might – if the right woman came along." They both then sat there in silence for several long seconds, simply staring at each other.

"And where do you want to live once your divorce is final? Will you stay on here in Portugal?"

"Oh, I can be happy almost anywhere, as long as there's sunshine for at least a good part of the year, but if given my first choice, I would live in Rio de Janeiro."

"That wouldn't be awkward, having your ex-husband around?"

Olivia laughed. "There are five million people in Rio. I think he and I can both live there without stumbling across each other too often!"

William became conscious of the fact that he was still holding her hand. He decided that it was time to change the topic of conversation. "I think we should go to Busaco this coming weekend. I'll talk with the head of my security detail tomorrow morning and see what we can work out. I've looked on the map and the hotel is only about two hours from Lisbon."

"Yes, this coming weekend would be good for me as well. I'm dying to see if we are right about the jewels being hidden somewhere at that hotel. Phone me once you've spoken with your security man and then I'll make the reservations, as we discussed. Could you get away by two o'clock on Friday, so that we arrive while there is still some daylight?"

"That would be good, so we don't get lost out in the middle of nowhere. And we'll take your car. Less conspicuous than my car with diplomatic license plates."

On Tuesday morning, just after a quick morning staff meeting for all Station hands, William was back in his office, preparing to have a second cup of coffee when in walked Corya, the head of his security detail.

"Ah," said William, "I was just going to go find you. I have a matter to discuss with you."

Corya dropped his body into the one visitor's chair in front of the desk. "Well, let me go first as there might be nothing for you to discuss with me."

William gave him a wave of his hand. "Please, go first."

"We just received a cable from Headquarters this morning. Unless Station has any further evidence about this assassination attempt, they're pulling me and my team out of here on Thursday morning. At the speed the war is going down in Kuwait, they figure we'll be setting up a new Station in Kuwait City within just a matter of a few days. My team is to go down there and provide security for those folks."

"Well, we've had no new developments on this alleged threat for several weeks, so I've got no objection. And as you know, I've never taken this threat too seriously all along, so I'd say you guys should definitely go where you're really needed. Have you spoken yet with Elliot?"

"I figured that is what you'd say, but I wanted to speak with you before I went to see the COS. The message suggests that the Embassy see if the Judicial Police might still give you some coverage. I also got a secure phone call this morning here at the Embassy from my boss back in Washington. He said to tell you that if you're interested in simply being pulled out of here since you'll have no coverage, he'll have Headquarters make that suggestion – that way it wouldn't look like it was you asking to be pulled out."

William laughed. "Thank your boss, but I won't give the COS the satisfaction of being rid of me."

"I suspected that would be your response. Well, I'll go see wunderkind up at the end of the corridor, and then get on with making flight reservations, hopefully for Thursday afternoon."

"Thanks for all your kind assistance while you've been here."

"Well, with us or without us, you should be fairly safe in your house now. We've made all those improvements to the doors and windows, and put in the motion detector sensors on the outside."

William stood up and stepped over to shake Adam's hand. "Thanks again for all your efforts."

"That's what we get paid for." He shook William's hand and then started to leave, but stopped. "None of my business really, but will your 'house guest' be staying on, now that we're leaving? She's mighty pretty and very charming."

William nodded in agreement with his assessment of Olivia. "I'm not sure, perhaps. By the way, I'll probably just be staying at home both tonight and tomorrow night. The heating unit at the jazz club has died, so it will be closed for a few days."

"Good to know. A couple of my guys have been wanting to get out and see the city like tourists before we left. This might give them that chance." He started to leave the office, but then stopped. "Oh, you had something to discuss with me?"

"Since you're leaving town, it doesn't matter."

"OK, see you later."

William then phoned Olivia. "I'm available for this weekend. Go ahead and make that call."

"I'll do that right now. Will you be home by six?"

"Yes, I'll see you this evening when you get home."

William sat there at his desk and rubbed his right hand over the back of his neck, as he often did when thinking. He wasn't sure if he could honestly say he was in love with Olivia, but he admitted to himself that it did sound very nice knowing that she would be there waiting for him at the end of the day. At his age, perhaps that was love.

The Embassy Security Officer Alex Wilson came by William's office in the afternoon. "I just got off the phone with the Judicial Police. They're pulling their people off as of Wednesday. They said that if the Embassy no longer considered there to be a serious threat to you, neither would they. Their men are needed in a number of other places, with enhanced security being implemented at various Portuguese governmental facilities around the city."

"Makes sense. Next time you talk with anyone over at the JP, please pass along my personal thanks for all their efforts."

"I'll do that." Wilson started to leave, but then sat back down. "By the way, while talking with the JP, they had a little news about the Libyan Embassy for us."

"What's that?"

"You remember all that esoteric brouhaha about what verb exactly had been used concerning some Libyans entering Portugal – and if that intercepted message confirmed that terrorists were coming to town?"

"Yeah, I remember that. I didn't understand the intellectual argument, but I remember the controversy. What about it?"

Wilson smiled. "Well, it turns out that the Embassy is bringing in three construction guys to make some repairs. Their DCM contacted the owner of the building that they lease to see if he could get a set of architectural plans and told him that they were bringing in three guys to do some work."

William laughed. "Ha, so much for that message being proof of a Libyan terrorist plot!"

Wilson shrugged his shoulders. "You just never know. You look at the facts you get and guess at what they mean in that very moment. See you later."

William then turned his mind to planning his exit from Lisbon on Friday afternoon as quietly as possible– at least so that Herr Müller wouldn't be aware of the trip to the Busaco Forest Hotel. William hoped there would be no trouble out there, but it would be nice to have a little back-up available, just in case. His mind drifted to the Gunny and he wandered down to his office for an off-the-record chat.

"Gunny, you got a minute?"

Gunny looked up from the Time magazine he'd been reading. When things were running smoothly, many hours of his day were spent just waiting for something to go wrong and then to take action to correct the problem.

"Sure, William, come on in. What you need?"

William closed the office door behind him and took a seat on the uncomfortable, straight-back metal chair in front of Gunny's desk.

"Does the Marine Corps own you 24/7, or can a Marine take a part-time job on say the weekend to make a few bucks, as long as that job isn't in conflict with U.S. Government interests?"

Gunny smiled. "You mean, could I work Saturday afternoons at McDonalds?"

"Something like that."

"I suppose I could, but I already have a steady job for which I earn a few bucks now. Not sure it would be worth tying up my Saturdays to only make a few dollars more."

William stopped smiling. "I've been conducting some private research into the possible location of a small treasure left over from WW II, which legally probably doesn't have a rightful heir to whom it could be returned, if found. Thus, if I could locate it, it would be mine, except for the part I'd share with somebody who might care to assist me some weekend."

"That's an interesting hypothetical situation you've laid out. You are speaking in purely hypothetical terms, aren't you?"

"Yes, I am."

"And just how could a tired, old Marine assist you in this private research?"

"Well, there could be a fellow or two who are modern-day neo-Nazis who'd like that treasure for themselves. So, it might be a wise, precautionary step if I had a friend come along with me this weekend who knew how to throw a punch, or even use a gun I'd loan him, if it came to that. In any case, someone with experience and maturity, who'd stay calm in any situation."

"Fellows like that in Lisbon are rather rare, and probably expensive. And just where would this weekend be spent?"

"There's a nice hotel a couple of hours drive north from Lisbon. I'd pay you $1,000 cash and cover your expenses if you came along, even if absolutely nothing happens and I find nothing. If anything happens, or if I find even a bit of treasure that amount goes up to $10,000. If there's a real pot of gold waiting for me, then I'd give you $50,000. That might help you set up a nice massage parlor down in North Carolina in your retirement next year."

"Yes, I expect that would. Any other details I should know in order to make an informed decision."

"Olivia and I are going out to this fancy, old hotel in Busaco this Friday afternoon to spend the weekend. Maybe, we've solved an old riddle as to where this wartime treasure is hidden – maybe not. We're going to try to discreetly slip out of town, but if by chance a few bad guys who apparently are also looking for it do show up, you'd be real handy to have just down the hallway."

Aloysius remained silent for several long seconds, clearly calculating several angles of the proposal. "Oh, what the hell. I haven't done anything stupid in years and just sitting around here guarding this ugly building is boring me to death. Plus, $50,000 would indeed help me open a much nicer massage parlor next year than my current bank account would allow for. So, count me in." He reached across his desk and shook William's hand.

"And I assume the only people knowing about this little weekend excursion will be you, me and Olivia?"

"Damn, you are pretty smart for a jarhead," William replied with a grin.

The two then spent the next fifteen minutes discussing details and contingencies.

William and several other officers sat in the Station's small conference room most of that afternoon where the Admin officer had managed to set up a TV with a link to CNN, which was giving fulltime coverage to the fighting down in Kuwait and Iraq. The Station was also receiving a few sit reps out of CIA Headquarters on the course of the war. There appeared to be nothing but good news.

The Coalition's armored attack across the northern desert of Kuwait seemed to have taken the Iraqis completely by surprise – as they sat waiting for the U.S. Marines to make an amphibious landing from out of the Gulf. The official news briefer for the Coalition Command had made great emphasis in the days just before the war began of the readiness of the Marine Expeditionary Force already out on the sea, waiting to storm ashore. All of that talk had simply been a deception. William had also learned at the Station that the Russians had kept their promise that they would cut off all intelligence support to Saddam, which included satellite imagery. The Iraqi Army was thus basically blind and deaf and had no idea of the massive swing northward and then the dash across the desert. Not only had the Iraqis been taken by surprise, but a number of American journalists bitterly complained that they too had been deceived by the daily official press briefing. How were they to keep the American public informed, they argued, as to what was happening in the war, if all the military secrets weren't shared with the journalists? In other words, they hadn't been able to leak in advance to the world where and when the secret ground attack would take place. Journalists always amazed William. They seemed to have the idea that it was their God-given right to publish over the airways secrets they managed to get one way or the other, regardless of the consequences.

CHAPTER 12

O n Wednesday night, Duarte, one of the younger Judicial Police officers who'd been working with the CIA security team for the past several weeks, took three of the Americans out for a farewell night on the town. He spoke reasonably good English and was still a bachelor, so he knew some of the more "lively" spots in town. The three Americans were also bachelors, at least while they were out of the country. They began with a nice seafood dinner down near the docks. They all swapped stories of their past careers over dinner and then Duarte suggested he take them to a "private" club in the city. Lisbon didn't have strip clubs, as in America, but they had places for similar entertainment, known as private clubs. In such a place, a customer paid an annual membership fee and could also then purchase an entire bottle of alcohol, which was kept in a small, locked cabinet for the member between visits. No individual drinks were sold. The alcohol was quite expensive. The lowest price for a bottle of average Scotch was US$250. This particular club had dark wood paneling on the walls, elegant light fixtures and genuine leather-covered chairs and seat benches.

However, the reason for the high price of alcohol was not because of the décor, but because the club featured a number of very attractive, scantily-clad, young, female "hostesses" who delivered your bottle to your table. If invited, one or two of the lovely ladies would then also gladly sit with the members and guests and drink with them. Most were attired in sheer negligees that left little to the men's imagination. Neither of the two ladies who joined Duarte and his three guests spoke any English, but that caused little obstruction to an enjoyable visit.

An hour later, the JP officer suggested that they move on to another club, which he described as being "more exciting." None of the Americans objected to his proposal, but they did buy Duarte a new bottle of Scotch for his cabinet, as a "farewell gift", before they left the first place. All four of them also left each girl generous tips, placing the folded paper money at strategic locations of their costumes.

The next club was only four or five blocks away, so they left the car parked where it was and started walking till about halfway there, when Chuck realized he'd left his nice lighter back at the first place. The other two Americans sat down on a bench to have cigarettes while waiting for Duarte and Chuck to return. Half way through their cigarettes, they noticed a fellow in a rain coat walk up to a bus stop at the intersection about thirty yards from them. They were seated in a fairly dark area of the street, but the bus stop was under a street light, which gave them a good look at the man standing there.

Bill nudged Tim with his elbow and nodded down the street and spoke softly. "That guy by the bus stop — isn't that the insulting, little prick who spoke to us at the Embassy on our first day here?"

"You mean the COS?"

"Yeah, Elliot was his name."

Tim stared hard at the corner and waited till the man turned so that there was a better view of his face. He was wearing a fedora, but the two men could still get a good view of his face.

"By golly, I do believe that is him. "You think he's out here tonight doing a little spying?"

Bill chuckled softly. "Maybe he's just down in this part of town visiting some of the clubs we are."

"May be," replied Tim with a grin.

They sat in silence for another full minute. Suddenly, a full-sized Mercedes sedan came slowly past them and stopped at the bus stop. The COS-look-alike walked over and got in the passenger-side back door. They noticed that the inside dome light didn't come on, as most cars do when you open a door. The vehicle then quietly and slowly pulled away from the curb. The two men then looked at each other and made faces of curiosity. Both then pulled out small notebooks and pencils and noted down the license plate number of the Mercedes. They'd noticed that the plate number started with a CD, meaning it was a diplomatic plate for an embassy.

"Beats me," said Bill.

"Strange," replied Tim.

A minute later, Duarte and Chuck finally returned.

"It took you two long enough," commented Tim. "Did you two stay to have another drink?"

"No drink, but Maria needed help adjusting her costume and Duarte being a gentleman, helped her," replied Chuck. All four laughed.

"Say, Duarte, do you carry around with you a chart of which countries have what diplomatic plate numbers?" asked Tim.

"Of course." He reached into his pants pocket and pulled out a small, notebook. "What was the three digit number right after the CD?"

"One hundred and forty two," simultaneously replied both men.

"Let's see … that's the Soviet Union. Why?"

"Oh, nothing special," replied Tim. "We saw a nice Mercedes drive by here a minute ago. I was just curious. Let's get on to that next club."

When Duarte dropped the three Americans off at their hotel about midnight, the three stopped at the lobby bar for a nightcap.

Once the waiter had delivered their beers and walked away, Chuck spoke. "OK, what was with the Mercedes Benz and the Soviet plate number? I'm betting there's more to the story than it just happened to drive by you two."

"Well, it's pretty strange," replied Tim with a low voice as he leaned forward and gave Chuck a precise accounting of what happened while they were minding their own business having cigarettes on that bench.

"Shit," was Chuck's one-word response.

"Yeah, shit with a capital S," replied Bill. "Who do we go tell that we just saw the F-ing Chief of Station getting picked up in a Commie's car, in the dead of night on a back street?"

"And you're sure that it was that jerk from the first day?"

Both Bill and Tim nodded in the affirmative. "No doubt whatsoever," said Tim.

"Corya's on duty all night tonight at the house. "Let's go tell him and he can decide what to do," proposed Chuck. Whatever this exactly is, it's way above our pay grade." The other two concurred. They went down to the garage and took the rental car they had parked there for the team's use. Fifteen minutes later, they pulled slowly up to Wythe's house. Mike was in a car out on the street. They found Corya drinking milk in the living room. William and Olivia were asleep upstairs.

"So, how was your night out on the town with Duarte?" asked the team chief. When he first saw only two of them coming through the door at such a late hour, he assumed something terrible had happened during their night out on the town, and one of them had been arrested. He was greatly relieved when he saw the third team member appear a moment later.

Tim had been appointed spokesman for the three. "You're not going to believe this shit boss!" he began. For the next five minutes, Corya listened in silence to first Tim and then Bill, before he started asking clarifying questions.

"And there's no doubt in either of your minds that it was the COS? You only ever met him once for like an hour."

"I'll remember the face of that arrogant twit till the day I die," replied Tim.

"Ditto," said Bill.

Corya finally ran out of questions and just sat silently staring at the ceiling with his elbows resting on the arms of his chair and the fingertips of each hand pressing against the other one. A full minute later, a big smile slowly came to his face and he mumbled, "Poor bastard – caught by blind, bad luck."

The other two thought Corya was losing his mind. "What the hell is so funny?" asked Bill.

I was just remembering something that one of the surveillance training course instructors told me several years ago. He'd asked me what the greatest threat to a street operation was if a case officer was operating in Moscow, or anywhere for that matter?"

"And what was the answer?"

"I made a few guesses about static surveillance or street cameras. He kept shaking his head and then finally, he smiled and told me that it was blind, bad luck. He explained that you can cleverly plan against all the opposition's measures, but you never know when some off duty KGB officer, policeman or simply a bored, concerned citizen will just happen to be sitting on a bench some night and see what you're doing." Corya laughed loudly. "Think of that poor, dumb bastard Loken. He'd probably driven around the city for several hours doing a surveillance detection route, then he dumped his car and walked another half hour and seen nothing suspicious. Yet, who's sitting on a street bench thirty yards from his car pickup point but a couple of CIA officers – who are only on that street because they've just come out of a titties bar? I mean, what are the odds of you two being there that night, right during that two minute window? Like I said, poor bastard – caught by blind, bad luck."

All three of them starting laughing.

"So what do we do with that sighting? We can't exactly report it to anybody at Lisbon Station."

"Given the time difference to Washington from here, I probably need to wait till about 1400 hours to call HQS. After lunch at the Embassy, I'll go into the Station and arrange to use one of the secure phones back to HQS. I'll tell whomever necessary that I need to talk to my boss back at Headquarters about our upcoming transfer to Kuwait."

"OK, but exactly who are you going to tell?"

Corya stared some more at the ceiling. "There'll be a record of the number I call, so I probably don't want to dial directly to the Counterintelligence Staff. I'll have to call the usual number back in Special Activities Division. Hopefully, MacGregor will be sitting there, doing nothing and drinking coffee. He knows I'm not insane. I'll tell him that I have something super-hot shit and for him to run down the hallway and find whoever is Head of Security for our Division. I'll tell him and then that guy can do the heavy lifting back at Headquarters in figuring out who to go to next. They can call my hotel room number thirty minutes later and simply tell me whether to come back to the Embassy, or to send a post card to Santa Claus – whatever you do when you have something so sensitive, you can't tell anybody. I mean, if the Russians have recruited the bloody Chief of Station, who the hell can I trust? In the meantime, you three tell nobody nothing. You got that?"

"Right."

"Now, go back to your hotel rooms, get some sleep and be back here at 0730."

The day passed like molasses for Corya. He did get airline reservations for himself and his four team members made. They'd been told to fly to Venice, Italy, where a van would meet them and take them up to the Aviano Airbase. They would then catch a U.S. Air Force flight out of Aviano on Saturday directly to Kuwait City.

He killed an hour up at the cafeteria and then came back to the Station at 1400 hours. He told Johanna, the cute Admin officer, that he needed to make a secure phone call back to his home office in the Special Activities Division about his team's onward travel – and that he needed some privacy. She kindly offered him to use her office, as she was about to go up to the small military PX on the grounds of the Embassy to buy a few things. He closed her door and dialed his northern Virginia number. Adam waited till the red light on top of the phone turned to green, indicating that he was connected in "secure" mode.

A gravelly voice answered and simply said, "Special Activities, MacGregor speaking."

"Hey, Mac, it's Corya out here in Lisbon."

"Hey, good to hear from you. I heard that you and your team are about to go down to Kuwait, you lucky bastard."

"Yeah, we leave here in the next day or so. Listen, I have a super secret shit issue to discuss with Security. Will you quickly jog down the hallway and find whoever the head dog is for Security in the division – and don't tell anybody else what's going on?"

"Sounds serious. OK, hang on, I'll go see if I can find the guy. His name is Fernandez. Be right back."

"I'll be right here."

About five minutes later, he heard a voice saying, "This is Ben Fernandez. How can I help you?"

"You're head of Security for the Division?"

"Correct and I take it you're Corya, calling me from Lisbon Station?"

"Yes, listen, here is the deal. A very sensitive security/counterintelligence matter has just come up and I need to speak to whomever handles that sort of thing. Probably over in CI Staff, and I don't want some GS-9."

"Probably be best if you sent in a cable. I can give you all the proper routing slugs to get it to the right people."

"I guess I need to explain the words 'very sensitive' to you – as in, nobody in the Station here can be trusted."

"Holy shit."

"Yeah, holy shit with whipped cream and a cherry on top. So, whatever you guys do back there, do not, repeat, do not send any cable out here to Lisbon Station about this matter. I know it may take you a little while to find the right super spook over in CI, but I can't sit around here on this phone in the Station much longer without people starting to wonder what's going on. So, I'm going to give you my hotel phone number and room number and somebody can call there and tell me what to do next – like come back to the Embassy, or wait till someone knocks on my room door, or whatever. If I'm to call back to HQS again, it should be this number there in SAD, so people in the Station won't wonder who I'm phoning. Got that?"

"I understand."

"I'll be back to my hotel in about thirty minutes."

"OK, got it. It might take me that long to find who to speak to over in CI. Anything else you want to tell me, so I'll know what section I should be contacting?"

"I'd rather not. Just tell them over in their front office, that this is bad with a capital B."

"OK. Somebody will call that number in thirty minutes, even if it's only me to say I'm still looking."

"Thanks."

Corya gave Fernandez the hotel phone number and repeated once more that under no circumstance to send a cable to the Station. He felt that had gone reasonably well and hung up. He then opened the office door and departed the Embassy. He took one of the rental cars his team had been using and headed over to the nearby Sheraton where he was staying.

Promptly thirty minutes later, his hotel room phone rang.

"Hi, Adam. This is Landy. My friend Ben told me that you might be able to pick up some Portuguese pottery for my wife while you're there in Lisbon."

"Yeah, I can probably do that. What does she want?"

"Well, I have a friend who happens to be passing through Portugal right now and she can come by yet this afternoon and give you a couple of pictures my wife had cut out of a magazine. That will give you an idea of what is wanted. Will you be around there in your room for the next hour or so?"

"Yeah, I always take a nap about this time of day."

"OK, thanks a lot for helping me out. Oh, her name is Jane."

"My pleasure. Look forward to meeting her. Goodbye."

Corya liked Landy. He could tell he was a sharp dude. He wondered who the hell Jane would be?

Sure enough, about forty-five minutes later, there was a knock on the door. He peeked through the eye hole and there was a sweet looking grandmother sort of gal standing there, carrying two brief cases.

"It's Jane, Landy's friend."

He opened the door and pulled it back. "Welcome. I'm Adam, come in."

She noticed that he had turned on both the TV and the radio to provide background masking noise. She pointed at both and smiled.

"As Landy told you, I have some clippings of Portuguese pottery so as to give you an idea of what items his wife is wanting." She then opened the briefcases. The first contained a laptop upon which he could type a message, which would then be encrypted and sent directly to the Director of the CI Staff. The second case contained a small parabolic antenna that could be unfolded and expanded. It had a cable so that it could connect to the laptop. She walked over to his room window.

"Let's see if we're lucky and your window might actually be pointed towards the right satellite." She turned on the laptop and hit a few buttons. A minute later on the screen appeared a graphic needle, which indicated a strength of nine out of a possible ten. "Ah, our lucky day."

Corya felt he should say something in response, so he replied, "great."

She typed in a few commands and up came a cable format, to which she typed a few words. She then stood up and pointed at the keyboard. "OK, sit down and type up whatever you want to tell the CI Staff at Headquarters. And don't worry, no other office will receive a copy of this message. It will also erase itself as soon as you hit send, so remember what you wrote."

Corya sat down and mumbled, "Nice toy." He'd been mentally

composing all day what his message would say, so he had it completed in about twenty minutes.

He turned back to Jane. "It's ready to go."

"OK, just hit that red button up in the right-hand corner that says SEND. It will be on somebody's desk at Headquarters in just a few minutes. Is it something that they can likely answer right away, or might it take a while for them to come up with an answer and send instructions back to you?"

He smiled. "I suspect that this will require some serious thinking by a number of people."

"In that case, we'll probably just first get a brief message confirming that yours was received and they're working on a full reply."

He walked over to a small couch in the room and plopped down to get comfortable. "Did you just happen to already be in Portugal? Is that why they could put us together so quickly?"

"Yes, I was already here for another reason."

"Do you need to know about what I just sent to Headquarters?"

She shrugged her shoulders. "Maybe not. If I'm supposed to know anything, they'll instruct you to tell me when you get a reply." She then sat down in a side chair in the room and took out a cheap, romance novel from her coat pocket and started to read.

Almost two hours passed before a little chime sounded on the laptop. Jane came over and hit a button and up came a response from Headquarters. "There you go. Your answer." She returned to her chair, but didn't return to her paperback book. She just stared sweetly at Corya.

He quickly read through the message and then looked over at her. "It says you should read this message, as it impacts on you as well, but first I should tell you what I sent Headquarters."

He gave her a quick summary of his outgoing message and then she read the Headquarters reply.

After she'd read the message, she looked up and said, "Oh my, you've certainly set off some firecrackers at Headquarters this morning, haven't you." She then gave him a big grin. "I see that the others will leave tomorrow for physical examinations at Aviano Air Base in Italy. In the meantime, they want you to go around and inspect the home security systems of all the Station personnel before you leave town on Monday. Do you actually know how to do that sort of thing?"

"Yes, well enough. As you read, the real purpose is to see if the memory record for the COS' system shows whether he was at home or not on Wednesday night. If not, that at least partially confirms that it was him that my two guys saw in downtown Lisbon around midnight."

"Well, his being at home might make it seem less likely that it was him they saw in town that night. However, his being out just makes it possible, not a confirmation." She shrugged her shoulders.

"I suppose so. It all gets very complicated doesn't it? I presume the scheduled physicals in Italy will give some big shot time to fly out to Aviano Air Base to debrief Bill and Tim."

"Very likely, but who knows. Try not think about it too much," replied Jane. "At times, God and Headquarters move in mysterious way. So I suggest that you just sit back, relax and enjoy a few days of paid vacation here in lovely Lisbon."

He grinned. "I can do that."

"As for Aviano, I'm sure they'll want to go over and over what Bill and Tim saw out on that street corner. Do please emphasize to all three men that there must be absolutely no discussion of that night or these subsequent events with anybody else."

"No worry on that point. We're all former military men. When we get an order, it's an order."

"Good. I suspect Headquarters might want to try to do something very clever with this opportunity, which will require total secrecy."

Corya nodded in agreement. "So, you'll be staying on here indefinitely?"

"Hard to say. "Will you be ready to send another message to Headquarters with the results of your checking the COS's security system records by Friday evening?"

"Yes, I'll do his system first thing Friday morning, then the DCOS' and so on down the ladder. If necessary, I can finish the other staff on Saturday and Sunday. How about we meet back here at my room on Friday at say 1600 hours?"

"That will be fine. I'll see you Friday. I'll go ahead yet today and advise Headquarters to expect your next message on Friday around 1630 our time." She then packed up her two briefcases and departed.

He gave her a fifteen-minute head start and then he left to return to the Embassy. Shortly after his return to the Station, the Admin officer found him to show him a cable just in for him. He was stay in Lisbon till Monday while he checked the workings of the home alarm systems of all Station personnel. His team were to go ahead and leave for Italy as planned, where they would undergo medical exams at Aviano Air Base before everyone would proceed on to Kuwait.

"Got it."

"Doesn't seem to make much sense, does it," Johanna observed to Corya.

"No, ma'am, it doesn't, but then I don't get paid to understand the thinking of great minds back in Washington."

She laughed. "That attitude does keep your blood pressure low, doesn't it! I'll let you know the details once I have your plane reservations made for Monday."

Given the Soviet connection, the Director of the CI Staff immediately passed the incoming Eyes Only cable from Corya to Paul, the head of Committee XII. He read it three times before he stood up to go gather all of his team. A smile also came to his face as he thought about how he could tell Harry in a few days when he came back from vacation that he'd been wrong about GOLDFISH. The agent had told them that Parshenko would be traveling to Portugal in January in connection with an important case against the Agency, and sure enough, they'd caught Elliot Loken in an agent meeting in January with the Soviets. Granted, the CIA mole hadn't been Wythe and they'd caught the real one through pure luck, not skill, but it still counted and GOLDFISH had been vindicated! He would propose to C/SE Division that a significant bonus be passed to the agent in his next scheduled dead drop to keep him motivated in providing further travel information on Parshenko. Thinking of Parshenko, Paul would like to task Lisbon Station to ascertain which Soviet travelers were in Portugal in January, but he couldn't risk alerting the COS that there was any special interest right now in Soviet travelers to Portugal. Perhaps in a few months such a check could be made in a low-key fashion.

The committee members were kept busy at Headquarters all that day and late into the night, finding every piece of paper with Elliot Loken's name on it from the first day he applied to the Agency while still in graduate school. Paul was hoping that they could somehow determine with divine hindsight just when it was that the man got himself recruited by the KGB. A meeting with the Chief of the CI Staff, the DDO and the DCI himself was already scheduled for 1000 hours the following morning. Paul wanted to have as many facts ready at his fingertips as possible because there would certainly be lots of questions.

He was also already working on a little idea in his mind as to how they might possibly be able to run a clever operation of their own against the Russians and thus make some lemonade out of the big fat lemon they'd just discovered. If the KGB wasn't aware that the Agency had tumbled to Elliot's treason, then the Agency might be able to use him to feed false information to them. Even better, if the Agency brought Elliot back to America ahead of his planned rotation in eighteen months, on a believable pretext, they could force the KGB into handling him in the D.C. area. This could provide a windfall to the FBI's Counterespionage Division in learning how the Russians communicated with a sensitive asset in America. Eventually, the Bureau could make a few arrests, expel some Russian diplomats/intel officers and have some splashy headlines. The Bureau always liked to generate splashy headlines making themselves look good – even if a success actually had had little to do with their own efforts!

How to transfer Elliot back to Headquarters without making the mole suspicious as to why he was being recalled so far ahead of schedule was the first intellectual hurdle. Paul called Domino's Delivery and ordered an eighteen-inch pizza with every meat product they offered. It would give him indigestion, but such fare in the past had frequently given him creative thoughts.

CHAPTER 13

By Friday, it was clear that the war was going very well for the Coalition and William decided that it would be safe to leave early that day for their exploratory trip out to the Busaco Forest Hotel. He'd bid farewell the day before to the security guys who'd been carefully watching his back for several weeks. They'd been true professionals and good guys as well. He hoped that no harm came their way down in Kuwait. He'd drafted up a short cable Thursday afternoon to send to HQS, complimenting the five men. The DCOS signed off on it, but the COS, never passing up an opportunity to prove he was a horse's ass, rejected sending it. His note back to William said that while they'd carried out their assigned duties in a professional manner, there had been no outstanding performance to merit such a cable to Headquarters. William wondered if one or all might have merited a complimentary cable had they been killed in the line of duty.

The Busaco Forest had been a nature preserve of the Catholic Church since a Papal Bull of 1643. Later, the King of Portugal built a "hunting lodge" in the middle of it. Most would have called it a small castle, but he called it a lodge. When the people of Portugal overthrew the king in 1910, the head chef at the facility "seized it in the name of the people." He quickly forgot about the "people" and turned it into a hotel for the wealthy, owned and run by him.

Olivia made their reservation in her name, so as to keep William's planned presence hidden. When she'd phoned to make the reservation, she asked what was the "best room in the hotel" and been told it was the bridal suite. "Best room" was the description in Braganza's diary, so that was what she figured they should explore first. Around two o'clock on Friday, William took a taxi from the Embassy to a hotel, where he caught another taxi to a second hotel. He then walked for 45 minutes and still saw nobody following him. Olivia had gone to her dress shop that morning with one suitcase that had clothes in it for both her and William. After lunch, she took a cab to her apartment and picked up her car. She then drove to a small hotel out at the far end of Cascais and waited for William to arrive. He arrived shortly after three. They then drove out to Busaco, with him behind the wheel, so that he could keep an eye out for anyone following them.

Despite being told the reservation was not actually for a wedding couple, the hotel management had placed several lovely arrangements of fresh flowers in the room. After exploring the suite, William sat down and said, "OK, tell me now, what's the price for this suite? Should I start looking for a part-time weekend job to pay for our stay?"

"Not to worry. I booked it in the name of the owner of the dress shop and they gave her a very nice discount. Besides, this is my treat to you."

William and Olivia then turned their attention to the corner of the room where there was an old-fashioned "royal safe", which the last king of Portugal had had built into a wall. There was a plaque on the wall by the safe in both Portuguese and English.

King Dom Manuel II had this safe added to his bedroom when the building had been his personal hunting lodge. It was opened shortly after the fall of his kingdom and several more times in the following decade just to make sure there was nothing in the safe. It has not been opened since 1929, as the combination was lost.

They both stared at it with great expectation for several long seconds before William spoke. "Well, this is hopefully the room to which Tristan brought Horthy's treasure to hide it and this safe would be the logical place. Plus, we now know why Tristan didn't have to worry about anyone noticing that it suddenly had a different combination, but how do we open it?"

"That's perfectly obvious," replied Olivia. "The diary said that Miklos Horthy Jr. would know how to open the safe." She went to her suitcase and brought out all the notes she'd made while doing her research. She leafed through the pages till she found Miklos Jr.'s birthday. Try this – 7-25-10."

They both were tingling with anticipation in hopes of having found the missing treasure. William turned the old dial with the given numbers, paused for a second while looking over at Olivia, then pushed down on the handle. It moved and there was that wonderful metallic sound of the round safe door unlocking. William pulled the door open and then slowly reached into the opening. He found only two sheets of paper inside, no jewels. William pulled them out and read the first one aloud:

"Dear Regent Horthy,
Even if the Germans didn't shoot you, these jewels don't really belong to you and I have a much better use for them.
Tristan"

William spoke first. "Well, we found the correct safe. Unfortunately, we're forty-five years too late."

"But Tristan supposedly died in Hungary in late 1944," replied Olivia.

"It was wartime. It wouldn't have been that hard for him to fake his own death back in Hungary, then return to Portugal and steal the jewels. And from what Colonel Clarke told me of Tristan's likely past, stealing the jewels for himself once he believed Horthy was dead would certainly have been within his skill set and his character."

"But then what became of him?"

"I fear we'll never know. Towards the end of the war, I'm sure there was a brisk business in providing people new identities. Tristan probably took a new name and he could have moved almost anywhere in the world with all those jewels."

"And what's the second piece of paper?" asked Olivia.

William unfolded it. It was a brief personal letter, handwritten in German. "It's in German. Perhaps you can read it."

She took the sheet from his hand. After a minute of silence, she mumbled, "Wow!"

"What is it?"

"It's a personal letter to Regent Horthy from Raoul Wallenberg, a Swedish emissary to Hungary in 1944. The letter thanks Horthy for his secret assistance to Wallenberg in preventing thousands of Hungarian Jews from being shipped by the Nazis out of Hungary and off to German 'final solution' camps in Poland. Who was this Raoul Wallenberg?" asked Olivia.

William looked at his watch. It was almost eight o'clock. "I'll tell you about Wallenberg shortly, but why don't we go on down to the dining room and talk there. I'm not sure how much longer they will be serving dinner and frankly I'm starving."

"Good idea, but give me a quick minute to change into a nice dress I brought with me from the shop to wear to dinner."

"Sure," replied William with a smile. "Say, does Simone know that you're always borrowing dresses from the store?"

"Of course. She thinks it makes good advertising."

Two minutes later, Olivia returned from the bedroom, wearing a beautiful red cocktail dress. It covered most of her shoulders, but plunged deep enough between her breasts to cause William to stare.

"Do you like it?" she asked with a large smile on her face.

"What's not to like and I'm sure we'll get excellent service down in the dining room."

The dining room was itself beautiful. The entire, high ceiling was of hand-painted wood panels. Each was about three feet in diameter and of various woodland scenes. The walls were of dark, wood paneling and the carpet quite plush.

After they'd ordered, William returned as promised to telling her about Wallenberg. "He was a neutral Swedish diplomat assigned to Budapest, quite famous for helping tens of thousands of Hungarian Jews survive in the last years of the war, but then the Red Army took him prisoner at some point in 1945. He probably died in a Soviet prison in 1947, although there were rumors and alleged sightings of him in prison camps for many more years."

"Why on earth did the Soviets imprison him?" she asked, while taking the first sip of her caiparinha.

"No one's sure, since the Russians denied for decades that they knew anything about Wallenberg, but they were always a paranoid bunch. They probably suspected him of something, even if they couldn't prove it. One book has claimed that Wallenberg was also spying for the Americans or the British while in Budapest, and thus the Red Army arrested him – never mind his diplomatic status from a neutral country. Another theory is that the Red Army simply didn't want any such person around as a witness to the atrocities it was committing as it captured Budapest."

"Sounds like a bit of history that will forever remain a mystery, but back to our letter, why would Horthy have sent it along with the jewels?"

"He probably figured such a letter attesting to his helping save Jews might save his own life if there were any war trials after the end of the war – and he was right about the trials. So, even more reason he was probably going crazy right after the war, wondering where were his jewels and that letter!"

"No doubt, but at least he didn't wind up in a prison and being executed, even without this letter. What should we do with it?"

"Good question. It would be a little difficult to explain how I got hold of it and there would be the whole question of its provenance, as they say. And at this late date, it's not needed for any legal issues."

"True, but I suspect Horthy's descendants would appreciate some confirmation that their father or grandfather wasn't a totally evil man."

"You have a good point, there. Let me think about what we should do with the letter. Anything with Wallenberg's name on it is of historical importance. At least something good can come out of our search."

"Oh well, it was an exciting game," replied Olivia.

"It was. Too bad we found nothing of real value."

"You found me," replied Olivia with a smile as she reached across the table and took his hand.

"I did, didn't I," he responded with a large grin. "I think we should get some champagne to celebrate. We've brought our investigation to a close and I found you." William discreetly raised a hand and signaled to the waiter.

"Why don't we drink it up in our room," suggested Olivia. "Where we can get more comfortable," she said with a suggestive smile. "If you've liked this dress, wait till you see the negligee I brought for tonight."

"An excellent idea." When the waiter arrived, he requested the wine list. After its arrival and a minute of study, he told him, "We'd like a bottle of the 1980 Dom Perignon Champagne, and please have it sent up to our suite. And then bring me our check." William figured, what was another

$400 for champagne, given what they were probably paying for the bridal suite!

"Yes, sir. The champagne will be up to your room in about ten minutes. We'll have to retrieve it from the cellar and start chilling it."

"That's fine."

After signing the check, the two then departed the dining room and headed for their suite. "I'm surprised we didn't see my Marine friend in the dining room, though he might have just had food sent up to his room," commented William.

The champagne arrived just a few minutes after they reached the room. The middle-aged waiter in a tuxedo pushed the small cart, covered with a white table cloth, over near a couch. The bottle was in an elegant silver chilling holder and surrounded by four tall, crystal champagne flutes.

"It may need to chill for another five or ten minutes, before it's down to the proper temperature," advised the waiter.

William signed for the bottle and included a generous tip. He then pointed at the four glasses. "Perhaps he thought we were going to have company."

Olivia laughed and stood by his side as he started twisting the bottle neck back and forth in the ice with the palms of his hands so as to make sure it was good and cold. Just as he began doing that, there was a knock on their door.

"That must be Gunny. Why don't you let him in while I'm tending to this cork." She went over and opened the door. There was a large mirror on the wall ahead of him, in which he could see the front door. As soon as the door was half-way open, he saw that it was Müller and two others. He had a Lugar in his right hand.

William's immediate reaction was to reach into his side coat pocket to bring out his 9 mm Browning, but he resisted that urge as Olivia was right in the line of fire between Müller and himself. Instead, he continued twisting the bottle with his left hand, while he discreetly reached up and pulled out the gun with his right. His body shielded his right side from view by Müller. He then smoothly slipped it down into the ice of the bucket. If the Germans patted him down, they'd find no gun on his person.

Müller indicated with his gun that Olivia should back up into the room.

"William, we have guests," she calmly stated.

He slowly turned around and saw the three Germans. "I take it from the gun in your hand, this is not a social call."

A thin smile came to Müller's face. Despite it technically being a smile, it gave the unwelcome guest a rather sinister look. "I think you know why we're here, Mr. Wythe."

Müller gestured with his Lugar for Olivia to go stand over near William. "A very nice suite you have here."

"Thank you. It's well decorated. I think you'll particularly like the wall safe, over there by the desk."

Müller rushed towards the safe. The look on his face showed his anticipation. The other two also had big smiles on their faces. Müller's smile quickly vanished when all he found was the note from Tristan to Horthy. Müller read it two or three times and repeatedly looked deep into the safe. Finally, he managed to mumble, "But where are the jewels?"

"Yes, we're just as disappointed as you are. As you can see from the note, there haven't been any jewels in that safe since probably late 1944."

"And why should I believe this note, or you?"

"Well, feel free to search the room. You obviously know that we just arrived here at the hotel and wouldn't have had time to do anything with them if we had found a safe full of jewels." The German remained silent. William shrugged his shoulders and gestured around the room. "Please, look anywhere you like."

Two of the Germans did just that while Müller kept a gun pointed at William and Olivia.

When they'd finished their fruitless search, William spoke again. "I only tumbled onto this hidden treasure story a few weeks ago when I was reading through Mrs. Braganza's diary. She had a brief description of how a British SOE officer named Nigel had tried impressing her in late 1945 with a story of treasure that Admiral Horthy had given him to take to Portugal for hiding until after the war. He did this to assist his effort at seducing her, so there was no way of knowing if his story was true. The rest of the paragraph in her diary simply said that an SOE officer named Tristan had taken the treasure to Portugal for hiding, but when he returned to tell Horthy where, the German Army had already taken him away as a prisoner."

"That much I know already. What happened after Horthy gave the jewels to the British?"

"Well, Tristan was supposedly killed on his way out of Hungary that second time and Nigel presumed that by late 1945 Horthy was dead as well. The diary noted that Nigel was killed in an automobile accident at the end of 1945, and thus both British officers who'd known about the treasure and its location were dead. Now Tristan had left a few clues with Nigel to pass to Horthy that would mean something only to Horthy, should he ever see him again, but that of course never happened. Through some luck, we actually figured out the clues Tristan had left with Nigel and the latter had then quoted in England to Gabrielle. She had written them down in her diary, which I read the night I'd met her. We arrived here just a few hours ago, hoping we had correctly interpreted Tristan's clues. We had, but alas, there is no treasure. As to what happened to it, my best guess is that after hearing of Horthy's removal from office in Budapest, Tristan faked his own death on the way back to Portugal. He then returned here and removed the jewels he'd placed in this safe a few weeks before."

Müller had been nodding as he listened to William. "And where do you think Tristan went with the jewels?"

William shrugged his shoulders. "He could have gone most anywhere on earth. There was great confusion at the end of the war. He probably changed his name and simply disappeared with his newfound wealth. By the way, how did you get onto this trail of treasure?"

Müller saw no reason at that point to conceal his story. "My father had been in charge of the Gestapo troops guarding Horthy at Schloss Hirschberg in Bavaria for almost five months in early 1945. Probably out of boredom, Horthy finally told my father about how he'd arranged to have a treasure in jewels that had belonged to the last Hungarian King secretly shipped out of Hungary to Portugal. He offered my father half of that treasure if he would let him and his family slip away one night. My father was a very loyal Nazi and would have no part in such a plot, but he did later remember all the details Horthy had shared with him. As I was growing up after the war, my father shared those comments with me and he had a desire until his death in 1959 of finding that treasure and using it to help rebuild the underground Nazi party that still existed in many countries of the world. That has been my goal as well."

William managed to suppress his urge to laugh that anyone in 1990 still believed that there was an underground Nazi Party to revive. "I'm sure that you killed Duke Wilhelm, but I'm curious whether Mrs. Braganza's fall down the stairs was an accident or did you push her?"

Müller smiled. "Yes, I did kill the Duke. The old fool refused to tell me what he had told you over your dinner a few nights earlier. We'd been following you ever since you'd met with Braganza and went away with her attaché case. I guessed that since the Duke had been living in Estoril back in the 1950s he'd known Horthy and thus might have had some useful information."

William simply remained silent, but was impressed that the Duke had chosen silence and death over telling Müller anything. He speculated that had Müller simply played the role of a common thief, he might have talked, but he'd probably started talking about the new Nazi Party, which got the Duke mad. He was old enough to have seen the evil of the original Nazi Party and had no intention of helping in the remotest way to revive it.

"And what about Braganza?"

Müller laughed. "We'd talked with her in her room, but she was not being cooperative. We were leaving to take her somewhere where we would have time and privacy to get her to change her mind. And then do you know what happened? The old fool threw herself down that staircase! Perhaps she figured if she was simply injured, other guests or the hotel management would then save her. Perhaps she intentionally tried to kill herself. Who knows? In any case, I then only had you as a lead. Not only had you met with her the day before, but we saw you leave with that attaché case."

William suspected that Braganza had intended to kill herself. She was getting nowhere in getting back what she considered her family's property and she probably didn't think much of the Nazi Party either. Not many people who'd lived through WWII did.

"We became even more convinced that you were on to the trail of the treasure when just a few days later you started having that massive security detail around you. And then you sent your lady friend here to do research about 1936. We'd been following her for several days in addition to you.

Fortunately for us, we were following her and got rather excited when the two of you headed out of Lisbon to this hotel. I put two and two together as you Americans say and guessed that you were headed to this hotel because the jewels were hidden here."

"I didn't see any car following me for the last fifteen miles of our trip. I must be losing my skills."

"Well, there is nothing out here except for the Busaco Forest Hotel, so I did take a slight chance and didn't bother to keep your car in sight towards the end of your journey."

"Well, I congratulate you on your excellent analysis about the jewels and my possible role. Unfortunately, we're all several decades too late. Oh, and by the way, the security detail was because of an alleged terrorist threat against me. It had nothing to do with my private treasure hunt."

"Ah, my miscalculation."

"No matter. The only important question now is what do you plan to do with Olivia and myself?"

"Unfortunately for you, killing the two of you is the only way to tidy up loose ends, even if we didn't find the jewels."

William grimaced. "I was afraid you were going to say that. However, you should know that the Portuguese Judicial Police have your name. You were a bit sloppy the night you approached me at the club and they noted down the license plate of your rental car. So, if I die this weekend, or even just disappear, the legal finger is going to point directly at you."

Müller smiled. "You wouldn't just be making up that story to try to save your lives would you?"

"Well, I might, but I don't have to be that clever. Through the car rental company the JP traced you to the Hotel do Mar of Sesimbra. Also, you should know that while my security detail promised me that they weren't going to follow me all the way out here to Busaco, I suspect they lied and one or two of the guests are actually plainclothes JP officers. Now, I do have an alternative suggestion to your killing us – and then probably being caught and convicted of several murders. Would you care to hear it?"

"By all means."

"Look, no one other than Olivia and I know of this whole fanciful treasure story and hunt, which is now over. You three could just go your way and we'll forget all about your visit with us tonight. We'll have a nice weekend of good food and wine before we return on Monday to our regular lives in Lisbon and your group will have plenty of time to leave the country. It's a shame that Braganza and the Duke died, but I'm no longer in the business of righting all the wrongs of the world. How does that sound?"

"You make an excellent argument Herr Wythe, but I think it's still safer if you are dead. Now, as for Frau Olivia, there might be another option, given her honored past."

Müller turned to Olivia. "You see, I know about your father and the excellent work he did for a number of Nazi officials after the war. I really don't want to shoot the daughter of such a hero of the Third Reich. In fact, I'm hoping that you might want to join with my group and its work. We could use a good, strong contact in Brazil."

William looked puzzled as to what Müller was talking about.

Olivia smiled at Müller. "It would be an honor to help carry on my father's important work."

A smile of satisfaction came to Müller's face. Olivia turned to William. "It's too complicated to explain to you and it really won't matter to a man who will be dead in just a few minutes."

"No, I suppose it wouldn't." He picked up his empty champagne flute standing on a table next to him. "But before anybody shoots me, would you mind pouring me some of that famous Dom Perignon champagne for which I've paid $400? I've heard about it all my life. I'd at least like to taste it once before I die. Perhaps even Herr Müller would like to join me in a glass."

Olivia looked to Müller, who shrugged his shoulders and responded, "Why not?"

"Very well," replied Olivia, who was rather surprised at William's interest in champagne on the verge of his death. Her mind had been focused on how to somehow get word to Gunny in his room that his help was definitely needed. She then walked over to the silver holder for the champagne, full of ice to keep the bottle chilled. She looked down and saw the butt of the gun sticking up out of the ice. She had her back to Müller, as she looked over at William, with a calm face. His eyes met directly with hers for a long moment, but he said nothing.

She lifted the magnum of the expensive spirits out of its cooler by its neck with her left hand as she started to slowly turn her body counterclockwise, so as to face Müller and the other two Germans. With her right hand, she pulled William's gun up out of the ice. Her body served to block their view of her hand. As she came to face the three Germans some ten feet from her, she gently, but rapidly, pulled the trigger three times as she kept the gun down at waist height. The two assistants dropped instantly after a bullet entered their chests near the heart area. She'd also hit Müller in the chest. His face was full of surprise, but he hadn't collapsed yet, so she put one more shot into his sternum.

William had remained frozen in place, still holding his empty glass. He was truly impressed with her shooting.

"Kidnapping of the wealthy for ransom has long been a threat in Brazil. My husband and I have taken a number of shooting and defensive driving courses." She gave him a big smile.

"I take it you passed the shooting course?" asked William.

"I actually had a perfect score last year on the firing range."

"Gunny will be very impressed with you. Speaking of whom, I should phone and ask him to come here and give us a hand with the bodies, but first, do pour me some of that champagne."

"Certainly. I was a little worried that I might drop the bottle while shooting, but I didn't spill a drop," she replied with a lovely smile.

CHAPTER 14

Willliam started to pick up the phone and call Gunny, but then he paused and turned to Olivia. "Before I phone Gunny, would you like to tell me what Müller was talking about when he referred to your father?"

"Well, that question you jokingly put to me one day about whether I ran a neo-Nazi group like Müller was close to home. My father had been the representative of the Third Reich's Ministry of Finance posted to the German Embassy in Argentina during the war. He was also the head of the Nazi Party at the Embassy. As the end of the war neared, many of the German diplomats simply quietly slipped away from Buenos Aires."

"And your father was one of those?" "Yes, but it was the Ambassador who ordered him to leave and to take all the currency in the Embassy with him. I don't know how much that was, but my mother told me once that she thought it was at least the equivalent of two or three hundred thousand American dollars – a large amount for 1945. He was to go to Brazil and set up some place that could then help Nazi officials who might get out of Europe and reach South America. There was an underground network in several South American countries, including Argentina that would then send them on to my father in Brazil for new identities and relocation. He was the last stop of something called the Odessa Organization."

"And that's how your father came to run that large cattle ranch in the south of Brazil?"

"Yes. There was already an emigre community of several thousand people of German ancestry who'd been living in that area of Brazil for many years, so it was fairly easy to place fleeing Nazis into the country."

"And did he help any fleeing Nazis after the war?"

"I suppose he did, but he died when I was only five, so I never knew much of what he had done. He was simply my 'papa'. I do have some vague memories of strangers coming and staying with us for a few weeks on different occasions. Of course, to a small child, everyone who comes to your house is a stranger."

"And when did you finally learn what your father had been during the war?"

"When I was seventeen, my mother decided that I should know everything."

"And your reaction?"

"I couldn't believe that my father had been a Nazi. He had always seemed the nicest and sweetest man to me and to everyone who worked on our *fazenda*. My mother told me about his past, but then told me to never speak of it, which I never did. I have no idea how Müller learned about my father."

"The most logical guess is that one or more of the Nazi officials that your father had assisted to "disappear" in Brazil are still alive – and still in contact with various underground neo-Nazi groups of today.

"I suppose, but they'd be very old now."

"It's only been forty-five years since the end of the war. If someone had been thirty in 1945, he'd only be seventy-five now. Did your mother ever tell you how many Germans your father had assisted in Brazil?"

"No, not really. She simply used the Portuguese word 'many', but for a Brazilian that could mean anything from ten to hundreds."

"And these Nazi officials who managed to get to South America really thought they could someday resurrect the Nazi Party?"

"That might have been how this escape network justified the funding for its efforts, but I suspect most of them were mostly just interested in avoiding prison or saving their own lives."

William remained silent for many seconds, before he spoke again. "Or, perhaps your father didn't really die when you were five years old?"

"I suppose that's possible, but I haven't used my maiden name of Wagner in over twenty years. How would Müller know about me?"

"Perhaps your father was more important to the post-war Nazi cause than you were aware."

"Perhaps, but he died in 1952. Even if he had been important, that was decades ago."

"You're sure he died in 1952?" asked William with a large grin on his face. "If he'd been in the business of setting people up with new identities, maybe he needed to disappear and 'reinvent' himself in the early fifties."

"I guess anything is possible, but he seemed to truly adore my mother. Hard to believe he would just move on and leave her and me behind."

"Probably not, unless he felt he had to do so. The state of Israel was created in 1948 and the Mossad service immediately began searching all over the world for former Nazi officials, particularly down in South America. If he'd felt they were closing in on him, maybe he believed he had to disappear a second time and not only for his safety, but for your mother's and yours as well."

"That sounds plausible. I must admit that there was no grave for him there at the fazenda. Mother told me that his small plane had crashed on a business trip up in the Amazon jungle and neither his plane nor his body were ever found."

"Hmm," was William's mono-syllabic response, which implied that he thought that the story of a plane crash death up in the Amazon jungle could mean several things. It might have truly been an accidental fatal crash. The Mossad might have sabotaged his plane. Or, perhaps her father had felt it was time, for whatever reasons, to reinvent himself. William decided not to voice to Olivia his thoughts.

Olivia spoke again. "Of course, if he did intentionally disappear as you're suggesting, he left behind all of his notebooks and journals. I remember my mother packing up all of his personal papers after his death. They're still in a metal foot locker in the attic of her small house in Rio in which my mother has lived for many years."

"Well, enough about your past. We'll probably never know how Müller knew that you were Herr Wagner's daughter." William went over to the phone and asked for Gunny's room.

A few minutes later there was a knock on the door of the suite. William confirmed who it was and then opened the door. Gunny immediately saw the three bodies on the floor.

"Wasn't much point in having me along since you managed to kill them all yourself," joked Gunny.

"Actually, it was Olivia who killed each one with a single shot."

She smiled at Gunny and then pointed to the one closest to him. "Well, actually, it took two shots to bring down that one."

From the look on Gunny's face, she could tell that he was quite impressed. "We were just having some of this wonderful champagne. Would you like a glass as well, before we bother dealing with the bodies?" She was holding up an empty flute and offering it to him.

"Sure." He stepped over one of the bodies to take the flute from her. She then retrieved the bottle from the cooler. He noticed that somebody had wisely placed bath towels under each body so that blood wouldn't stain the beautiful, light blue carpet. He went over and opened a window wide, so as to help remove the smell of gunpowder from the room.

Once they all had their glasses filled, they sat down and William briefly told Gunny what had happened.

"You two seem to have handled everything just fine without me," observed Gunny.

"Well, we still have to dispose of these bodies before the maid comes in the morning. We also don't know if Müller has any more companions here at the hotel."

Gunny nodded silently, then went to a glass doorway, which led out onto a small balcony facing out from the building. He opened the door and stepped outside for a minute, before rejoining them in the suite.

"Nothing but grass down there. Not even any plants that would get crushed." He checked his watch. "Around 2300 hours, let's just drop them off the balcony. I can fit all three in my vehicle. I'll then drive them away and dump them in the woods ten or fifteen miles from here. By the time the police find them, hopefully, no one at the hotel will even remember them being here."

"Sounds like as good a plan as any," replied William. "Let's go through their pockets and remove their wallets, car keys and papers. We don't want the police to find anything on them that mentions us, or even this hotel. Hopefully, they all came in only one or two cars and we'll move them elsewhere as well." Olivia hadn't had a problem in shooting them, but she demurred on going through the pockets of dead men.

A thorough search performed by William and Gunny turned up the keys to two rental cars. Fortunately, both keys had an attached tag with the make, model and license plate number, so it would be easy to identify their two cars out in the car park. William used his handkerchief to pick up the German's weapon and then he carefully placed the Lugar back in Müller's pocket.

"I noticed when we arrived that there didn't appear to be any video cameras in the parking lot, so there'll be no record of who drove off the cars."

"Good," replied Gunny. "You two can drive their rental cars and follow me. We'll find somewhere to leave them and once we've tossed the bodies, all three of us will come back to the hotel in my car."

"Perfect," replied William. "That only leaves the question of whether there might be any other associates of Müller here at the hotel."

None of them had any insights as to that question. Finally, William shrugged his shoulders and said, "I guess we'll just have to take our chances – and be a little more careful when we open our room door the rest of the weekend."

The three of them finished off the rest of the champagne, while William and Olivia gave Gunny a short version of the clues found in Braganza's diary and of their pointless search.

"Too bad the safe was empty," commented Gunny. "It would have made for a much better ending to your story."

At eleven o'clock, they decided that the few other guests would be asleep and what staff who were on duty all night would have settled down somewhere in the hotel. Gunny picked up each dead body in turn and easily carried it out onto the balcony as if it was a mere ten-pound bag of flour. Each body simply made a dull thump as it hit the ground below, but no other hotel room lights came on, nor did anyone open a door or window. They waited five minutes before going downstairs via the stairwell and out a side door. Olivia drove Gunny's car over to the edge of the parking lot while William and Gunny carried the bodies to the lot. All went as planned.

Wearing gloves, William and Olivia then got into the two rental cars and the caravan of three headed off into the night. About fifteen minutes away from the hotel and close to a major road, they left the first rental car, with the keys still in the ignition, near a closed gas station. Gunny then found a quiet spot he liked and dumped the three bodies some fifty feet into the woods. William left the second car on a side street on the outskirts of a nearby small town, again with the keys in the ignition. William and Olivia then joined Gunny in his car for the return trip to their hotel. Forty-five minutes later all three were back in the hotel. William had placed a coin in the frame of the small side exit door from the hotel, so it wouldn't lock and thus they could return without passing by the front desk. They then bid Gunny goodnight and he returned to his own room.

Once they were back in their suite and seated comfortably on the couch, Olivia said, "Before Müller showed up, it seemed that you were about to tell me something important."

"Oh, yes, well I was thinking I might propose to you, even though we found no treasure." He saw no reaction in her face. "You know, propose as in marriage."

"Yes, I know what a proposal is. So why don't you?"

"Because I've thought more about it since earlier this evening. I've concluded that marriage is an option for a man with sufficient money. I may be very much in love with you and I think you might even be in love with me, but I have several obligations. I can't afford to marry you. If I married a foreigner, I'd be sent home almost immediately and you know why I need to stay abroad for several more years."

"Well, you're right about my being in love with you, or at least I think it's love. You and I have had very different lives, but there's a certain feeling I get when I'm near you. I simply feel very safe and comfortable when with you and miss you terribly when I'm not. But I can understand about your financial concerns regarding your children. Tell me truthfully, had we found the jewels and you suddenly had money, you were going to propose to me? I mean money's the only cause for hesitation now on your part?"

"Yes."

She hesitated several seconds before speaking. "I haven't been totally honest with you about my background."

"You told me you're married, but a divorce is coming and you told me about your father. What else could you be hiding?" He tried to grin, but was in fact a little worried about what he was about to hear next.

"Actually as of this morning, I'm officially a divorced woman. I met with my husband's lawyer who'd flown over to settle things. Not only am I divorced, but I have forty million American dollars in my bank account."

"You have what?" he sputtered, despite his attempt at remaining calm as his eyes opened wide.

"Forty million dollars and also, I own the dress shop where I work – there are also shops in Rome, London and several Brazilian cities and I own them all."

"So, there is no Simone?"

"Well, there is that brand name, but she is me. So, I think we could cover all your financial obligations to your daughters and still have a few dollars left for us to live on. Unless you're one of those old-fashioned gentlemen who doesn't want to be supported by his wife's money."

William laughed as he pulled her close to kiss. "No, I have no such objections at all." After a long kiss, he finally did get the words out, "Will you marry me?"

"Sim, meu amor. Do you think there is any way we could get married here in Busaco this weekend? That would be such a nice ending to our search."

"Sadly not. I actually looked into that possibility a couple of days ago and there are various forms to be signed and filed, especially for two foreigners. But by the end of this coming week back in Lisbon we can certainly have everything arranged."

"Oh, by the way if you're wondering if any of that forty million dollars came from my father's Nazi funds, it does not. It's either from my dress shops or it's money that my now ex-husband stole from people in his banking business."

William smiled. "Well, as long as he stole it from other rich people, then I'm OK with spending it. Different topic. Where do you want to go on a honeymoon and for that matter where would you like to live?"

"Unless you want to stay on here in Portugal or go back to America, I'd love to go live in Rio de Janeiro. I wasn't born there, but I've been there for more than twenty years, and I think of it as home."

"Rio would be fine. I presume there are bars or restaurants there where I could make a living as a piano player?"

"There might be one or two such places," she replied with a laugh. "But can we discuss such things tomorrow? Right now, why don't we go to bed!"

"An excellent idea." They headed for the bedroom.

The bedside table lamp was on her side of the bed and she started to reach over to turn it off after letting her negligee fall to the floor, but then paused. "Oh, I forgot to mention that I also get to keep the summer beach house just outside of Rio, so we don't have to immediately go house hunting when we arrive in Brazil."

William's attention was totally on her beautiful, naked body just before the light went out. He never heard a word about a beach house. As he crawled under the covers, he thought briefly about the fact that he hadn't been with a woman for a long time, but then remembered the old saying that once you'd learned how to ride a bicycle, you never forgot how to – and he was about to enjoy a twenty-speed Pinarello. Brazilian girls grew up in a culture that was all about physical pleasure.

During the night, William woke up in the middle of a pleasant dream, which truly surprised him, as he never had dreams. At least, he hadn't had any since the day his wife had died in Malta. Since then, William had just tried to get through life with as little pain as possible, till one day he'd die and it would be over. That was what a couple of KGB officers who'd tried to befriend him at two different posts over the past decade, with an eye to recruiting him, hadn't understood. They'd seen his heavy drinking and assumed there must be some problem or anger over something with which they might be able to help him in return for his spying for the KGB. Such attempts had stopped in more recent years. Perhaps, they'd finally come to understand that there was nothing they could offer him because there was nothing on this mortal coil that he wanted. Having himself read a number of the great Russian literary works, he thought that if any ethnic group should have recognized profound sadness and hopeless despair in him it would have been a Russian. His mind then moved on from Dostoyevsky and Tolstoy to thinking about what had changed that had brought dreams back to his nighttime sleep cycle? Obviously, it was Olivia, mostly – though he admitted to himself that the thought of what he could do with some of her millions of dollars might be playing at least a small part in having dreams back in his life.

His mind then drifted to the peculiar thought of what it would be like living in the same city and maybe even in the same home for the next thirty years. For most of his adult life, he'd moved from place to place every two or three years as he'd been assigned to different countries. Would he get bored from simply living in the same place year after year, even in as exciting a city as Rio de Janeiro? Only time would tell. It was also going to be strange for the first time in thirty years that when living abroad, he would not be busy assessing everyone he met as a potential recruitment. He was an excellent conversationalist, but from now on he would have no hidden agenda while talking with people – looking for vulnerabilities and determining their access to secret information. He could just chat with people for the pleasure of chatting with interesting people. He wondered if he would enjoy talking with people with no hidden purpose.

He finally fell back asleep as he was contemplating how and when he should break the wedding news to his two daughters.

They both woke up Saturday morning with big smiles on their faces; he clearly still enjoyed riding a bike! They spent most the day making plans. William phoned to Rodrigo, the head of his former JP security detail, and gave him the news that he was returning on Sunday morning instead of Monday. Even though they too had dropped round the clock coverage of him, William had agreed that he would keep Rodrigo apprised in general of where he was, in case a security incident came up and the JP needed to respond quickly.

Gunny came by the suite in late morning to announce that he needed to get back to Lisbon. "Sorry to cut out on you early, but one of my Marines had a little fender bender this morning with the duty car and I probably ought to get back and see if anybody needs his ass chewed out."

"Well, thank you for coming out here this weekend. It looks like all the excitement is over anyway. By the way, did anyone else at the Embassy know where you were headed Friday afternoon?"

"No, the men of the detachment have to tell me if they're planning on leaving Lisbon, but I don't have to tell anybody anything. I just told a few of the guys that I was going fishing on Friday and not to bother me unless the Embassy was being overrun by Iraqi ragheads."

William and Olivia smiled. "Alright, I'll see you back at the Embassy on Monday. Drive safe."

Gunny came over and gave Olivia a big hug. "You'll have to come out shooting with us some Saturday when we do our monthly practice. No, on second thought, the way you shoot, you'd just embarrass my Marines!" They both laughed.

He shook William's hand and bid him farewell.

After the door had closed, Olivia commented, "What a nice man."

"Indeed, and I must remember on Monday to give him the $1,000 I promised him."

Olivia smiled as she gave William a hug. "I think we should give him more than that for all that he did to help us last night."

"Probably so, I'll think about that today. You think we should have told him about our getting married?"

She grinned like any newly engaged woman would have. "No, just surprise him on Monday along with everyone else."

They were having exceptionally good weather for a January day, so after an excellent lunch in the hotel's restaurant, they went for a walk in the garden and surrounding forest for which the hotel was named.

"Now that you are about to retire, will you miss your work with the CIA?" asked Olivia as they walked along hand-in-hand, like two teenagers in love. There was a lovely crunching sound to the pea gravel underneath their shoes.

"Oh, like any job that you've done for almost thirty years, there are aspects of it that I'll miss and some that I won't. I've always enjoyed the 'game' — the challenge of meeting foreigners and finding ways to get into their heads to find out what it is that might be lacking in their lives. If a fellow is pretty well satisfied with his life, his job, his family and the politics of the country in which he lives, I'm not going to be able to recruit him to spy for America. Now, if he's lacking something and I can figure out what that is, then maybe I can make him an offer to provide what is lacking in return for his giving me secrets."

"I guess from the spy movies and novels I've always thought it was simply for money," replied Olivia.

"Money may be part of it, but often there's a factor of ego or revenge, or ideology involved. I've always enjoyed that intellectual chess game, but after so many years, the novelty has begun to wear off. And I'm certainly tired of dealing with jerks like Elliot who are always just calculating what steps to take to promote their careers. But to be fair, I haven't been worth much as a case officer this past decade because of the drinking, so nobody's going to particularly miss me."

She gave his hand a squeeze. They stopped and he stared into her eyes.

"Anyway, I'm already a new man, as of these last few weeks because of you. Otherwise, I wouldn't have asked you to marry me. I'm sure I'll be perfectly happy simply playing the piano several nights a week in some smoky nightclub in Rio and in the daytime helping you spend your money." He gave her a grin and then kissed her. "As of Saturday afternoon, the old William Wythe will be dead and gone and the 'new' one will be sailing with you to Brazil."

Olivia spent several hours that afternoon on the phone talking to her dress shop manager. William had told Olivia to make all the decisions in regard to the wedding on Friday and then a nice reception afterwards for maybe thirty or forty, depending on how many people she would care to invite. The shop manager would also go ahead and arrange for the tickets for Saturday when she and William would sail for Rio de Janeiro.

Late in the afternoon, she was giving him an update on all the plans. When that was done, she told him, "I also have one more important thing I should tell you."

"Beyond your father having been a Nazi and that you're worth millions, you mean there's more?" he asked with a grin.

"Just one small thing and I only learned it by accident on Friday morning when I met with my husband's lawyer back in Lisbon. Hopefully, you'll find it amusing."

"You have my full attention."

"Friday morning, after the actual divorce business was over, just the Brazilian lawyer and I were left in the conference room. I've known the man for almost twenty years and he's always been very kind to me. He expressed his regrets that my marriage had ended in a divorce, but he wanted to tell me something – strictly off the record."

"And that's what I'm to find amusing?"

"I hope you'll see some humor in it. The lawyer apologized for all the trouble my husband had caused, not only for me, but for you as well. He said that my husband had hired a private investigator to check up on me here in Lisbon and had learned that I was spending a lot of time with you, though no actions had occurred that could help him in a divorce proceeding. Apparently, my husband still decided that if he could somehow get you out of the picture, my desire for a divorce might end."

William hadn't heard anything humorous yet. "And just how was he going to get me out of the picture?"

The lawyer said he didn't know all the details, but apparently the private investigator sent some crazy letter to the Embassy about a terrorist threat against you. My husband hoped that the Ambassador would send you back to America for your safety."

William let out a roar of laughter. "Well, thank God for that letter. If I hadn't had all those bodyguards around me the last few weeks, Müller might have had other ideas of how to deal with me!"

"Are you going to tell the Embassy the truth about the threat letter?"

William gave the matter some thought for almost a minute. "No, I don't think so. It would be too complicated to explain. And now the whole matter is over and I'm leaving the country anyway, so what's the point?"

"You're probably right. Well, you'll have until Saturday to think more about it."

The phone rang. It was the dress shop manager calling back to report on various preparations, so William went into the bedroom to take a nap. He closed the door, turned off the lights and lay down on the bed. It was relaxing, but he couldn't go to sleep. His mind was still thinking about how Müller and his neo-Nazi buddies could have known he was at the Busaco Forest Hotel. How could he have not spotted surveillance on him during the two-hour journey from Lisbon to the hotel? Müller's story of having dropped back towards the finish because there was only one place William could have been heading sounded a little thin.

It seemed much more likely that someone had told Müller in advance where William was headed for the weekend. He reviewed in his mind, who all knew or could have even suspected that he and Olivia were headed for the Busaco Forest Hotel? Or who might Olivia have told, even accidentally?

The only three people William could recall that knew where he was headed on Friday afternoon were Olivia, Gunny and Rodrigo of the Judicial Police. Olivia had her father's Nazi past and Müller did know about that, which would make her a prime suspect if he was being objective about it. However, the fact that she shot and killed Müller and the two other neo-Nazis would seem to clear her of suspicion. Gunny? What reason on earth would a twenty-year Marine of Irish ancestry have for cooperating with Müller?

That left only Rodrigo, presuming Olivia hadn't told someone else about her planned weekend getaway with William. He'd ask her about that in just a few minutes. Rodrigo had also been aware of William's dinner with Duke Wilhelm. But what motive would a career Portuguese policeman have for betraying him to a group of Neo-Nazis? His brain suddenly flashed. Rodrigo did feel he'd been screwed over by the JP in his career. Could that be at the heart of his actions? He'd have to give that angle further thought.

He gave up on trying to fall asleep and rejoined Olivia in the living room of the suite. "By the way, did you tell anyone, perhaps at work, that we were coming here this weekend? Or could anyone have overheard you making the reservation when you phoned here?"

"No, I don't think so. I definitely didn't intentionally tell any of the other ladies at the shop, and the door to my office was closed when I made the call."

"Are there other extensions in the store that someone could have used to listen to your call when you made the reservation?"

There are two other phones, but you usually hear an obvious click if someone picks up one of them while I'm on my office phone."

A smile came to William's face, as if he'd just had an epiphany. "You brought that special dress from the store that you wore to dinner Friday night. Did you discuss with anyone the need for a dress for a special occasion over the weekend, and with whom you might have just accidentally mentioned where you'd be wearing that dress?"

She returned his smile. "Nice try Sherlock, but I didn't discuss with anyone my clothing needs for the weekend."

His smile disappeared. "Hmm. I guess I'll have to reconsider how Müller might have known in advance that we were coming to this hotel."

The rest of the weekend sped by and at 1000 hours on Sunday morning, they went down to the front desk to check out. William started to take his credit card out, but Olivia stopped him. "I've already charged everything to Simone," she whispered with a grin.

"We're checking out of the bridal suite," she said to the handsome young man behind the front desk. "And just charge everything to the credit card number that you already have, including four bath towels that we've taken from the room as souvenirs of our wonderful time here."

The clerk was quite astounded. In his twelve years at the reception desk, never had a guest voluntarily told him that they had stolen one of the hotel's monogrammed towels!

As Olivia was dealing with the bill, William started staring at a sheet of the hotel stationary laying on the counter. He noticed at the bottom of the high-quality bond paper that the Busaco Forest Hotel was a member of the Lewis Group. It listed luxury hotels in Rio de Janeiro, Sao Paulo and Forteleza in Brazil, plus a hotel in Miami and one in Johannesburg. He found that an interesting coincidence that someone named Lewis owned the Busaco Hotel and asked to speak with the Manager. A minute later, Mr. Silva appeared in front of the registration desk from a corridor that led back to an Administrative Section. Having been told that it was the gentleman who'd stayed two nights in the wedding suite who wished to speak with him, the manager arrived with a wide, artificial smile on his face. He was a young man in his early thirties, well-groomed and who spoke several foreign languages. He was actually only the weekend manager, but he would do.

"Good morning, Mr. Wythe. I trust you've had a pleasant stay with us," he began in perfect American-accented English.

"We've had an excellent stay, in all regards, and I wanted to pass along my compliments to you. The room, the food, the service – everything was a delight. It requires a good staff of course, but a good staff starts with good management."

Silva's wide smile became even wider and genuine. "We are so glad that you have enjoyed your time with us and we shall see you again in the future."

"Indeed, you shall. By the way, I noticed on your hotel stationary that you are part of the Lewis Group. Please tell me about this company."

"It's a chain of prestigious, luxury hotels located on several continents. The Busaco was added about seven years ago."

"Have you ever met Mr. Lewis?"

The Manager smiled and said no. He took William aside. "Apparently, hardly anyone has ever met Mr. Lewis. He is a very private man – a Howard Hughes of Brazil who has owned expensive hotels back to just after WW II. There hasn't been a photograph taken of him in decades."

"How mysterious," replied William.

"One of the corporation lawyers who comes here for the annual audit told me once that Lewis wasn't even his real name. It's just the name of his corporation. He's not a native Brazilian, although he speaks excellent Portuguese. Supposedly, he arrived in Brazil right after the war and being one of the few people around with money was able to acquire a number of luxury hotels. One rumor has it that he is the illegitimate child of some Hungarian nobleman."

"So how old do you think the man is?

"Oh, he'd have to be in his mid-to-late seventies, if he got his start in the late forties. He's been married to a Brazilian woman for many years and has children and grandchildren. That lawyer had joked with me that with the Brazilian wife and children Mr. Lewis couldn't be extradited to another country. If a person has a Brazilian spouse and a child, he can't be extradited for any reason."

"Very interesting. Thank you for your time and our excellent stay."

When he went back over to Olivia, he was laughing like a fool. "You won't believe who owns this hotel!"

"Who?"

"I'll tell you in the car. Let's get headed back to Lisbon."

Once out on the highway, William told her what he'd just learned of the Lewis Group of hotels.

"You really believe that the owner could be our missing Tristan Lewis?"

"Well, the facts I was told by the hotel manager certainly fit our allegedly dead SOE officer. If he'd assumed a new identity, I wonder why he would use the name Lewis in the company title, but perhaps he just couldn't resist the humor of it. Same thing for the rumor that he's the son of a Hungarian nobleman. Who could have started such a rumor except himself?"

"True, but he was taking a certain risk by such actions."

"I guess that's just his personality. It's quite funny when you think about it, particularly his buying the hotel from where his wealth came."

Their conversation returned to preparations for leaving for Brazil on Saturday. "Do you think we can really get everything arranged in just five days?"

"Well, I'll just need to arrange for the packing of my clothes and personal items I want to keep. And of course, I'll have to tell the COS of my immediate retirement. I hate to give him the satisfaction of getting rid of me, but what the hell, now that my wife has forty million dollars, I can be big minded!" He smiled.

"Yes, I'd think you can. Just forget about him and your entire past. You can concentrate on how you're going to show me your love every day for the next several decades."

"I can do that." They were both silent for several seconds and then William asked her, "When we get to Rio, should we call on Mr. Lewis – just to hear his side of the story?" He grinned.

"Why not?" she replied and laughed.

"Oh, I'd also like to discuss with you my spending some of your money this week, beginning with Gunny."

"That's fine," she replied. "I still think Gunny deserves more than just a thousand dollars for all he's helped us with this weekend."

William smiled. "I think so too."

Several thousand miles east and north of Portugal on that same Sunday, a Russian couple were having a conversation in their one-bedroom apartment on the south side of Moscow. He spread on the table the two thousand rubles he'd picked up in a hollow rock early that morning.

"Look at how much I received this time," he exclaimed to his wife. "We'll be able to afford one of those excellent Polish baby cribs by the time our baby arrives in May."

"Yes, that will be very nice." She tried to smile, but she was worried. "But if you're in prison by then, you'll never get to see our son in it!"

"I've told you, there's nothing to worry about. I'm not even giving the Americans real information, so no investigation within the KGB could ever lead back to me as the person within the KGB who gave such information to the CIA."

"So why are the Americans paying you so much money? You're a lowly personnel clerk in the KGB. You make sure people get their paychecks and their vacation time. You don't even know any secrets!"

"That's the beauty of my plan. I've told them that there are several penetrations of their Service by the KGB and that they are handled by a super spy named Parshenko."

"And is there such a person at the KGB?"

"Yes, he's in our chess club. I know him from there."

"And what does he do?"

"I don't really know. I don't think it's much of anything, but his uncle sits on the Central Committee and so he's treated with great respect. Another player told me last year that Parshenko is an annoying bore at Headquarters and so the General in charge of his department often sends him abroad on pointless trips just to be rid of him for a few weeks. And the General also figures that giving Parshenko such nice trips will curry favor with the uncle."

"And what does he do on these trips he makes?"

"Nothing really. They are called 'inspections of opportunity' and make so little sense that all the KGB rezidencies he visits think he's really carrying out some super-secret mission on the side. And that's what I told the CIA he's been doing for several years, meeting with a penetration of their service. I presume the CIA has started some big investigation looking for a mole within their ranks, based on where Parshenko has travelled and when. It's perfect! And even if the KGB does have a mole or two within the CIA who is telling the KGB about there being a secret agent for the CIA in Moscow, the information he's reporting can't lead back to me because it's all imaginary! I make money for us and the baby and I'm not even hurting the Motherland!"

She counted the money once more and smiled. "Alright, but don't go outsmarting yourself and get us arrested!"

CHAPTER 15

First thing Monday morning, William went into the COS's office to give him the news of his retiring, but before he could get to that issue, the COS asked him to have a seat and started talking.

"All Stations in Europe have received a request as to who can they spare to go immediately to Kuwait to beef up our presence there and in anticipation of possibly having to open a Station in Iraq as well. The preference is for bachelors and Arabic-speakers. You don't have the language, but otherwise, you going to Kuwait for a few months would be the least disruptive for any of the officers here in Lisbon. This is on a voluntary basis of course, but I knew you'd be willing to go – you being a team player."

William smiled. "No, sorry, I won't be available for Kuwait. You see I'm retiring this Friday. I know you'll miss me terribly, but that's the way it is." William stood up to leave the office. For once, the COS was speechless. William stopped at the door, turned back to Elliot and said, "Oh, just one more thing. I wanted to tell you before I left that you are without question the greatest horse's ass I've ever met." William then closed the door behind him and continued on down the hallway to find a cardboard box into which to put his few personal items to take home.

After packing his few mementos, he went down the hallway to tell the Admin Officer of his plans.

"Hey, Johanna. Did you have a good weekend?"

"Nothing special. How about you?"

He smiled. "Well, let's see. I decided to retire this coming Friday and I also decided to get married on Friday afternoon as well. So, not a bad weekend."

"Good God," she practically shouted and then came from around her desk to give him a hug.

"Would you please send in my request to retire and then start figuring out what forms I have to sign to make that happen?"

"Of course. So who are you marrying?"

"The woman I brought to the Ambassador's dinner recently. Her name is Olivia and she's from Brazil."

"Oh, I heard about her. All the ladies who'd been there that night talked about the beautiful dress she wore." She then gave him a quick grin. "And all the men talked about how beautiful she was!"

William laughed. He'd been doing that more often in recent weeks. He started to leave her office and then turned back to her. "Oh, and keep Friday afternoon free so you can come to my wedding. I'll get back to you shortly with the details."

The smile suddenly disappeared from her face. "Different topic, you probably haven't heard, but Mr. Corya got hit by a car crossing the street yesterday afternoon near his hotel."

William's own face turned hard. "How bad is he?"

"Apparently, not too bad, but he'll be stuck here in Lisbon for a few more days instead of immediately departing for anywhere."

"What happened? I mean, are we sure this really was just an accident?"

"According to Mr. Corya, it was all his own fault. He was just looking in the wrong direction and stepped out into the street. The nice old couple driving their car couldn't stop quite in time and hit him, but not too hard. They even drove him to the Emergency Room."

"Is he still in the hospital?"

"No, he went back to his hotel last night with his broken leg in a cast and I believe he'll be in here this afternoon."

"Well, thank goodness it wasn't really serious. If you see him when he comes in, please ask him to come see me."

"I'll do that and I'll let you know by tomorrow morning about the forms you need to sign."

"OK, thanks."

From Johanna's office, he headed down to see Ted Ellis in the Consular Section to ask about what paperwork would be needed to get Olivia officially registered as his wife and to apply for American citizenship for her.

"Ah, so for once the Embassy rumor mill is correct," was Ted's initial response. "Congratulations! My secretary, Jackie, told me you were getting married when she brought in my morning coffee. Not much happens around here that she doesn't learn about instantly."

"Yes, Jackie has it right. The lady I took recently to the Admiral's dinner will be Mrs. Wythe as of this Friday afternoon and I wanted to get the paperwork started for her legal status as an American."

"Well, nothing moves that fast in the U.S. Government bureaucracy as you well know, but we can at least get all the applications filled in and signed before Friday."

"Great, I'll just leave you an address in Brazil where you can mail her documents when they're ready."

"Brazil?"

"Yes, I'm retiring this Friday as well. Didn't Jackie know that?" William asked with a little smile.

"No, she didn't."

"Well, there you go Ted, for once you have news before Jackie does! We're honeymooning down in Rio de Janeiro for a month, maybe more, and then we're headed back to America."

"That's wonderful. Listen, normally, there'd be weeks of preliminary background investigation and checks with our Embassy in Brasilia, but…" Then Ted smiled. "Since you actually gave us notification of this coming wedding a month ago and we've already completed all the background checks, come next Monday I can simply send off the completed request to Washington. I can even ask for expedited service on humanitarian grounds."

"That's very kind of you Ted. I should have passed you gossip months ago. OK, I need to get back upstairs and you need to go whisper in Jackie's ear before she hears of my upcoming retirement from someone else! I'll send you a memo tomorrow with the details about the time and place for the wedding and reception on Friday afternoon."

Ted gave William a hearty handshake. "All the best in the world to you and this young lady."

About ten, William finally got around to turning on his computer and found a cable from the Bulgarian Desk with instructions on what they wanted him to do with Yordan.

Given the dramatic changes underway in Bulgaria and the end of Communist Party rule, it is questionable which DS officers will even survive the transition and remain members of the service in the future. Our State Department is currently reaching out to the new government in Sofia in instituting a new relationship. They don't want any flaps in the coming months suggesting that we don't trust the 'new' Bulgaria. Besides, we anticipate that the new regime will make us aware of any ongoing intelligence operations that are of interest to the U.S.G. Therefore, if Case Officer still feels it worthwhile, he may offer Yordan a one-time debriefing fee of USD 1500. However, we are not interested in an ongoing relationship with him.

William just sat there for a full minute, staring at the screen and thinking how short-sighted that position was. He predicted that within six months, Headquarters would be telling all Stations to immediately start targeting officials of the "new" Bulgaria. All governments lied when it was in their interest to do so. The new Bulgarian Government would be no different and the American White House would be demanding that the CIA find out what's really going on within Bulgaria. Oh well, he was retiring. Not really his problem anymore. He phoned Yordan and made plans to meet for dinner the following evening at a small Italian restaurant by the Bull Ring in the old part of the city.

Olivia made a brief visit to the Embassy just before lunchtime to drop off a small package for William. A few minutes later, William then went down to the Gunny's office. "Did you get the car accident all straightened out Saturday?" asked William.

"All straightened out. How did the rest of your weekend go? All peaceful and quiet?"

"Yes, not another Nazi showed up all weekend," he replied and laughed. He closed the office door and took from his small briefcase a large manilla envelope of money — all crisp, clean hundreds. He laid it in front of Gunny. "Here's $50,000 for your assistance over the weekend. You can put it into the Marine Ball fund if you wish, your own retirement account, or just tuck it under your mattress."

Gunny was speechless for several long seconds. "Thanks. This should help quite a bit in opening that Thai massage parlor next year." He opened the envelope and took a quick look at all the Ben Franklins. "It's not that I doubted your statement as to the amount, it's just that I've never seen that much money at one time in my entire life and couldn't resist."

William smiled. "This will be my last posting as well. I just turned in my retirement papers, effective Friday."

"You don't waste any time once you make up your mind."

"No, I don't. Also, hopefully, you can be free Friday afternoon to come to my wedding with Olivia and a small reception afterwards.

"Man, that's two good decisions you're making. What happens after the wedding?"

"We're sailing for Rio de Janeiro on Saturday on our honeymoon."

Gunny tapped the envelope full of money. "I guess you came into some money this past weekend after all," commented Gunny with a grin.

"I'm doing it the old-fashioned way. I'm marrying it. It turns out Olivia is a multi-millionaire!"

Gunny stood up and came around his desk so he could shake William's hand. "Damn, you're getting a good woman and money. I'm glad you've found a new purpose in life."

"Yeah, it was a pretty good weekend! Sorry I'm leaving you stuck at the bar with that brand new case of Oban single malt. I doubt if anyone will ever order any of it after I leave."

"Don't worry about it. The Detachment will give it to you as a wedding present, as long as you promise to serve it at the reception on Friday." Gunny gave one of his famous wide grins.

Shortly after the lunch hour, Corya stuck his head into William's office.

"I heard you were looking for me?"

"Good lord, how you going to survive Kuwait? You can't even get across a street in Lisbon without getting hurt!"

Corya laughed. "Ah, but you should see what I did to the hood of their car," he replied with a big grin. He then told the whole story to William.

"Actually, there will be no Kuwait for me. I'm to fly back to Washington as soon as some doctor says I'm good to travel."

"Well, that makes for a good story of how you spent your weekend, but I just might have you beat."

Corya smiled. "Yeah, Johanna just told me. My team left you alone for just a few days and you decided to retire and get married. Unbelievable!"

"Well, if you can manage to not get run over by any more cars between now and Friday, plan on attending my wedding at 1600 hours that day."

"I'll be there, even if on a stretcher."

After Corya left, William spent several hours cleaning out his safe, with some folders going to other officers and some just straight to the shredder. Around 1600 hours he headed to the music club to see Nick. The owner always came in early on Mondays to do whatever he did with the accounting books. William was fairly certain Nick kept two sets of books. One was real and the second one was what would be shown to any governmental tax auditor who came by. William needed to speak with Nick alone.

When he arrived, there was Nick sitting at the bar with two accounting ledgers open before him. He didn't have an actual office anywhere. The only lights burning in the bar were the small spot lights above the bar. One burned directly over Nick, which highlighted him against a black background and gave him a rather dangerous appearance.

Nick looked up from his accounting. "You're here on a Monday. Did you come in to practice some new tunes?"

William tossed his rain coat and fedora on a table and headed straight behind the bar to fetch himself a Coke. Nick was surprised that he hadn't poured himself a Scotch.

"I came in to tell you I'm leaving."

"You're leaving my bar, or you're leaving Lisbon?"

"Both. I'm also retiring from the Agency. I'm getting married Friday afternoon and we're sailing for Brazil on Saturday evening."

The older gentleman gave William a broad smile and put down his pencil. "The bride-to-be wouldn't happen to be that lovely woman Olivia who's been in here quite often on the evenings you were playing?"

"Good guess. You're still pretty sharp for an old guy," teased William.

"Hey, remember, I was trained by the U.S. Government to spot the obvious."

William then spent ten minutes explaining his future plans and also a brief accounting of his run-in with the Neo-Nazis over the weekend.

"You remember the unpleasant German that night at the piano, when you came over?"

"Yes, don't tell me he's a wanna-be Nazi?" replied Nick in mock surprise.

"Well, he and his two friends used to be. And it's all so silly, because there was no hidden treasure to be found."

"A treasure?" asked Nick while opening his eyes wide.

"Perhaps once there was. What I actually found was the hiding place, but the Hungarian jewels that had allegedly once been there have been gone since late 1944. It looks like an old British SOE officer decided he had better use for them than Admiral Horthy of Hungary would – at least he concluded that after the Nazis hauled Horthy off to a German prison in October 1944."

"All very dramatic, but you wound up with no treasure and three dead bodies for all your efforts?"

"That's about it, except it turns out that Olivia doesn't work in a dress shop, she owns it, and several more. She's also worth tens of millions of dollars, so I can retire in style."

"My, you did have a good weekend," teased Nick. "Marriage aside, you may be choosing an excellent time to retire from the espionage game – seeing as how the Cold War is coming to a close."

William laughed as he sat down on one of the bar stools and sipped on his Coke. "You mean I should just declare victory and go home?"

"In a word, yes. Look, I was in the OSS in the closing years of WW II, which was the last war for which just about everybody in the world who wasn't a Fascist agreed upon as being a 'good' war. Then we began the Cold War, in which at least most Americans initially agreed that we should be doing something to stop the further spread of dictatorial, Commie countries. That consensus certainly faded after Vietnam. With this imminent end of the Cold War, there'll now be worldwide euphoria for a year or so, and then we'll discover that certain countries still don't like other neighboring countries. And there will be regional conflicts when one jerk leader wants more. This mess with Saddam Hussein over Kuwait, which America has been sucked into, will be just the first of a string of problems. America never knows when to simply stay home and let nasty people fight it out between themselves."

"My, you've gotten cynical as the years have gone by! But I see your point. Declare victory, move on and I'll be much happier is what you're saying."

"Exactly. Listen, you told me once that your mother named you after her favorite actor, William Powell, right?"

"Correct." William had no idea where Nick was headed with that fact.

"You remember all those great Thin Man mystery movies he made with Myrna Loy?"

"I've seen all six of them, sure. He was the detective Nick Charles and she was his wife, Nora. Your point being?"

"You remember his repeated line when somebody wanted him to get involved in solving some crime? He'd reply, 'No, I'm too busy spending my wife's money to do any detective work.' Take that advice. Go with your new wife to Brazil and enjoy your golden years spending her money. Find some piano bar in Rio and amuse yourself a few evenings a week, work on your tan and grow old in comfort."

William laughed. "Not bad advice. Say, I do want to ask you a question before I leave town."

"Sure, shoot."

"What brought you to Portugal long ago and what's kept you here all these years?"

Nick laughed. "Well, by the mid-fifties, I'd drifted out to Kansas City and found steady work doing little things for a group of guys with broken noses, if you get my drift."

"Understood."

"Things got kind of nasty one night in the summer of 1972. The other guys shot first, but I shot better and needed to leave America. One of my bosses had a cousin here in Lisbon, so here I landed."

"And then?"

"Well, in that first year, I met a really nice girl and she convinced me to get out of the business with that cousin. I stumbled into the night club world and here I still am almost twenty years later."

"So, typical case of a good woman straightens out a bad guy?"

"Something like that. And speaking of the effects of a good woman on a man, I'll comment that I've never seen you as sober since I met you as this last week or two. Might I assume that Olivia has had something to do with that as well?"

"No doubt. It's not that I still don't love and miss Mary Beth, but I've finally realized that I need to get on with what's left of my life. And Olivia deserves something better than the drunken piano player I'd become, so…" He held up the Coke bottle and shrugged his shoulders.

Nick grinned. "So, another case of good woman straightens out a guy. I just hope that you play the piano as well sober as you do drunk!"

William laughed. "I hope so too. Say, how come after all these years in Lisbon you don't speak Portuguese better?"

"The locals understand me, sort of. Why should I care what tense I'm using?"

"Good point."

"While we're swapping questions, I've always been curious since that first night back in February when you walked in here and sat down and started playing the piano – why had you chosen my place? Had somebody told you about my club?"

William laughed softly. "No, I knew nothing of your club. I was just out wandering around one evening here in the Bairro Alto, drinking, when I saw that dilapidated old sign over the entrance. I said to myself that this looks like my kind of bar, and I walked in. I saw the piano sitting there and no one playing it, so I just took off my coat, sat down and started playing – just pure, good luck."

"Yeah, I remember that night. It was a day early in the week and only a few customers in the place. I was going to come over and tell you to stop using the piano, but then I heard how well you played and figured, what the hell."

"I'm glad you didn't. I just sat there playing and ordering drinks. And then a couple of folks had a waiter bring me a free drink. What more could I want? And almost a year later – I'm still coming in and playing."

"Many of our regulars are glad you did. You've had a place to hang your hat these many months and play the piano, and eventually meet the next Mrs. Wythe. We'll miss you, William, but I'm glad to hear that you're leaving because to be honest, you don't fit in here anymore."

William gave him a puzzled look. "Meaning?"

"I mean when you first came in here back at the start of the year, you were a drunk, but more importantly, you were a man who'd given up on life. You were just sleep walking through it and didn't much care what happened. Now – you're drinking less, but more importantly, you give a damn. You see something to achieve or do in life again. That's what I mean when I say you don't fit in with the rest of the losers working here, including me. Whether the change has come because of Olivia who knows for sure, but I suspect it did, so I'd recommend you work hard at holding on to that woman."

William laughed. "That's the first time I've heard in a long time that I'm not enough of a failure to fit in somewhere. But I agree with you that I need to work hard to be the man that Olivia thinks that I am – and deserves."

"Good. I'm sure you two will be very happy down there in Brazil, especially with all that money." He grinned.

"Hey, I do need to ask you for one last favor. There's a JP Captain, named Rodrigo Santos. He's been part of my protection detail in recent weeks and I think he's been tied up with these Neo-Nazi clowns, providing them information on my movements."

"You have actual proof you could take to his superiors?"

"Of course not. It's just my educated hunch. Besides, I'd just as soon not discuss with the police my weekend out at Busaco. Anyway, I'm not sure if there are more of those thugs around or if they're the type that will seek revenge once somebody finds Müller's body after the 'accident' he had out there in the woods. You see my dilemma."

"I presume you have a plan?" asked Nick with a smile.

"Yes, I'm going to invite Rodrigo to a one-on-one dinner this week, in order to say goodbye. At that dinner, I'm also going to tell him that I know he was connected with Müller and providing information about me. I'll tell him that I'm not going to the police, but if I ever see him again, I'll kill him." There was no smile on William's face. "I'd like you and two or three of your waiters to be seated at a nearby table that I will point to when I explain that I will still have friends in Lisbon who will not take kindly to anything happening to me in the future."

"I like that. Say, if you ever want to live in Kansas City, I still know a few guys who would be happy to employ you! Only one change for a better plan. All my waiters are pretty boys. I have three acquaintances with broad shoulders in the city who will look much better in that supporting role to me. Just tell us where and when you need us to be for this dinner."

"Your call on who to have dine with you. And just tell the waiter to bring your check to me."

Now Nick smiled. "No check. We'll call that my wedding present to you and Olivia."

"OK, I'll phone you as soon as I have a fixed dinner date with Rodrigo. I'm thinking the Clube dos Empresarios would be a nice venue."

"An excellent choice," replied Nick, who then stood and gave William a farewell hug. "You enjoy life down there in Brazil! You deserve it after all these years in the Great Game."

That evening, William phoned Rodrigo of the JP and asked him to meet him for dinner on Wednesday at 7:00 p.m. at the Clube dos Empresarios, so as to pass along some news. Rodrigo readily agreed, as that exclusive restaurant was way above his monthly paycheck.

There was a light, but cold drizzle Tuesday night when William met Yordan for dinner. As William entered the small Italian restaurant in the old part of the city, he saw that Yordan had already arrived and chosen a table off in a corner. He had taken the chair which put his back into the corner and gave him a nice view of the front door. It was also secluded from the other tables, so they would have privacy in their conversation. William quickly thought to himself that it was nice having a "working" dinner with a fellow intelligence officer; he knew how to choose a good table.

William saw that Yordan had a full-sized, black umbrella hung over the corner of his chair. He couldn't resist a comment, as he pointed at the umbrella and smiled. "Do I have anything to worry about?"

Yordan laughed. "No, this one only repels rain."

After the opening amenities and the ordering of food, Yordan said, "I don't suppose you have any secret information about the war down in

Kuwait, do you? I hate to ask, but the head of the DS overseas division is desperate to show to the new government that the service can actually learn a secret now and then – and thus we might be worthwhile maintaining in the new scheme of things."

"Sofia doesn't understand very well how the American Government and military works if they think that the Pentagon would share with inconsequential Lisbon Embassy any war secrets. Sorry."

Yordan shrugged his shoulders. "I just thought I'd ask. I don't have any secret sources I can ask, so I figured I'd check with you."

William was somewhat amazed. "You don't have a single clandestine agent that you're running in Portugal?"

Yordan snorted. "Who would want to work for the Bulgarian Intelligence Service? Communism is dead and we have no money. The Ambassador just sent a memo around our Embassy yesterday reminding us to turn off all the lights that aren't absolutely needed, so as to lower our monthly electric bill!"

"I guess that means that the DS isn't secretly running any moles within the American Government?"

"Not unless they're willing to work for free!" They both laughed.

"Different subject. Have you gotten things worked out for your daughter to get the medical treatment she needs back in Bulgaria?"

The smile disappeared from Yordan's face. "No success. Everybody, including the state hospitals and doctors now want hard currency in their hands to do their jobs. One of the latest jokes going around in Sofia is that the good news is that the wait time to get medical treatment has been greatly reduced to just a matter of a day or two. The bad news is that the wait lines are so short because almost no one in Bulgaria can afford to pay for any treatment."

William didn't know whether to laugh or cry at that joke.

"You know, the Stambolovs have been serving mother Bulgaria for over a hundred years, but rulers always have very short memories."

William leaned forward, lowered his voice and a serious look came to his face. "Tell me, my friend, how much would it cost today to get your daughter the best treatment there is in Bulgaria for her cancer?"

Yordan sat silent for several long seconds. It isn't that he hadn't expected some sort of pitch to come from William – and he had even inquired "on the left" as they said in Bulgaria, what such treatment would cost – but the directness still took him by surprise. "You Americans do get directly to the point. So, if I become a spy for the CIA, you will give me the money I need to save my daughter's life? Is that the bargain?" There was no bitterness in his voice, but perhaps just a touch of sadness.

"That isn't my offer at all, Yordan. In fact, my Agency isn't interested in you for recruitment. The management back at CIA Headquarters thinks that by the end of this year, we will all be sitting around the campfire and singing Kumbaya in universal friendship – that we won't need any spies within the new Bulgarian government coming into power."

Yordan just snorted in amazement.

"No, the offer I'm making you is a personal one. I am a very rich person and I want to help a fellow intelligence officer who is in need. We were on opposite sides of the Cold War, but you worked for your country with honor. My side has won and the war is over. I'm sad the way your government is treating you and your daughter and I want to help as one man to another. So, tell me how much would be needed for her full treatment in the coming months?"

Yordan had to fight to hold back tears before answering. "Perhaps US$8,000, $9,000 at the most. I know that is a lot of money, but…"

William held up his hand for Yordan to stop. He then took a used copy of War and Peace, in Russian, from a small cloth sack he'd brought with him. He'd hollowed out the pages and placed $10,000, all in hundreds, inside the famous book. He placed the book on the table and slowly pushed it across the table while looking straight into Yordan's eyes. "This will cover her medical needs and a few extra dollars so that you can frequently send her flowers. And on her birthday, send her several dozen roses from me." William had wanted to give somebody money in such a Hollywood fashion his entire career. He'd finally achieved his fantasy with only three days to spare.

"Next, you told me last week that people in your apartment bloc in Sofia will soon have the right to purchase their apartment, correct?"

Yordan was afraid to even touch the book on the table. "Yes, but the amounts they are asking for each apartment will guarantee that only the bigshots who can steal money out of the current government before it collapses can afford to buy their apartment. Those big time *Mafiosi* will buy up entire floors of apartments – and eventually resell them to foreigners."

"How much do you need for you to buy your apartment?"

Yordan didn't even have to pause to calculate from the Bulgarian lev to dollars, as one had to pay the purchase price in Yankee dollars and so he already had it calculated. "It will cost right now almost US$6,000."

William reached again into his sack and brought out a used Russian copy of Crime and Punishment, also hollowed out with another $10,000 inside. He sat that on top of the first one. "This will cover the purchase price, plus any bribes necessary and keep you in plenty of tasty *banitsa* for the first year or two."

Finally, Yordan smiled. "You're turning me into quite a literary specialist!"

William, grinned, turned his head slightly and shrugged his shoulders. "Well, this way you can retire in the comfort which you're entitled to after your many years of service to your country."

Yordan raised his glass to the American and said in English, "Thank you."

Conversation ceased for a moment as the waiter delivered their food and brought two more Italian beers.

"I also have a little news," began William. "I'm retiring from my government on Friday and getting married that afternoon. I'll be gone from Portugal in just a few more days."

A big smile spread on Yordan's face. He raised his beer glass and shouted "*Parabens!*" He immediately waved for the waiter and told him to bring a bottle of his best champagne. "We must toast this occasion properly! And the champagne is on me – now that I am a man of wealth. So, tell me about this foolish woman who is willing to marry such an old man as you."

An hour later, the two old Cold Warriors called it an evening and made their final farewells.

"I hope that your daughter recovers from her cancer and that things turn out well for your country."

"There aren't words in any language to thank you enough for what you have done this day for me and my daughter. I wish you a happy second marriage and a good retirement, wherever that will be."

They stood and Yordan reached for his umbrella. "Here, take this as a remembrance of our friendship here in Lisbon."

William smiled broadly and then headed out the door. It was still raining softly. He popped open his new umbrella and walked off into the night down a narrow street. The corner street light from behind him glistened on the wet cobblestones and briefly cast his shadow on the street as he walked away. His shadow grew dimmer with each step. How fitting, he thought, as he completed his last official act of espionage. He reflected on his peculiar profession of the last thirty years – one in which, like tonight, he'd often said goodbye to people he'd genuinely liked and knew that he'd never have contact with again.

When he got back to his house that night, Olivia was still up and waiting for him. William was taking no chances with the German crowd and had insisted that Olivia stay on with him until they left the country on Saturday. She couldn't wait to hear how the dinner had gone with Yordan. They sat down together on the living room sofa. He reported the conversation with the Bulgarian in fullest detail.

"Oh, that was the sweetest gesture on your part. I know you play a very tough guy, but at heart, you are really such a sentimental fellow."

He smiled. "Well, I can be, with your money."

She leaned in closer and gave him a kiss.

"Come on, it's late. Take me to bed," she said in a sultry voice and with a provocative smile.

On Wednesday morning, William prepared a very short message to Headquarters stating that he'd raised the idea of a one-time debriefing session with Yordan in return for US$1,500 and that the Bulgarian had politely, but firmly said no. William also reported that Yordan was retiring in the coming summer and stated that there would be no point in any officer bothering to recontact Yordan in his remaining months in Portugal. It would have been nice to have had one last "notch" on his recruitment belt as he retired, but this was the best way to end the Bulgarian caper. Besides, he really didn't want for it to appear that a "success" had occurred under the command of the COS.

Wednesday evening, William drove to the Clube dos Empresarios for his planned dinner with the suspected neo-Nazi informant on the Judicial Police. His security detail was gone, but he did conduct an hour-long surveillance detection drive, just to make sure no one was following him. William was already seated in one of the large leather chairs in the lounge area and sipping a Sagres beer when Rodrigo arrived. He looked very elegant in his formal captain's uniform. Normally, he was in civilian clothing when working with the Hostage Rescue Team. William had rarely seen him over the past year in his uniform.

"Some special occasion, Rodrigo? I've rarely seen you in your uniform." William pointed at the chair next to his own and signaled for the elderly waiter in his tuxedo to come over to take his guest's drink order. Saying, "elderly in a tuxedo" was redundant because all the waiters matched that description. Rodrigo also ordered a beer.

"I dressed up because there is a rumor going around that you are retiring very soon and leaving Portugal. Is that true?" he asked with a knowing smile.

"Goodness, secrets don't stay secrets very long in this city."

"So, you're leaving us? Poor Elliot will be terribly upset that he is losing you," he said with a perfectly straight face. The dislike between William and Elliot was known throughout the Embassy and the various Portuguese security and intelligence services that had contact with the Embassy.

"Oh, I suspect he'll be able to control his grief over my departure, if he tries real hard. Anyway, I wanted to tell you I'm leaving, so you won't need to worry about me or my whereabouts after this Sunday when I depart for Washington."

"Well, we shall all miss you, but that does solve the possible assassination threat against you." He shrugged his shoulders. "I guess we'll never know if that threat was genuine or not."

"No, I guess not. In any case, I had a very quiet and relaxing time out at the Busaco Forest Hotel."

"Good, I've heard that it's a very lovely place and a beautiful hotel."

William took a sip of his beer and then just stared for several long seconds at Rodrigo in silence, before finally speaking. "So, what did Müller give you in return for keeping him alerted on my whereabouts these last few weeks?"

Rodrigo's face froze. William hoped that Rodrigo never played card games for money because he certainly did not have a "poker face." Finally, he managed to sputter, "What are you saying?"

Until that moment, William had only been about eighty percent certain that Rodrigo had been the leaker of information to Müller, but his response to William's allegation clinched it.

"Don't worry Rodrigo, I'm not going to report you or even harm you. You are a very lucky man. I'm retiring and so I just don't even care anymore, but if I ever see you again anywhere in the world I shall immediately kill you."

Rodrigo could think of nothing to say in response and just sat there motionless and in silence.

"And one more thing. You see those four gentlemen at that table over in the corner?"

Rodrigo looked over in the indicated direction. In fact, he'd noticed them when he'd first walked into the cocktail lounge area of the club. He'd thought that he recognized the face of one of them from a wanted poster. Rodrigo nodded acknowledgement to William that he saw the four men, but said nothing.

"They're friends of mine and they live here in Portugal. If anything happens to me in the coming years – anything at all. If I have a car accident. If I slip on a bar of soap in the shower, anything at all, then they will come kill you. So I suggest that you simply forget you ever knew me and the same advice for any of Müller's acquaintances as well."

Rodrigo saw no point in responding to the threat. He simply stood and wished William a "Bom voyage", as he nodded slightly with his head. He then turned and left, staring down at the floor as he walked away, so as not to make eye contact with any of the four men in the corner.

William sat there, finishing his beer and pondered why Rodrigo had cooperated with a neo-Nazi like Müller. Perhaps it was as simple as money. Perhaps it was at least partially related to Rodrigo having been screwed out of a promotion six months back when the position of head of the Counterterrorism Division had been given to an African emigrant from Angola so as to make the Judicial Police appear more "diverse." Anyway, not his concern anymore. William smiled to himself. He thought about the fact that even though he was retiring, he had still just lied to Rodrigo, without even thinking about it, when he told him that he wasn't leaving until Sunday and would be headed for America. Old habits of deceiving others just came automatically to him after all those years.

The waiter came over and asked him if he was ready to order.

"Yes, I'll start with the French Onion Soup and then I'll have the filet, done medium. I'll decide about dessert later."

"Of course. And for your friend?"

"Oh, unfortunately, he decided that he couldn't stay for dinner. It will be just me, dining alone."

"Very good, sir."

Unbeknownst to William, besides his three friends sitting with Nick in the restaurant, Nick had arranged for several more of his street-wise friends to be waiting outside in two cars with instructions to follow the JP officer when he left. They reported via radio to Nick just a few minutes later that Rodrigo had driven only five minutes after leaving the restaurant before he stopped to use a payphone. He had made a call of only a minute's duration and was then standing on a nearby street corner, as if waiting to be picked up. Nick instructed his man for them to forcibly take Rodrigo off the street before anyone else showed up. The first car would then drive south out of the city, go to the beach near Sesimbra and wait for him there. The second car would wait around and see who possibly showed up at that corner to meet the policeman and then discreetly follow that car wherever it went. Nick wanted to know who Rodrigo had phoned. The old OSS officer then immediately left the restaurant, leaving his companions there to enjoy their dinners. They had orders to follow William home and then to watch the house the rest of the night – just in case.

A half hour later, Nick rendezvoused with the others at a small parking lot near the beach. The lot and the beach were completely deserted at that time of night, especially in winter. Nick exited his car. His "friends" took Rodrigo out of the backseat of their car. He immediately began to vehemently protest. "You cannot detain a senior officer of the Judicial Police without there being serious repercussions."

Nick softly replied, "You were given a warning by William, which you clearly chose to ignore, for which there are also serious repercussions."

Rodrigo's last thought was that the man speaking to him had the worst foreigner's accent of Portuguese he'd ever heard.

Nick then took the small .22 caliber pistol out of his pocket with his hand covered in an expensive calf-skinned glove and put two shots in rapid succession into Rodrigo's heart. With his other gloved hand, he then took a small plastic bag containing cocaine, leaned over and placed it into one of the policeman's pants pockets. He then commented to his friends, "Ah, another good policeman has tragically gotten involved with narco smugglers." He then gave the gun and his gloves to one of his men with instructions to toss them into the ocean on the way back into the city. "I really liked those gloves. I'll miss them," was his last comment.

As he drove back into the city, he knew that William would be upset with his action that night, but he knew from his years in Kansas City that you shouldn't leave loose ends in any business. Hopefully, William would be out of the country soon enough that he would never even hear about the tragic shooting of a corrupt police officer.

He met later that night with the two men who'd tried following the man who showed up at that street corner about fifteen minutes after Rodrigo had made the call from a pay phone. They reported to Nick that a man had waited several minutes at the deserted intersection, clearly looking for someone. Finally, he drove off in his large, top-of-the-line Mercedes.

"We tried following him, but you'd told us to not get spotted and with only one car, we had to break off after about five minutes. He was heading north out of the city, and was clearly checking to see if he was being followed."

"Did you get a good look at the driver?"

"We'd say he was about fifty, with short hair and a neatly trimmed, dark-colored mustache and goatee. There was only a dim street light nearby, so we couldn't get a good look at him, other than to say he was a white man."

"And the license plate number?"

"It was a German plate. We'll make some calls in the morning to a friend in Germany and see if we can unofficially learn anything that way."

"Alright, good job. Let me know if you learn anything through the license plate tomorrow."

Nick didn't like the indication that there were yet more Germans in town and interested in William.

CHAPTER 16

As William left his house on Thursday morning he noticed a gray-colored Renault with two men in it sitting across the street from his house. He would have gotten worried, except for the fact that they both smiled and gave him a quick wave as he pulled out of his driveway. They didn't follow him, but rather continued to watch his house. He checked carefully on the way to the Embassy for any signs of surveillance, but saw no one who appeared to be following him.

As soon as he reached his office, he phoned Nick Haber.

"Did you enjoy your dinner last night?" asked William.

"Pretty good, although I had to leave a little early when something else came up."

"Well, thank you for your assistance. Hopefully, my ex-friend got the message."

"Oh, I'm sure he did," replied Nick, glad that his friend couldn't see through the phone line the wide grin on his face.

"Say, you wouldn't know anything about a gray-colored Renault with two men in it who were sitting in front of my house this morning?"

"As a matter of fact, I do. I figured that just to be on the safe side, why not have a couple of my friends keep an eye on your house and your lovely *Brasiliera* these last couple of days – until you get on that ship on Saturday."

"OK, I suspected your hand, particularly since they waved as I drove off."

Nick laughed. "I only employ the most polite sort of people."

"Right, I'll see you at the wedding tomorrow."

"Till tomorrow."

As soon as he hung up, Johanna, the Station's beautiful, thirty-year-old, single Admin gal entered his office. She'd brought in to him a number of retirement forms for him to sign, prompting William to joke, "I don't remember having to sign this much paper when I joined the Agency!"

"Things have changed in thirty years," she replied with a mock stern face. She then gave him a big smile and said, "We'll miss you, William. Well, most of us will anyway." They both laughed. "Are you sure we can't hold a little farewell party for you this afternoon?"

"No parties. And remember, the story, even around the Embassy, is that I'm retiring in America."

Her face turned serious. "You hiding from someone?"

He grinned. "I just don't want Gunny to know where to send my final month's bar bill."

"Well, good luck in the future. I'm sure you and Olivia will be very happy for many years to come. I'll see you at the wedding tomorrow."

"You better. Olivia told me that it's an old Portuguese wedding custom that you have to have at least one virgin at your wedding to ensure happiness in the marriage."

She threw a pencil at him, then left with all the signed forms.

He spent much of the rest of Thursday morning taking phone calls from various diplomats around Lisbon who'd somehow gotten the word that William was getting married and leaving Portugal. Diplomats were worse than the fabled housewives in small towns over backyard fences. He'd miss that camaraderie that existed in a diplomatic community, even between representatives of political opponents. All diplomats were living away from their homelands, often from members of their family, so they all had much in common, despite their cultural, food and language differences.

He'd also miss the game of espionage that he'd played for so long, but as with all careers, sooner or later, there comes a time to retire and leave the work to a younger generation. Besides, the Cold War was quickly coming to an end –that was the only game he'd ever known. Nick was probably right. Declare victory and move on. To exactly what, he didn't know yet. Hell, maybe he'd get involved in the dress business with Olivia. He laughed out loud at that thought. No, probably not the dress game, but he was sure he'd find something. Maybe life could imitate art and he'd become a private investigator while spending his wife's money like Nick Charles had in all those *Thin Man* movies. William still loved and missed his first wife, but he was glad he'd found someone with whom to share a new life down in Rio. He'd definitely have to find a small, smoke-filled bar where he could play piano a couple of nights per week.

At 1100 hours, the COS called everyone together for a brief meeting in the Station's conference room. He was holding a paper copy of an EYES ONLY cable that had come in that morning from Headquarters. "It's to me from the DDO."

He wet his lips and began to read it out loud:

"I know you will be sad to leave Lisbon early where you have been doing an outstanding job, but for needs of the service I'm having to ask you to return immediately to begin a new job. This will be as Deputy Chief of a task force I have just created to prepare plans for the entire Agency in this new Post-Cold War era we're about to enter. Commensurate with this new position you are also immediately being promoted to the super grade level of GS-16".

Elliott then just sat there with a wide smile on his face. "Chuck here will serve as Acting Chief for the next few months until a replacement can be found for me."

The clapping for the fact that Elliot would immediately be leaving was genuine. The idea that the man was being moved up in the world to some prestigious position and given a promotion was almost so incongruous as to be unbelievable. Corya simply sat silently in a corner of the room, with the faintest smile on his lips, as he guessed at what was afoot. He gave Elliot maybe six months before he was in a federal prison, twelve at the most, no matter how clever was the deception that the CI Staff had clearly just set in motion.

As William would officially be retired in less than five hours, he didn't even have to pretend to be happy with such an outrageous announcement and didn't applaud, even insincerely.

Lieutenant Fonseca of the Judicial Police Lisbon Division tapped on the outer door of his superior's office on Friday morning and after hearing a faint grunt of an answer, entered the office of Captain Abreu. "I just got off the phone with Inspector Schultz of the Bavarian State Police of Germany."

Abreu looked up with his very sad eyes and asked, "Yes, and what does this Schultz want?"

"He said that we may both be interested in the same person and he would like to come by this afternoon to discuss this German citizen who had recently been in Portugal."

"I see, and why does he think that the JP has any interest in this man?"

"Apparently, we put in a request to Interpol a couple of weeks back about this person and that somehow generated a request down to Munich for information."

"And have we received a formal request from the Bavarian State Police for a name check on their citizen?"

"No, this Inspector who just phoned here ten minutes back, said he was in Lisbon and asked if he could just drop by for an informal chat this afternoon. I told him I would gladly meet with him, but I wanted to make you are aware of his coming by, in case you wished to meet with him yourself. He'll be here in fifteen minutes."

"Did he give you the name of this person of joint interest?"

"Said he'd prefer not to over the phone."

"Hmmm. Don't suppose he speaks Portuguese? I hate trying to speak German."

"As a matter of fact he does."

Abreu smiled. "Well, since finally there's a German official who's bothered learning anything but German, why not. I've nothing special on today. Let me know when he arrives."

"Yes, Captain."

Fifteen minutes later, Lieutenant Fonseca returned with Inspector Schultz and after the obligatory introductions, Schultz, in his passable Portuguese, began to explain the reason for his visit that day.

"Your Agency sent a request a couple of weeks back to Interpol about a German citizen named Jurgen Müller of Munich. Interpol inquired of the Bavarian State Police and that is what has brought me here today. We've been interested in Müller for many months for possible car theft activities associated with his large automobile dealership in Munich. I was down here on vacation and thought I'd just informally drop by for a little chat."

"Very good. Give us a few minutes to pull up our records on this Müller. Lieutenant, why don't you take our guest to see our small museum, while we're waiting for my secretary to do the search – and I need to make a phone call on an unrelated matter."

Inspector Schultz stood. "I would be honored to see your museum." He then turned and exited with Lieutenant Fonseca. Abreu smiled after the German was out of his office, as he thought to himself that the German had almost clicked his heels when he'd stood up. He'd also never known a German official of any rank who would let anything interfere with his beloved vacation time. He buzzed for his secretary and gave her the task of pulling up any records on Jurgen Müller. He then placed an international call to the Bavarian State Police in Munich, Germany to ask to speak with Inspector Schultz. Abreu felt a little more at ease when told that there was such a person, but that he was away on vacation. Still, the whole affair struck him as odd.

A few minutes later, he read the printout his secretary had brought him on Müller. One of his officers assigned to a VIP security detail with the Americans had sent in the name request to Interpol. It was simply that he'd appeared to have had an "unpleasant" conversation with the American diplomat who was under protection. Interpol had come back with only a few details about the man. The most interesting was that he was suspected of involvement with an underground neo-Nazi group in Munich. "Hmmm," was his one-word mental reaction to the report.

He'd just finished lighting a cigarette when Fonseca returned with the German.

"Yes, we had sent in the request to Interpol. However, it was simply in connection with a small altercation one night in a local nightclub. Nothing linked to automobiles in any way." He shrugged his shoulders. "I'm afraid sometimes a few of our junior officers get carried away with wanting to check on international connections of any foreigner who comes across our path."

Inspector Schultz smiled. "Ah, so nothing of real interest about the man?"

"No, not really."

"And he's not been encountered subsequently here in Portugal?"

Captain Abreu pretended to look for a moment at the one-page report and replied, "No, nothing further."

"So, my visit has been for nothing today, other than a chance to see your fine museum."

Abreu stood up and extended his hand. "We always welcome visits by our German colleagues."

Fonseca returned to the Captain's office after escorting the German out of the building. "So, there was really nothing more in our files?"

Abreu handed him the single sheet of paper.

Lieutenant Fonseca smiled. "You didn't think it worth mentioning to Schulz that our inquiry was in connection with a VIP protection detail?"

"I find the whole visit by Schulz 'while on his vacation' strange, and it's none of his business what we and the Americans are doing in Portugal. It's also odd that he didn't mention anything about the alleged Neo-Nazi activities of Müller."

"No, he didn't."

"And did you notice that silly mustache and goatee of his. He must be fifty and yet he has them dyed the pure, dark color of a twenty-year old!" The Captain shook his head and then returned to reading a report on his desk.

Friday passed quickly. The intimate wedding in a small, old neighborhood Catholic Church, which the manager of Olivia's dress shop had arranged for, went smoothly. As the couple walked out the front door of the church, they were hit with much rice. That, William expected. Finding ten Marines in their dress blues, standing at attention on the pathway leading from the church to the decked-out honeymoon car was a nice surprise, courtesy of Gunny. The reception was held in one of the small banquet rooms at Le Meridien Hotel. Nick had booked for them the bridal suite that night in the hotel. He'd also arranged for two of his "friends" to be outside their door all night long – just in case.

Everyone from the Station, except for the COS, was at the reception. Despite William's own judgement, Olivia had insisted that everyone at least be invited, including Elliot, whether they were particularly wanted or not. The DCOS came up to William at the reception to pass along Elliot's regrets, claiming that he'd been called to the Portuguese Defense Ministry at the last moment that afternoon. Neither Chuck nor William believed what had just been said, but pretending it was true was the proper thing to do.

Yordan had not been at the wedding, but did make a brief appearance at the reception. He simply came up to the couple, kissed Olivia's cheeks, shook William's hand and wished them much happiness in the future. He also leaned forward and whispered in William's ear, "Her surgery yesterday went well." The Bulgarian then just disappeared into the crowd.

As the reception was winding down, William found himself seated alone off in a corner. His first quiet moment all day. Corya wandered over on his crutches and joined him at the deserted table, which was full of plates of partially eaten cake and dirty glasses.

"Just wanted to express my congratulations on your wedding and your retirement," began Corya.

"Thank you. It's been a pleasure having you around for the last few weeks. Has the doctor told you when you can travel?

"Probably on Monday, if there's a plane seat available to get me back to Washington."

"From what I've seen on the news, the fighting is just about over, unless Bush wants to drive all the way to Baghdad," speculated William.

"That's not going to happen. If we took the whole country, then what are we going to do with it? So, are you looking forward to retirement?"

"Yeah, it's been thirty years. Anything I'm going to contribute to world peace and prosperity, I've done it by now. Time to move on and make room for younger officers.

"You mean like wonder boy Elliot?" asked Corya with a smile on his face.

"Bah, don't get me started on that twit," replied William with a disgusting scowl on his face. "I'm having such a nice day."

Corya realized too late he should never have mentioned Elliot's name. He leaned in closer to William and lowered his voice. "Listen, for your ears only — that news about Elliot's promotion and immediate recall to home for a new job may not be all as it seems. Agency management isn't as dumb as they sometimes appear."

William gave him a puzzled look. "So, what's afoot?"

"I can't say any more and shouldn't have even said what I did, but I couldn't let you go away thinking that that walking idiot was actually rising to the top."

"So, what's going on?"

"All I'll say is that sometimes the guys on the seventh floor can be very clever. You're a bright guy. I'll leave to you to speculate while sitting on the beach in Rio in the sunshine as to why Elliot is being made to feel that all is well as he's being brought home early for an important new job. I suggest you watch the American newspapers in the coming year." Corya stood up and extended a hand. "You go have a great life in retirement."

"And you stay safe."

They shook hands and then Corya left. Another parting after which William would probably never see the other person again.

Master Gunnery Sergeant Aloysius Murphy looked great in his dress blues, with all his ribbons and awards as he came over to kiss the bride one more time and make his farewell.

"Man, Gunny, they should put your picture on a recruiting poster," proclaimed William.

Olivia told him, "Aloysius, pay no attention to William. I think you look very handsome today."

He extended his hand to William. "You two have a good life down there in Brazil. Nobody will ever know all that you did for your country during the Cold War, but you definitely deserve a good retirement."

William gave him a big smile. "Yeah, both of us old Cold Warriors do. I'm going to come visit that Thai Massage parlor someday, so it better be nice!"

"You'll always be welcome – as long as you have a permission slip from Olivia." Gunny then stepped back, pulled himself up to full attention, gave William a salute with his white-gloved right hand and said "Permission to disembark, Sir."

"Permission granted, my friend. Stay safe."

Gunny then smartly turned and moving smoothly past people and tables, headed for the exit. Once again, William was amazed at how that large of a man could move so gracefully.

Le Meridien Hotel owned a classic, black Rolls Royce, which they made available for special guests. This included for guests of the Wedding Suite. William and Olivia rode in style to the docks that Saturday afternoon. Per William's request to the driver they went down the grand Avenida da Republica – just to have one last fond memory of the ancient city that had had such an impact on his life.

"A penny for your thoughts," said William.

"Actually, with the hyper-inflation these days in Brazil, that will cost you several hundred cruzeiros," she replied with a smile.

"I'm good for it."

"OK, for some reason I was just thinking about what sorts of things we may find in that foot locker of my father's that's sitting at my mother's house."

"Might be nothing, but who knows. We'll definitely check it out. I think we should also arrange a visit somehow with 'Mr. Lewis'. We can assure him that we don't want any of his money, but I'd love to hear the full story of those Hungarian royal jewels he stole."

"Indeed, and for all we know, there might have been other interesting items in Horthy's secret shipment destined for Portugal."

"True, very true."

Arrival at the dock brought an end to their conversation about future activities in Brazil. Having arrived in a Rolls Royce, the Customs officer and the ship boarding officials assumed the couple must be important and not to be trifled with during the boarding process. Having reached their small suite, William marveled at the three large shipping trunks belonging to Olivia that had already been placed in their cabin.

"I see you're traveling light this trip," he said pointing at the trunks."

"That's nothing. The other five are down in storage. I'm taking all the fashions of Casa de Simone for the new season with me to wear in Rio. Hopefully, to stir up demand for next year's line of clothing."

"Quite the business woman, aren't you?"

"I am and speaking of business, when my store manager contacted the cruise line to make these reservations, she found out they'd already been made and paid for by you."

He took her into his arms. "That's right. Once we reach Brazil, I shall happily become a kept man living on your money, but I at least felt I should pay for our honeymoon cruise to get to Rio." They both laughed, which was followed by a long kiss.

At 1700 hours, the newlyweds' ship left the harbor and sailed due west into the sunset. The couple stood arm-in-arm, up in a forward lounge, watching the sun just starting to dip down into the Atlantic Ocean. William thought that it was a perfect metaphorical ending to his days in Lisbon and his career with the CIA.

"I saw on the ship diagram that there's a bar somewhere up on this deck. "Let's go check it out," suggested William.

A few minutes later, they entered a small, cozy lounge and headed for the bar. A Germanic-looking gentleman about fifty, with a neatly trimmed mustache and goatee dyed jet black in color entered the bar just a few seconds after they did. He took a seat at a small table in the corner from where he had a good view of the bar.

Sometimes, sending in the official paperwork to the CIA Headquarters to retire didn't mean that one could actually retire from the game.

TO BE CONTINUED

Made in the USA
Monee, IL
06 November 2022

17264545R00128